I0638117

THE MAN OF A THOUSAND FACES

Volume One

Airship 27 Productions

TM

SECRET AGENT X: VOLUME ONE

"Secret Agent "X" and the Skeleton-Men of Calcutta" © 2008 Kevin Noel Olson
"Secret Agent "X" and The Cult of the Walking Dead" © 2008 Mark Justice
"Secret Agent "X" and The Cold Touch of Death" © 2008 Brian Meredith
"Secret Agent "X" and The Icarus Terror" © 2008 Andrew Salmon

Cover and interior illustrations © 2008 Rob Davis

Editor: Ron Fortier
Marketing and Promotions Manager: Michael Vance
Production Designer: Rob Davis (2025 Edition)

Airship 27 Productions
airship27hangar.com

ISBN: 978-1-953589-98-9

Third Edition

Produced in the United States of America

10 9 8 7 6 5 4 3 2 1

SECRET AGENT "X"
Volume One
CONTENTS

The Agent X-Files **5**

Norman Hamilton

SECRET AGENT "X" *and the* **SKELETON-MEN** *of* **CALCUTTA......9**

By Kevin Noel Olson

An ancient race of cave dwellers threatens the surface world and only Agent X can foil their plans of conquest.

SECRET AGENT "X" *and the* **CULT** *of the* **WALKING DEAD.........46**

By Mark Justice

Banker Augustus Wellington was murdered before Agent X could save him Now a mysterious oriental cult is going to resurrect the dead man in front of an entire city.

SECRET AGENT "X" *and the* **COLD TOUCH** *of* **DEATH...............82**

By Brian Meredith

Agent X must protect the President of the United States from an unknown assassin who uses vanishing bullets.

SECRET AGENT "X" *and the* **ICARUS TERROR........................129**

By Andrew Salmon

Agent X must find the mysterious "Number One" and somehow thwart his plan to disrupt the World's Fair.

The Agent X-Files

NORMAN HAMILTON

At the height of their popularity, the hero pulps starred half a dozen heroes whose main ability was the art of disguise; to be able to change their appearances and become someone totally new. Of all these masters of the personal camouflage trick, none was more adept or successful at it than Secret Agent X –The Man of a Thousand Faces. During his long run he was published by Periodicals House Inc., and his stories attributed to writer Brant House; a wry in-joke as it was obviously a house name. Most pulp historians believe many of the Agent X adventures were written by veteran wordsmith, Paul Chadwick.

As a hero, Agent X was a strange oddity. His real name and background were unknown to most people, but one such individual was K-9, a very high government official in Washington. Unlike the typical, chisel jawed; gray-eyed hero of his era, Agent X was for all intents and purposes a faceless protagonist who invariably is hounded by the police because his rather daring methods brought X into conflict with the law. He was an enigma to them.

What was gleaned by the readers over countless issues was both fascinating and equally mysterious. He was clearly a young man, in the prime of life. While doing research to write the new tales you are about to read, the four writers of this volume amassed a good deal of information and shared it with each other. Under Ron Fortier's guidance it became the Agent X Data File and is presented for your edification here.

1 – As a young man he spent many years in the Far East and learned many Oriental languages. He became a member of the Mint Tong Brotherhood and was known by them as Ho Ling. It was during this part of his life he also mastered the fighting arts of judo and ju-jitsu.

2 – He joined the Armed Forces in World War I and served in France as a flyer for the 151st British Camel Squadron. Besides his missions as a skilled pilot, he also had a fancy for fast motorcycles and was often drafted as a dispatch rider. He once performed a mission for Lawrence of Arabia. During the war he traveled extensively from Russia, to Mongolia and even had assignments in Mexico.

3 – He was severely wounded in France. A piece of shrapnel pierced his side and almost killed him. When the field doctors stitched the wound shut, the resulting scar was in the form of an X and it would forever cause him mild twitches of pain whenever he over-exerted himself in later battles.

4 – Upon his discharge, he was recruited by K-9 into the Government's Intelligence Department to become an independent agent able to confront any and all threats to the welfare and security of America at a given notice.

5 – Agent X's operations are funded by 10 wealthy men. He has never met any of them or vice versa. He is subscribed to an unlimited fund which is on deposit to him in the name of Elisha Pond (one of X's two permanent false identities) at the First National Bank. As the fund is depleted, the 10 replenish it so that X is never without money he needs to maintain his vigilant war against crime. As Pond, X is a doctor and millionaire philanthropist. Eventually as time went on, crooks that had run afoul of Agent X in the past began to suspect the Pond identity.

6 – Although he is an independent agent, X does not work alone and has created an extensive network of very special operatives under the bogus cover of the Colonial Research Foundation managed by Harvey Bates: a powerhouse of a fellow, rugged, six feet tall and fiercely loyal to Agent X.

Jim Hobart is a chief operative, but doesn't know it. The red-headed Private Investigator was once a police officer who was framed for corruption. X helped to clear his name and now employs the Hobart Detective Agency as its number one client.

Lastly there is the lovely Betty Dale, the daughter of a police chief murdered by underworld gunmen. Blond, blue-eyed, with a knock-out figure, this gorgeous spitfire is a crime reporter for the Herald and one of the few human beings in the world who knows the history of Agent X. She is in love with him but is willing to defer marriage and a normal life together until the day X puts aside his make-up kit and retires.

All of X's operatives were required to use ID papers and ever-changing passwords to identify themselves to each other.

7 – Other recurring disguises used by X in his exploits are, A.J.Martin, a reporter for the Associated Press. This persona allowed him access to news conferences and contact with many of the people involved with the cases he investigated. By far his most daring ruse was portraying Charlie Foster, Police Commissioner. The bravado by which he donned this face and entered the very den of the men hunting him was pulp panache at its most colorful.

8 – Because he abhorred deadly force, Agent X armed himself with a collection of gas guns. His suits always were sewn with many hidden pockets in which were hidden chemical pellets used to drug unsuspecting enemies. Even his right shoe contained a tiny air gun that fired a non-lethal dart when a certain pressure was applied to the heel. And as mentioned before, X was a master of empty-handed martial arts.

9 – Among X's many other fantastical abilities were his talent for hypnotizing animals with his gaze or affecting them with a high pitched whistle. Besides his linguistic expertise, X was a genius in cryptanalysis and toxicology. He had also made extensive study of electrical components and his radio equipment was far superior to that of the regular law enforcement agencies. The guy was a veritable one man army if he had to be.

10 – Finally the remaining regular cast member was the honest, hard working, ace of detectives, John Burks, who had made it his personal mission to capture Secret Agent X. Though he could never prove X had ever murdered anyone, Burks automatically suspected X was behind every new crime wave he investigated. In the end he was considered an expert on Agent X by other agencies and often called upon as a consulting figure.

And there you have it, the incredible dossier on one of pulpdom's most enduring heroes.

What is most ironic is that most pulp historians consider Secret Agent X as a low level hero in the pantheon of the great pulp characters. Granted he's not as famous or popular as the mighty trio of the Shadow, Doc Savage and the Spider, but I would argue that he very much deserves to be listed among the second tier of notable crime-busters along with the Avenger, G-8 and Operator 5. Simply by the sheer longevity of his own title and his continued appeal to a majority of veteran pulp enthusiasts. Surely this must stand for something. In fact, Fortier says that no other character in this new series of hero anthologies has generated as much buzz among readers as Secret Agent X. "At the mention of his name, people look up and then smile," he said after attending his first Pulp Con earlier this year in Dayton, Ohio. "I soon realized Secret Agent X still has a very large following among fans."

Thus this grand collection of four brand new, fast paced stories from the files of America's number one defender, the Man of a Thousand Faces. One of the unique challenges it presented was to artist Rob Davis who found himself having to draw a hero whose face was always different. The problem was how to let people know which figure in his dramatic, action scenes was actually the redoubtable hero. He solved that dilemma in a most ingenious fashion, by adding a very small letter X somewhere on the character's body. He leaves it up to the readers to spot the telltale mark of the super spy.

For many, many years the adventures of Secret Agent X thrilled his fans all across the country. Get ready to join their company as the faceless avenger once again leaps into mayhem and action as only he can!

FINIS

PROLOGUE

My friend,

It has been too long since we have spoken. It is for necessary expediency that I hope you will understand I must forego all pleasantries to relay a recent adventure so that you are aware what fate threatens the citizens of my beloved India. Indeed, what fate threatens all humanity with death, and at worst, slavery under the most extreme brutality and degradation ever seen upon the face of the glorious Earth.

I discovered the pall that now hangs over our collective race under the most unassuming circumstances. At the behest of five American adventurers, I found myself visiting a small village deep in Kashmir in the interest of studying certain documents contained in the home of a holy man living there. My American companions and I became aware of an extraordinary mystery.

As you are aware, unique scriptures containing ancient histories are often contained deep in the basements of houses.

Many of these documents are utterly unique in their existence and contents, and there are untold numbers of them. Many have not been read by a living soul in several centuries. The largest portion of these scrolls and their contents remain entirely unknown to the Western world.

Upon arriving at the village riding on our finest Arabian horses, we encountered a plume of what we initially thought to be smoke. We thought nothing of it, supposing a villager engaged in burning an offering to any one of the plethora of Hindu gods. As we got closer, however, we readily noted the earthen tone of the cloud and its lack of the black hue often associated with animal sacrifice.

When we reached our destination, the house of a holy man in the center of the village, we found the structure relocated an indeterminate distance beneath the surface of the Earth. We gathered from the villagers the structure disappeared the night before into a gaping hole now residing in its place. The plume we took as smoke was a cloud of dust that accompanied the deafening sound (so described by the villagers) of the Earth opening its maw to swallow entirely the house, its basement full of scrolls, and the holy man. The cloud diminished overnight with its remnants being what greeted us over the Kashmir sky that morning.

The party, supposing the scrolls could have survived the plunge downward with a minimum of damage, immediately decided upon an investigation into the hole.

It was not an easy descent, my friend, utilizing the mountain climbing equipment we carried with us. Traversing such a treacherous cavern would have proved entirely impossible without the proper tools.

We utilized electric torches to light the way. Adding to our artificial means, luminescent lichen on the walls of the cavern aided in illuminating the cave's interior.

The cavern system we entered amazed us all in its enormity. Every man in our party carried an accomplished history in mountain climbing and cavern exploration, but this construction of gods or devils found no home in any of our previous experiences.

Our first, unexpected loss of a member of our party occurred when Saul Wakely's rope failed and he plunged to the darkness below. Characteristic of brave Wakely's strange humor, he yelled to us as he fell, "Take heart, gentlemen! I have expected my demise for years!" The depth of the cavern was such as to not allow us to hear his body strike anything.

Our expedition might have wisely been cut short right then, but it emboldened our sense of determination and adventure to continue in the memory of our fallen brother. With much effort, we made our way to one of the several ledges on the side of the cavern. Inside the wall next to the ledge, we found a small hole large enough for us to crawl through. Using a mountain climbing device peculiar to Tibetan Sherpas, we unhooked our ropes from high above us and recovered them to continue our travels.

Moving through the hole, we found a smaller cavern leading downward, likely as deep but not so wide. Ledges and outcroppings in the new cavern allowed for easier climbing, and we continued.

Despite the loss of one of the party, we necessarily retained good spirits. After much arduous travel downward, we encountered creatures entirely beyond the description of words. If you will accept an insufficient but expedient description, they appeared as tiny, emaciated corpses. The skin on their faces, if you can call them faces, was pulled taut. The pale, yellow color of their translucent skin allowed display of their skulls beneath. Oh, the horror of such an initial encounter deep below the surface! We faced the undead crawling from their graves!

With the celerity of spiders on their webs, and as easily as a man traverses a boardwalk, the hideous beings came. Their long, thin fingers found handholds where none could be found by the thick hands of a human.

Climbing upward for escape was not possible given the creatures' speed. This fact did not deter Johnson, as stark terror made the usually stolid man lose all reason. As the remainder of the party watched his frenetic climb and pleaded with him to return to the ledge we had found with yet another egress, we barely made out the skeletal figure hanging impossibly from the roof where we had tied off the ropes on sturdy stalactites. With a gleaming knife, the skeleton-man cut Johnson's rope and sent him careening downward as the outcroppings battered him to death. His screams did not last long, and, praise the gods, Johnson's death proved a blessing compared to what shortly befell others in our party.

The creatures offered us no respite or time to contemplate the fine man that Johnson was while yet alive. We hurriedly moved through the small hole into yet another side-cavern. Using all our strength, and some given to us from the gods-know-where, the four of us lifted one of the massive stones littering the floor of our new surroundings and pushed it into the hole we had just entered. Just as we prepared to fill the hole, one of the creatures stuck its head into it. The eerie light from the lichen illuminated the wicked grin of the creature, almost disrupting our resolve as we shoved the rock violently into the hole. From the scratching sounds on the rock, we knew it purchased us only temporary respite.

Please do not judge me harshly for what I will tell you next. The others rushed down the tunnel as the creatures prepared to tumble the rock inward. Quickly taking stock of my surroundings,I discovered a small hole, barely large enough to fit a single man, next to the passage. I knew, given time, it could easily hide and save one of us. One of us, yes, but only one. Call it fear if you will, call it cowardice if you must, but I chose the hole as my salvation and damned each and every man in the remainder of our party. I prayed they might find their own salvation as I slid feet-first into the coffin-like aperture and covered my head and face with dirt.

Like the lowliest worm, I crawled into the hole just in time. The rock tumbled to the cave floor. I watched with one eye. My heart fell as I saw my companions against a wall. The cave was a dead-end. No escape remained to them as the terrifying horde approached. I cannot tell you how horrifying it was that occurred next to such fine men as I shall ever hope to know! Seeing they had trapped the rest, the creatures surrounded them and, they started biting and scratching at them with their bared teeth and needle-like fingers! They tore my companions apart with their bare hands and teeth! Impossibly, I held my urge to vomit. To further their ignominious and painful murders, the skeleton creatures, oh gods!, they started eating them alive! Those screams carry on in my ears even now as an opera of pain!

As I observed this abomination, I wished to stand up and join my friends in death. I wish I had let those abominable creatures tear me asunder, limb from limb, and devour me alive. It would likely be more bearable than the shame that I felt, but I could not move. Eventually, they slaked their inhuman thirst for flesh and moved out of the cavern of death.

I lay there for an interminable time after the skeleton-men finished their gruesome feast. When I finally moved, it was not entirely on my own volition. Hearing a voice coming from behind me in the diminutive hole caused me to rush out of it in stark fear. The voice said, "Please sir, can you help me?"

I picked up a rock as a skeleton-man's face appeared from inside the hole. I meant to throw the rock, but the repetition of the entreaty stayed my hand. "How is it you speak English?" I asked.

The creature crawled from the hole. For the first time, I saw one of them with clarity and with unease rather than terror. His size gave the impression of a pre-pubescent child. His wide-eyes did not have lids of any kind, and his translucent, pallid skin displayed his wiry muscles along with his bones, organs and veins. He wore a diaper to hide his shame, as I noted now the others had as well. Something primal attempted to rise in me and strike the creature down, but I subdued the urge.

"My people live a subterranean existence," he explained. "My name is Levech. I ran away from my people for a time. I lived in the streets of Calcutta, pretending to be a homeless orphan begging for change from the British. I wore dirty clothes to hide my frame, and very few bother to even look at a street urchin. I learned quickly how to speak English from listening. My race has a unique ability to adapt. After some time and further education about humans, I returned to my people. A hatred of mankind runs rampant in our society, but I found humans to be exactly like us. The

potential for good and evil is as inherent in our history as it is in humans.

"*I returned to try to teach my people a way to cooperate with humans and understand them. Unfortunately, my efforts made me a monster by one among us named Pemerach. He hates humans with a passion, and has remarkable powers of persuasion. He sought objects he assured the people would devastate the human race.*" (*I will not here describe the objects lest this message fall into hands other than your own.*)

"*Pemerach discovered where the man lived with these objects. A holy man lived in the village above us, who belonged to a secret society that kept the objects hidden for centuries. Last night, my people excavated under the holy man's house and sent it plunging to the bottom of the abysmal cavern. They are now searching for the objects amongst the ruins.*"

I swallowed, entirely engaged in the creature's narrative. "*Have they found them?*"

He shook his head and reached into his pocket. "*They have not discovered both. I have discovered the one they have not, and both might be vital to the dark designs of Pemerach.*" *Levech held the object out to me.* "*Will you help me, sir, and take it to the outside world? If Pemerach gets a hold of both, your kind is doomed!*" (*I will explain further the dangers when we speak face-to-face, if ever the gods will such a meeting.*)

That is all of the information possible and necessary to relay concerning the uncanny adventure, of which I am sole survivor. The good skeleton-man helped me escape the damnable pit after ensuring his people did not suspect any had survived out of my party. Disguising myself as an indigent wanderer, I managed to travel virtually unmolested in this society with its phobia of untouchables. I made my way to Bombay, and eventually found passage to America. I dropped the object in my possession with a museum display shipment to your great land, although it will take investigation to discover the shipment's exact destination.

To answer one further question you may have with my limited time before departing India, I will tell you this. I did not destroy the object as it may prove vital in fighting the results if the object Pemerach holds is sufficient for his wicked scheme. I come to you, Agent X, because you are the only warrior I can imagine ingenious enough to defeat these unholy designs against my people, and all of mankind!

Yours truly,
Ambassador Casavis

Chapter One
THOSE WITH DEATH'S VISAGE

Betty Dale shifted in her chair. It was not an uncomfortable chair; far from it. In fact, she never experienced a more luxurious piece of furniture in her life. An ornate design complimented the dark wood outlining the red velvet upholstery of the high-backed chair. No, it was not the chair itself that left Ms. Dale struggling for composure.

The man who sat across from her in an identical chair caused her to blush unwittingly with his suave features and charming voice. To say his impeccable gray pinstripe suit fit like a glove insulted the fine tailor work that paled such an analogy. His suit fit him as a coat of fur befitted a lion, and Ambassador Casavis exuded strength from his chair. His offered an easy smile, somehow making Betty feel entirely at ease.

"Miss Dale," the Ambassador said with a foreign accent nearly hypnotic in its naturalness, "Can I offer you something to drink?"

Betty looked at the four large Sikhs standing at attention behind the Ambassador. Thick, naked arms escaped their open shirts and their beards fell thickly around their exposed chests. Their long scimitars reflected the electric light about the room. She repressed a shudder and offered a smile to Casavis. "No, thank you very much. I am here to ask you some questions for the Herald."

The Ambassador opened his hands, indicating his openness to her questions. "I serve at your pleasure, Miss Dale."

"Well," Betty began, "I understand your life is endangered?" She halted as she saw Casavis' smile falter slightly. "Oh, I am so sorry. I did not mean to offend."

Casavis waved his hand dismissively and stood to his feet. "Not at all, Miss Dale." His smile returned as he put his hands behind his back. "I presumed you would ask that question, although it came rather early in the interview. I appreciate your candor. Most reporters would try to skirt the issue, when they knew all along that there was only one question people want to know about. You are a strong woman, and a man of my stature can appreciate that."

It was not often a man made Betty feel something akin to a swoon. In her past experiences with the Ambassador, he had not affected her as strongly as he did tonight. "If you feel this line of questioning too forward…"

Returning to a full smile, Casavis splayed his fingers questioningly. "What is too forward when a man is faced with death at every turn? Indeed, you are very correct, Miss Dale–could I presume to call you by your first name?"

"Of course. My name is Betty."

"Betty," Casavis let it drip off his tongue. "It always reminds me of a flower. Yes, Betty. I live under the mounting threat of death. I can trust no one, and regret placing you in danger just by your presence here."

Betty shook her head. "It's not your fault. I practically demanded this interview, and you were kind enough to agree."

"Kind enough?" Casavis let out a long sigh. "I do not know of kindness any longer. When I became ambassador to America, I did not expect what has been placed, unwelcome, at my doorstep. You see, it is not just my life that is in danger. No, I could easily live with that. Nor is it even the threat of civil war that concerns me. It is the future of my countrymen and all of India. I can trust no one to keep me safe."

Betty wrote the information on her pad as quickly as she could, her pencil scratching across the paper. "This will make for a very good story."

Casavis nodded. "Of course, of course. The Herald readers will be enthralled. Yet, my country continues to be endangered with my life."

"Oh," Betty said. "I did not mean to infer…"

"I am well aware of your good intentions. That is why I agreed to this interview. Now, I will reveal to you what I can reveal to none for fear of my life."

As he said this, one of the guards pulled a slim pistol. Before the other guards could react, the guard with the pistol shot them all with tranquilizer darts. They all three fell to the ground to the tune of Betty's scream. The guard pulled a scimitar from beneath his belt and moved toward Casavis. The Ambassador did not seem surprised. "Hide behind the chair, Betty!" he ordered in a voice distinctly not belonging to Ambassador Casavis. It was a voice only Betty would recognize, and delivered for her recognition. It was the voice of Secret Agent X!

Betty obeyed the orders and slid behind the ornate and substantial chair, though keeping an eye on the action. The guard swung his deadly blade at X, but the agent stepped deftly aside. He grasped the assassin's arm with inhuman speed and dexterity, only to watch as the thickly-muscled arm fell apart like so much wet putty. Beneath the thick muscles, there appeared to be a much thinner man! The bone-thin hand escaped the remains of the counterfeit arm that served as a sheath and delivered a solid blow that belied its emaciated appearance.

The unexpected strength of the blow knocked X backward. The skeletal man crawled from beneath the remains of his erstwhile disguise much as a snake crawls forth from its wasted skin. The figure's translucent, sickly skin pulled tight against his flesh and showed the reddish muscle beneath. As a finale, he tore off the artificial visage to reveal features of a corpse-like face displaying the skull beneath the tight, semi-clear dermal layer. The thin lips of the mouth failed to cover the teeth, leaving a permanent grin. Likewise, the eyelids remained wide and spread away from its fiendish, bloodshot eyes. The idea of a mummified body instantly impressed in X's mind.

With the speed of a tarantula honing in on its prey, the creature headed straight for X. The tiny man thrust himself violently at X, driving the agent toward the tall window behind him. X crashed into the glass and used his strength to avoid the largest pieces. The pair of combatants engaged in a battle of titanic proportions, despite the skeletal figure's apparent lack of physical advantage. The assassin tried

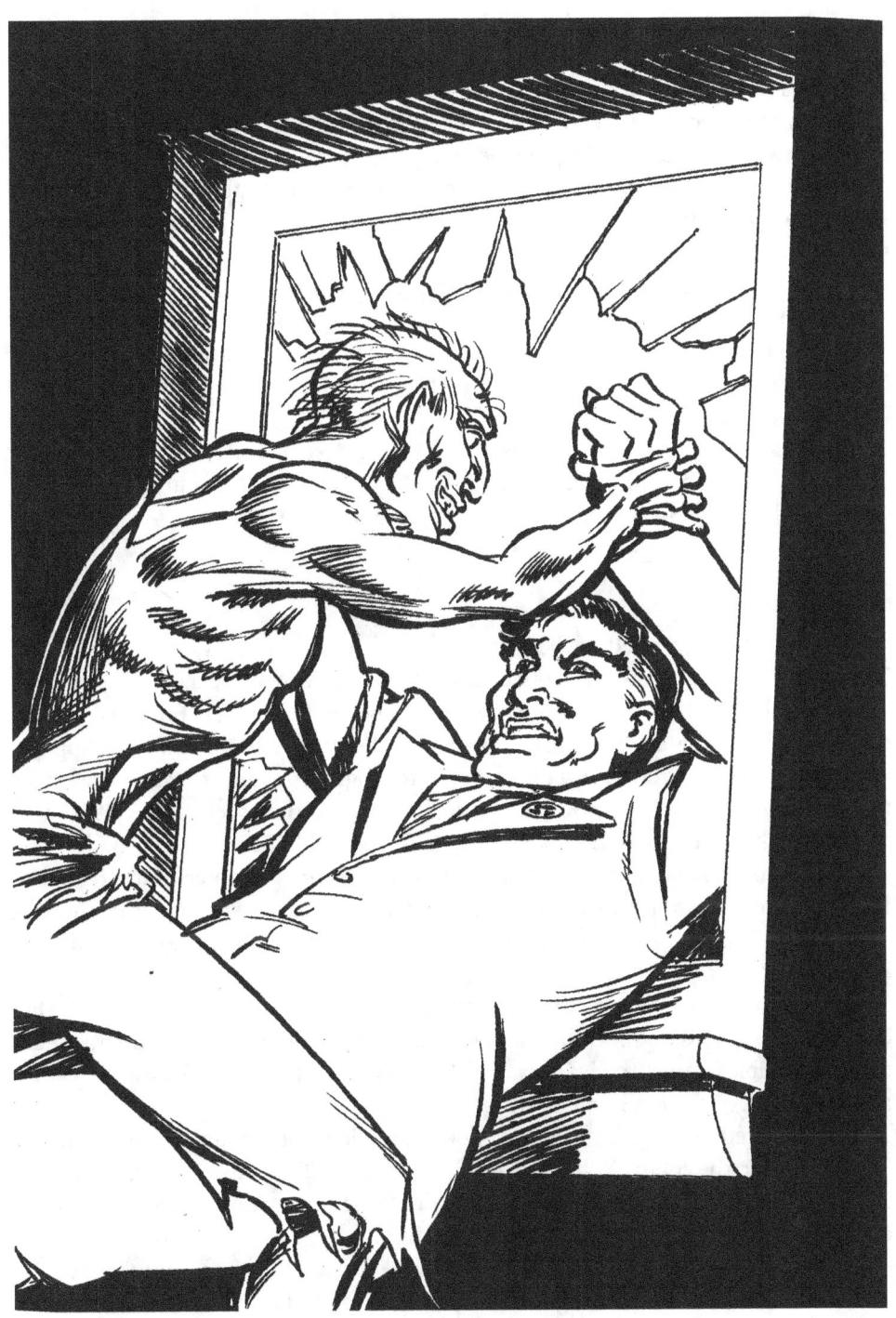

"The assassin tried...to push X out the window."

with all his impressive strength to push X out of the window. They tumbled against the broken glass on the sill, precariously battling on the edge of a five story drop. The assassin picked up a convenient piece of glass and thrust it at X.

Rather than avoiding the makeshift blade, X intentionally took the thrust in his arm and twisted quickly, using the piece of glass buried in his skin and muscle as a convenient lever to send the tiny figure off balance. Though not an intentional effect, the diminutive assassin rolled over the broken glass covering the window sill and out the window.

The assassin grasped the pointed glass remaining in the window sill and hung on. As X rushed to the window to offer his foe salvation, a shot rang out from across the street. The assassin's head exploded into bits of bone, brain, and blood as the limp body began its descent to the ground below. The window across from the one X stood near went dark.

"The shot came from the Kali Arms Hotel," X decided aloud. "The ruse was necessary, Betty. I had to pretend to be the Ambassador to draw out the assassins. Go home. I'm going to find the gunman-if it's not too late."

•••

The apartment emptied of the female reporter. Only Secret Agent X remained. The three body guards still lay comatose on the floor. Moving to a bookcase in the wall, he pulled out a rare and thick volume labeled Tabularis Smaragdus and replaced it in the same spot upside down. The bookshelf slid away, revealing an elevator. X knew the room, usually reserved for dignitaries and those who wished to hide indiscretions. His knowledge of such secrets in the hotels of the city made him a veritable Master of Trapdoors equal to Leroux's Phantom.

X slid into the small elevator and shut the door, leaving the interior utterly dark. He pulled the lever in the side, causing the contraption to move ruggedly downward in bumping, irregular motion. The device proved extremely utilitarian and without elegance or comfort.

With a clunk, the elevator signaled the abrupt end of its descent. Pushing the door open, X spilled out into the shadowed alleyway. After closing the door, which turned invisible against the brick wall as the door resembled seamlessly the rest of the wall, the secret agent rushed into the street.

People stared as the gape-mouthed doorman allowed the regal and unattended figure to enter the lobby. Whispers reached his ears. Time and its essence stood against X, so he moved to the elevator of the lobby before anyone could engage him, or rather Ambassador Casavis, in a conversation.

In a perfect accent attributable to India, X ordered the floor number to the young elevator operator. Though impressive looking, it became clear the teenage operator did not recognize the Ambassador's likeness. The unlikely pair completed the journey in silence, with X delivering a handful of bills as a tip into the grateful and bewildered operator's hands. "If you keep the elevator here for ten minutes," the disguised agent promised, "you will receive more."

Leaving the smiling elevator operator, Secret Agent X rushed down the hallway. He hoped he was not too late to catch the gunman. Arriving at the apartment, X tried the door. He found it unlocked and entered cautiously. With a cursory glance he satisfied himself that the gunman had left the room, although it would certainly require closer examination to be certain.

The room was small, consisting of a bed and a dresser with mirror and a door likely leading to a closet. Although it was clean and comfortable, it did not compare in lavishness to the room directly across the street. The room was empty of anything untoward such as an abandoned rifle or spent shell.

X moved to the most obvious place someone might hide and carefully opened it. Inside stood a skeletal figure nearly identical to the one X faced across the street. It wore a long white robe over its emaciated frame. The steely sinews of its taut muscles showed through its pale skin. Several red sticks of explosives were strapped to its chest with a leather belt. A small timer and wires decorated the deadly device.

It became apparent to the agent that the assassin did not wish to escape. Rather, all useful evidence would be destroyed in the blast and the ensuing incendiary fire. Instantly assessing the situation, X deftly pulled the wires out of the sticks of explosive. His knowledge of explosives made the crude device mere child's play for his keen mind. "None of that now," he admonished. "You will leave a mess for the maid."

The tiny figure's eyes widened impossibly, adding further to his skull-like appearance. His face fell, and the corners of his insufficient mouth bent awkwardly downward. With a snarl, the creature lunged at X.

His previous encounter with one of these men prepared X for its inordinate strength, and he let out a grunt as he avoided the lunge. Out of control and moving fast with momentum, the tiny ghoul ran into the mirror. The gruesome reflection greeted him before he smashed into the silvery glass and shattered it.

Retrieving the rifle from the closet, X spun about to face the creature. As the assassin struggled to its feet and gained its bearings, X pointed the rifle at it. "Give it up," the agent suggested. "There is no need for you to lose your life. I only want to ask you a few questions."

Without hesitation, the skeletal man thrust himself at X again. Agent X expected this, as the small figure showed full preparedness to die by explosives. He'd hoped he could save the poor creature, as its figure engendered pity along with repulsion. It obviously remained on a death-wish. Quickly, X raised the rifle at the figure's head and pulled the trigger. The silenced rifle made the sound of a *whiff*, and the tiny man fell prostrate to the floor.

Dropping the rifle, X rushed to the diminutive man's side and removed the explosives still strapped to his chest. If the agent wanted the creature dead, the drab wallpaper would be stained with new colors. Instead, the bullet merely grazed the skull in a spot where X knew it would render the man unconscious. Tearing some of the white material from the figure's robe, he carefully dressed the wound. He used some of the material to tie the man up as well before examining the remainder of the room.

Returning to the closet, X did a more thorough search than he had previously been allowed. He found a strange case about five-feet long and shaped like a cigar. Carved entirely from a single piece of a dark wood, the craftsmanship proved impressive. Opening its latch, X found a man-shaped indentation where the small man would fit perfectly. A rifle case was nearby, but that did not concern X.

Picking up the small figure, the agent set it gently inside the case and snapped it shut. He lifted it by its handle, surprised at its incredible lightness and well-balanced design. The emaciated man added about ninety pounds, but the weight was not unmanageable for someone of reasonable strength and size. Of course, X realized this meant at least one other conspirator besides the two encountered already, although he suspected many more.

X ran his hand around the outside of the case and felt an interruption in the wood. Under the English words Rabelis Import Company, someone had neatly carved an address, written in an ancient Sanskrit, into the side of the case. Out of the few people familiar with this form of writing, X counted among them. X noted the address in his photographic memory and carried the case into the hallway.

Returning to the elevator, he found the operator waiting patiently for him. "The elevator is here for you, sir," the operator said.

Smiling through his disguise, X pulled a wad of bills out of his pocket with no thought to the denomination and handed it to the young man. "Here you are. Thank you for staying."

The operator shut the door once X got inside and pulled the lever. "Pleased to be of service, sir." He looked at the unusual case X carried, but he didn't think it fitting to ask questions.

Leaving the hotel, Agent X put the case in the trunk of a black sedan waiting nearby. He started the car and pulled away from the curb.

Chapter Two
EYES OF THE MUMMY

The money wasn't great, but Gerald Dake enjoyed his job as night watchman at the International Antiquities Museum. Besides, the girls liked the uniform and it helped his social life. The job was pretty easy, and Gerald had no complaints. The boredom was the real problem for the young man. He job was to watch for untoward activity and to ensure the century-old building did not catch on fire.

He wished he worked for one of the larger museums. There would be more to see and think about. The I.A.M. pretty much received the dregs the bigger museums weren't interested in. A display on Eastern pieces was the newest feature display. The display contained lots of jewelry and papyrus scrolls; not to mention that tiny, creepy mummy in the corner that arrived in the morning shipment. Strangely, the Professor added the mummy to the existing display right away.

Gerald had always supposed mummies only came from Egypt, although he suspected many things he took as truth were erroneous. At any rate, it was the first time Gerald had heard of a mummy from India. Though he found it repulsive, he found it difficult to stop examining it. The black eyes stared out from the yellowed dressings as it leaned in its sarcophagus. The burial case looked quite uninteresting. No gold framing its edges and sides, only some cryptic carvings in the wormed wood. Gerald spent as much time away from the dried and wrapped corpse as the museum's diminutive size could possibly allow.

The museum's more boring, permanent displays showing devices and utensils brought back from Africa, most likely cheap tourist trinkets. Still, Gerald surmised they would impress the average Joe off the street.

Before the museum closed for the day, visitors would incessantly ask the museum's attendant Gina about all the objects. Gina with her bright blue eyes and dark hair would just make up interesting-sounding stories borrowed from an imagination filled with cheap magazine stories and the radio programs. He had to admit, some of the explanations seemed semi-plausible and very exciting. Not unlike Gina herself.

With nothing else to do, Gerald would even make up his own stories to pass the time. There was one particular fetish stick that pleased him to think belonged to Solomon Kane, and a large, scary mask made of wood he supposed to be based on an actual likeness of the chieftain of a bizarre tribe of inhuman, man-eating creatures. Gerald did his walk around the museum with hesitation every time he planned to enter the India display. He prepared to go there when he heard a knock on the front door.

He looked through the glass and saw Professor Fellows, the museum's curator. Since Gerald only worked at night, he knew the professor never came this late at night, and he seemed impatient. Gerald thought he should question Fellows more, but the look on the professor's face forbid. The young guard fumbled with the keys.

A kind, elderly man hunched with the weight of years, Fellows assumed the role of absent-minded and pleasant genius. He wore a black raincoat, a fedora over his graying hair, thick glasses, and an amicable smile; though the smile was conspicuously missing. "Gerald," Fellows exclaimed as he pressed the door open. "Jerry, I mean. No need to stand on formalities. It is imperative that the India display be examined. My apologies for not having my museum I.D. with me, but there is no time to lose!"

"Yes sir!" Gerald replied.

Fellows seemed to consider Gerald for a moment. "You better pull your gun as well," the professor suggested enigmatically.

Gerald obeyed unquestioningly and brandished his weapon. The security guard rushed after Professor Fellows, surprised at the speed and adroitness with the curator's movements. The sense of urgency with which the professor moved belied the scholar's advanced age.

The pair entered the room of bright-colored artifacts. Without hesitation, Fellows headed directly for the mummy's coffin.

"What are you doing?" Gerald demanded, but the professor continued on. Gerald lurched back as Professor Fellows approached the mummy in its coffin, and the mummy sprang to life and leapt at the pair!

Gerald resisted the urge to pull the trigger on his revolver. "What the heck is going on, Professor?" His question went unanswered.

The mummy delivered a powerful and violent blow to Fellows' chest and knocked the professor back. The mummy's wrappings unraveled to show more of the corpse's tight, pallid skin and emaciated figure.

Having never shot at a living creature, let alone a dead one, Gerald breathed deeply and pulled the trigger. The mummy let out a low, burping yelp as the force of the bullet carried it backwards. It smashed into a display case of rare stones and shattered the glass.

It lay still for a moment, although Professor Fellows never stopped moving. His neck taut and his temple reddened from the pressure of his gritted teeth, he rushed at the unmoving figure. Though nervous, Gerald remained ready. The mummy jumped to its feet suddenly before Fellows could reach it. "Holee mackerel!" Gerald exclaimed. "How can we stop it?"

Professor Fellows replied by delivering a rib-compressing punch to the mummy's torso. Blood flew from the bullet wound where Gerald had shot it, and the guard felt a little better. A corpse didn't bleed, he surmised. Whatever the heck else it was, it was alive. He fired another shot.

Although the shot barely missed the mummy, as it and the professor engaged in combat once more, it did find purchase in one of the lines that still fed the museum's antiquated gas lighting.

The gas ignited but did not explode. Instead, it spewed a stream of fire across the room, catching tapestries and mannequins on fire. The fire among dry and delicate artifacts quickly spread its tendrils about the room as the Professor and the mummy grappled in a titanic struggle.

Not daring to fire again, although he saw clearly the damage was done, Gerald rushed over to help the professor. Fellows pushed the mummy away once more with a powerful blow to its jaw. "Shoot it!" the professor demanded. "Shoot it in the head!"

Pulling the trigger, Gerald blinked. When he opened his eyes again, he saw the mummy's head exploding in concert with the echoes of the gunshot. Brain and bone arced through the air. Professor Fellows rushed heedlessly past the falling corpse, headed for the flaming pipe. "Pull the fire alarm, Jerry!" he demanded as he clambered onto a tall display to reach the broken gas pipe.

The red fire alarm lever rested in the wall. Gerald pulled the lever. Instantly, the bell rang with ear-bleeding volume throughout the establishment. He turned his attention back to the professor, struggling to twist the thin pipe closed.

As Gerald watched, the skin from Professor Fellows' face began to melt under the fervent heat of the stream of fire. Gerald rushed over as the professor twisted the metal of the pipe to choke off the rushing gas.

"You're not the professor!" Gerald shouted, pointed his pistol at Fellows. "Who the hell are you?"

The professor shook his head, flinging away his melting skin. "You better believe I'm Professor Fellows," he assured through a gruesomely melted features. "You are not prepared for the truth yet, Gerald and we must escape the flames."

Replying to his last statement, the false wooden wall separating the displays collapsed into a burning pyre, trapping the professor behind its infernal pile of wreckage.

Gerald turned his attention back to the professor. "You're not who you claim you are!" he demanded. "Tell me who you are!"

Professor Fellows nodded, causing the larger portion of his nose slipping away. "We must move, Gerald," he said in a voice not belonging to Fellows. "In the interest of expedience, I will tell you I am an agent working for the government. You have not heard of me; few have heard of Agent X. However, if we work together we can escape this hellish flame. All will be explained with patience Gerald. Are you willing to obey my explicit orders until we are free again?"

Gerald put the pistol back in its holster and nodded. "I'm with you, X. What's your first order?"

"My first order is," X replied. He paused to ensure Gerald's full attention. "Trust me."

Gerald nodded as X, with horrifically distorted facial features, leapt to the floor. "Put your arm over your face and follow me!" he shouted as he clambered expertly through the burning rubble, impossibly avoiding the everywhere-present flames.

With his arm around his mouth and nose, Gerald followed fully and willingly an erstwhile acquaintance who had now been transformed into an utter stranger. A man who mere moments ago he had thought someone else entirely, and a man he had no reason at all to trust except the direst necessity as now existed.

Coughing the smoke out of his lungs and wiping the tears out of his eyes, Gerald kept his eyes on the figure through the haze and blinding flames. X's footsteps released cinders and sparks as he stepped in the debris. Gerald could barely see, but watched his feet. Seemingly miraculously, blackened footsteps remained in the glowing coals where X passed by, leaving a clear pathway for Gerald through the broken and burning material.

Following the clearly-marked path, Gerald came to the other side of the rubble. Though still frightened, he was almost totally worn out when the devilish African mask he had spent so many nights musing about confronted him through a thick cloud of black smoke. "We are almost out of here," the mask informed with X's voice. "Keep your eyes on me. Smoke can become an impenetrable labyrinth very quickly."

"Mister X?" Gerald said tentatively as he followed the figure walking away from him. "Are you wearing a mask?"

"Yes," replied X as the sound of sirens filled the air. "As I must always. Nobody can see my face, or I might not be able to protect my countrymen and serve justice. Since Justice wears blinders it's often better that its enemies are kept in darkness."

Gerald did not respond, but saved his nearly-spent energy to ensure he did not

"...the devlish African mask ...confronted him..."

lose sight of the enigmatic X. Soon, the air improved and the smoke thinned. He watched as X nonchalantly pushed the door open and held it ajar as four firemen with axes rushed past. Gerald stood back as they came through, dragging a long hose between them.

X walked onto the soft grass of the lawn in front of the museum. The sounds of sirens filled the night, and Gerald finally took a deep breath of fresh air. It took him a moment to reflect before he realized Agent X had saved his very life! In the spur of the moment, he trusted the agent, and X did not fail him. He looked up to the figure wearing the strange mask. "X," he started, but the smoke retained in his lungs caused a coughing fit. When he looked up again, there was nothing there but the creepy African mask resting empty on the ground. Secret Agent X had disappeared!

Chapter Three
THE FACE OF X

Red rays of dawn moved through the streets and illuminated the museum with smoke escaping its doors and windows. Rubbing his eyes, Inspector John Burks moved across the museum's lawn. He stopped a fireman pulling a hose toward the truck and showed him his badge. "Inspector Burks," he said tersely. "I'm here to investigate the homicide. Where's the stiff?"

Shrugging, the fireman replied, "A stiff? Yeah, but it might be older than you, gumshoe. Looks to be a mummy, but it's burnt like my wife's meatloaf so you gotta take the kid's word for it. Police shoulda sent out an archaeologist instead of a homicide detective."

Burks pulled a cigarette out of its metal container and put it between his lips. "What kid?"

The fireman pointed to the museum steps where Gerald sat with a blanket over his shoulders. He held onto a steaming cup of coffee with an exhausted, nervous grip. A creepy African mask leaned against his knee. "That one sitting on the steps looking like he just pulled an all-nighter at the coal mine. Name's Gerald Dake, and he's had a hell of a night." Burks yawned. "Where'd he get the coffee?"

"Across the street at the Wild Goose Café. The owner lives above and opened early to make a noise complaint. I'll get you some coffee, but he wants his cup back when you're done."

"Done." Burks nodded. He walked over to Gerald. "Gerald Dake is it? I'm a police detective. I need to ask you a few questions, son."

Gerald nodded wearily. "Go ahead."

"Well, let's start by hearing your version of what happened here last night."

Gerald told the story to Burks, truncating it enough to finish before Burks got the welcome cup of coffee in his hand. "Secret Agent X?" Burks repeated. "I'm not surprised he's involved in this. Hah! An Ambassador goes missing, a little guy looking like your mummy except without a head paints the sidewalk, and a report of bullet holes in a hotel room across the street." Burks slapped his knee with his free hand, careful not to spill his coffee. "Yeah, this has X all over it. Did you see his car or which way he went?"

Gerald shook his head. "I'm sorry I can't help you more. I couldn't describe him, since he looked like Fellows before his face melted, and I couldn't see anything but a mess after that. He wore this mask, but I don't think it'll help."

Burks held his hand out. "Lemme see that." The detective looked at the creepy visage with its sharp teeth and narrow eyes. Burks frowned. He turned it over and dropped the cup of coffee. The cup shattered as a smile crossed his lips. A perfect impression of a face was left by the melted putty of X's disguise. "I'll be damned! This is X's face!" The aging detective gritted his teeth. "I've got the goods on you now, X."

aaa

After leaving the museum, Secret Agent X parked his sleek black sedan by the train yard. Pulling up the back seat of the automobile, he revealed a wardrobe of clothing with uncanny variety, all neatly folded. He removed one of the specially-tailored outfits and hung it on a hanger by the passenger door. He opened another compartment under the passenger's seat to reveal various bottles of makeup, bags of putty, wigs, and sundry items.

Taking off his worn and tattered clothes, he used water from a jug, soap, and a sponge to take a quick bath to remove the smell of smoke. He brushed his teeth and combed his hair. He removed from the specialized disguise kit from his pocket and applied the putty and face paint in appropriate amounts. He pulled and prodded the concoction until he looked quite different. He dressed quickly and smiled into the rear view mirror. He looked perfectly like A.J. Martin, press correspondent, photographer, and one of Secret Agent X's many disguises.

Closing the special compartments again, X opened a secret compartment in the dash to reveal a radio set. He pulled the bullet-shaped microphone out and spoke into it. "Calling station X, calling station X."

X did not wait long for a reply to come from the other end. The Colonial Research Foundation did actual charity work, and was highly beneficial to the community. However, its true purpose was as a front lead by Harvey Bates which disguised X's investigative operations. From inside a room filled with radio equipment and wires disappearing into walls and equipment like so many serpents moving into their dens, Harvey Bates replied. "Station X acknowledging. Awaiting orders." A tall and handsome man, Agent Bates stood at the center of X's operations.

"Report on the condition of our prisoner and the condition of our guest," Agent X ordered into the microphone.

"Our guest is resting comfortably and expressed the agreeability of his surroundings at our last contact. The unusual prisoner you brought is being well cared for in the holding cell, but is entirely uncooperative. It is this agent's opinion that he cannot speak in any language. He is eating food and continues in his pathetic attempts to break down the door, but of course to no avail."

Nodding, X responded with the microphone. "Our guest's information proved quite accurate concerning the events at the museum." It would not do for X or Harvey to use the name of their guest. If the assassins could discover where the real Ambassador Casavis was hidden, his life would be in danger.

"As informed, there was one of the men there, disguised as a mummy. He didn't complete his mission to retrieve the object in the display. In the confusion, I was able to abscond with it unbeknownst to the security guard. Fire destroyed the Indian display, so they will likely think it destroyed. Report on the research into the Rabelis Import Company."

"Rabelis Import Company is very new," Harvey informed. "That address is not for the company, either."

Agent X nodded without anyone to see. "I know. It belongs to the one person I did not expect to be involved in this affair. I can personally guarantee his innocence." X did not elaborate further. "Continue your report."

Harvey cleared his throat. "The address is to a vacant warehouse in Chinatown. The company recently had a shipment of crates arrive from India. Within the shipment, it seems possible at least that these small killers and their nutshell cases could have been shipped."

"I am going to investigate," Secret Agent X replied. "X out."

aaa

Knocking on the door of Gerald Dake's apartment, Betty Dale touched up her blonde hair and straightened her white blouse and matching skirt with a black-rose pattern.

Her smile sparkled with her blue eyes as Gerald opened the door, entirely unprepared to greet a lady. "Excuse me," he said in surprise as his wide-eyes drank in her attractive appearance.

Gerald rushed to the nearby kitchen table and pulled a dingy blue housecoat over his stained undershirt and guard's pants dirty with soot. After leaving the museum, he came home and crashed onto his bed, hardly managing to remove his shirt and jacket before falling onto the mattress like Prometheus thrust violently by the Gods from heaven. "You must excuse me, ma'am. If I'd known you were coming, I could have prepared, Missus…"

Betty offered her hand. "Betty Dale," she replied, before tersely but politely correcting herself. "Miss Dale." Gerald wiped his hand on his thigh and took hers. "I'm a reporter from the Herald, and my boss wanted me to ask you some questions about the museum fire last night."

Gerald ran his hand through his unkempt hair. "Well," he started hesitantly, "I'd like to help, but I really can't tell you much."

"Tell us all you can," said a man's voice as a figure appeared in the hall behind Betty. "We'll decide how big it is."

Though the voice instantly drew a picture in her mind, Betty had to turn away from Gerald lest the young guard see her surprised expression. The middle-aged man's simple grey suit quite matched the rest of his appearance. A sandy complexion decorated his very ordinary features.

"A.J. Martin!" Betty Dale exclaimed, barely managing to keep her voice at a normal volume. Martin was the one alias Betty knew for a fact belonged to Secret Agent X, and she found the plain-looking man highly attractive for that knowledge. "What are you doing here?"

A.J. smiled. "Why, chasing down a filler story for page nine," the reporter replied. Of course, Betty knew it to be a lie. If X came out for an interview with Gerald, something bigger was happening than a simple fire at a small museum!

A.J. brusquely pushed past Gerald and Betty. Testing the old wooden chair for strength first, he sat down and pulled out a pad and pen. "So, what can you tell us about last night Mister Duck?"

"Dake," Gerald replied with slight annoyance. "My last name's Dake."

It looked for a moment as if Martin lost Gerald's cooperation, but Betty sat down at the table and smiled at the young man. "Yes, Gerald Dake. What can you tell us Gerald?"

Gerald smiled back at Betty, overcome with her charms. "Would you mind if I made some coffee while I answer your questions? Last night really took it out of me."

Martin shrugged and offered a hand gesture toward the small apartment's stove. "By all means. I had a rough one too, let me tell you-but I'll let you tell us first."

Gerald told them the story as he lit the wood under the old burner and poured water from a pitcher into the teapot. It didn't take long for the water to boil, and Gerald used a strainer to make the coffee. He offered his guests hot cups of coffee. "Sorry, no cream. I can't keep it cool up here without an icebox."

Martin waved the issue away with his hand. "I take mine black. How about you, Betty?"

"Do you have any sugar Gerald?" Betty asked.

Gerald shook his head. "Sorry."

"That's fine." She smiled and took a sip.

"As I was saying," Gerald continued as he sat down with his coffee. "Professor Fellows fought the mummy…"

Martin shook his head as he wrote it down. "What kind of Boris Karloff story are you telling us, son?"

"It's the God's truth!" Gerald demanded. Betty smiled at him, and he calmed down. "Then, his face melted and he told me he was Secret Agent X."

Martin slammed his notebook shut. "Secret Agent X!? Now I know you're pulling our leg!"

Shaking his head, Gerald replied angrily, "That policeman believed me! Why can't you? Why should I care, you're just a stinking reporter!"

"What policeman?" Betty broke in.

Gerald rubbed his hands together. "That detective, Inspector Burks."

"John Burks? Not much of a detective, if you're asking me," Martin quipped.

Gerald nodded. "Yeah, that's the guy. He took the African mask X wore. He said it had a perfect impression of the agent's face. Between you and me, I hope they don't catch him though. He saved my life."

Betty sat forward. "Where is the mask now?"

"I don't know," Gerald admitted. "Probably at the police station."

Martin let out a howling laugh. "Probably. I wouldn't worry about Burks catching Agent X. The detective's been trying for longer than I've been writing for the rags!"

Betty had never seen A.J. Martin act so rudely, but she recognized the technique. Gerald disliked Martin by now, and was offering information just to be contrary. It was exactly what X wanted, although his initial supposition that the young museum guard knew little to nothing became apparent with every answer. "I'm sure the mask will help the detective."

Martin put a cigarette between his lips and lit it. "Faith in the authorities is a… what is that?"

"What's what?" Betty asked, but muscles steeled beneath X's jacket as he pushed her and Gerald to the ground.

"Get down!" Martin shouted as he shoved the table in front of the two prostrate figures. A grenade crashed through the window just as X joined the pair. Glass flew everywhere as the grenade exploded in a fireball, conjoined with the deafening sound of the explosion. Pieces of shrapnel dug deeply into the table's wooden top, pushing brutally through the thick pine, but lost all velocity and stuck in the soft wood. The pieces remained harmlessly embedded.

"What the heck was that!?" Gerald exclaimed. "I have a deposit on the apartment!" X pulled him down as he started to stand.

"That was a preliminary," he warned. "There's more to come."

"More what," Gerald asked, "and who's sending it?"

"Someone's here to get you, Gerald, and it's not the boogey man. Not literally, anyway. Maybe someone else thinks you know more than you're telling," Martin smiled. "That's why we're here, after all."

Three of the tiny skeleton-men crashed through the door as two more climbed through the window. X pulled a gun from his jacket and shot one of those arriving by the door before another blew into a pipe and struck X in the wrist with a dart and caused him to drop the gun. Taking the dart from his arm, X stood to his feet. The dart made his right arm completely numb as he drove into the fray with the two and drug them to the ground. "Get out of here," he commanded. "Get out of here now!"

Gerald grabbed Betty by the arm and pulled her past the violent tussle and through the door. X swung with his left fist, firmly planting one of the thin creatures on the ground. The two creatures from the window rushed over to help their beleaguered comrades. X felt another dart strike him in the neck, and he fell unconscious.

The remaining skeleton-men abandoned the incapacitated X and followed after Gerald and Betty. The pair ran down the steps and opened the door to the outside. A tall, stately Chinese man barred their way with three skeleton-men standing around him. The man had pleasing facial features and an overall gaunt build. He smiled beneath a long mustache. He wore a long robe of fine, green-colored silk with threads of gold accent throughout. A red dragon design decorated the back of the robe.

Three things happened simultaneously; Betty started to speak as Gerald took a wild swing at the tall man. The third event included the tall figure blowing a cloud of red dust toward the pair. All concluded with Betty and Gerald falling to the ground, unconscious. Heinous laughter accompanied their journey into the world of dreams.

Chapter Four
MARKING X

X awoke in the middle of the floor of the disheveled room. He rubbed his head and cursed softly. Taking a quick survey, it soon became apparent that he was alone. He picked up the dart from the floor and examined it. It was dipped in a type of liquid, some of which remained on the side of the tip. He pocketed it until he could get back to his vehicle and check out what the liquid was that made him numb, but he felt certain that it was not meant to kill.

Using the edge of the table, X stood to his feet. His arm remained numb as did part of his face, but it was little more than an annoyance now. He recovered his gun and put it back in his pocket. As a precaution, he checked his pockets. His makeup kit and all of the ordinary contents remained. He moved to a mirror hanging on the wall. His disguise remained undisturbed. A.J. Martin had not been compromised and could be used again.

X pulled out a piece of paper from his vest pocket. It had the address from the box; written in ancient Sanskrit like the original. He gritted his teeth and crumpled the paper. Either someone had a good deal of hubris, or lacked the proper information. X suspected and hoped for the latter.

X picked up his hat, crumpled during the struggle, and placed it on his head. He shut the door softly as he left the apartment. He had an unscheduled appointment with the fiend behind the complex conspiracy. X smiled. The man would not be prepared, he was certain of that. He had a stop to make first.

Tied to a chair, Gerald sweated under the bright light in the otherwise darkened room with rusting, grey metal as its main construction and decor. He could hear the lapping of water, and the air smelled of the sea. His feet rested in the inch of water covering the floor. Across from him, Betty Dale sat likewise bound to a chair. A gag kept her from speaking, though Gerald's mouth remained free. "Betty!" he whispered. "Are you okay?"

Betty nodded in reply. His gaze moved instantly to the thick metal door as it swung open. Two of the creepy-looking, diminutive skeleton-men dressed in small tuxedos walked through first, followed by the imposing figure of the Chinaman. He cradled in his arms one of the inhuman creatures like some sort of gruesome infant. "I trust you are well rested?"

"Let us outta here!" Gerald demanded.

The man smiled enigmatically. "I have a few questions for you first, Gerald Dake. It concerns an object in the India display at the museum you guarded last night. Apparently, it disappeared from the wreckage. Would you know anything about that?"

"What are you talking about?" Gerald asked, his face twisting into an expression of inquisitive anger. "I wouldn't steal anything!"

The figure smiled. "Of course not, Gerald. Of course not! Still, I have to be certain. As you have no doubt discerned, you are on a ship. A derelict World War One warship named the USS Swainford, to be exact. The Swainford's been decommissioned, and is resting here on the open water to be used for testing a new torpedo. They will begin firing precisely at Noon, which will be..." the man looked at his pocket watch, "...in about three hours. I will be drinking sherry about then. Of course, if you let me know what happened to the object, you can come with me."

"I told you, I don't know what you're talking about!" Gerald's face turned pensive. "Unless..."

The man's eyes narrowed. "Unless what?"

"Unless X took something," Gerald replied. Betty's eyes widened.

"X?" his captor inquired.

"Secret Agent X. He was there last night."

The man's face dropped. "Secret Agent X? That meddler!" He recouped quickly, his smile returning, the man took a deep bow. "Thank you Gerald. I am afraid this will be our final conversation."

Gerald could not control his rage. "What? I don't care if you kill me, but you're not going to kill an innocent woman!" Betty's eyes pleaded.

"I will not kill anyone," the man said with a shrug. "The United States military will send you to a watery grave through an impressive, though ultimately useless display of military prowess. When I recover the missing object from Agent X, all of the world's governments will bow before me. Do not question whether I can recover the stolen artifact. It is a foregone conclusion. Miss Dale has seen too much last night to be allowed to tell anyone, and you have seen much as well. Goodbye, Mister Dake."

The Chinese man shut the metal door behind him and the skeleton-men, producing a metal bang that resounded throughout the hull of the ship. Gerald fell silent as the sound of the slamming door sealed his fate.

After some moments of silence, Gerald heard a knocking sound on the wall. "Hello?" came a female voice, muffled through the wall. "Is anybody there?"

Gerald looked up incredulously. "Hello? We're here! Who are you?"

"My name is Gina," the voice replied weakly. "I work at the International

Antiquities Museum, and Professor Fellows from the museum is here with me. We're tied up. Can you help us?"

Gina! Gerald felt his heart stir. He gritted his teeth. "Gina, it's Gerald-the night watchman. I'm here with newspaper reporter Betty Dale. I don't know if I can help, but I will do everything in my power to try! You and Professor Fellows pray."

"Gerald?" Gina's voice came back. "Do you have anything to help us?"

What did he have? He was entirely incapacitated. Then, it came to him. Perhaps he was left with one tool he could use.

Using the weight of his body, Gerald bounced his chair over to Betty. "If you will excuse me, Miss Dale," he apologized. He moved his mouth toward Betty's face as she cringed and turned away. Using his teeth, Gerald gently bit the gag by her cheek and pulled it down. She spit out the piece of cloth in her mouth and coughed. "Thank you."

"I'm not done yet, Betty," Gerald replied. "I'm going to use my teeth to try and take the ropes off your wrists. Once you're free, you can untie me."

Betty nodded. Leaning his chair forward, Gerald went to work on the ropes around her wrists.

•••

The door to the police laboratory slammed open as Inspector Burks rushed in. A man with thinning gray hair and thick glasses wiped his hands on his once-white lab coat and stared at Burks. "I need you to look at something, Mike," Burks said as he held up the African mask. "I need you to make a plaster casting of the wax inside this."

Mike Lagwell took off his thick glasses and cleaned them with his dirty lab coat. "What is in it the wax?"

Smiling uncontrollably, Burks turned the mask around to display the wax impression inside. "Agent X's real face!" he exclaimed proudly. "Now, I can catch that fiend once and for all!"

Mike shrugged and took the mask from Burks's hands. "It'll take a while, but I can get the impression."

"Come on!" the inspector protested. "It takes like ten minutes in the field to take a cast of a footprint!"

"Yes," Mike agreed, "but there's a chance the wax could be destroyed if I do it wrong. We don't want that now, do we?"

Burks clenched his teeth. "No, we don't want that at all. Take all the time you need, Mike. I've been chasing this slug for so long a little bit longer won't hurt anything. I've got X marked down for a date with justice!"

Chapter Five
WEB OF DEATH

nside the office of a warehouse on the docks, the Chinese man sat at his desk. He contemplated the information garnered from his interrogation of Gerald Dake. He swirled around the tea leaves in a cup sitting by some papers. X! That blasted soul! He'd heard of X in whispers, and even doubted at one point the mysterious man even existed. Now, he could not afford to doubt it. The secret agent would not stand in his way, nor would anyone be strong enough to oppose him!

Without warning, the door opened. Carrying the smell of the ocean with him, a figure wearing a black robe strode in. The hood obscured the face as the figure spoke. "It is your time, usurper! Drop this charade!" it demanded.

The Chinese man smiled coolly at the surprising guest. "Usurper, you say? I am a simple business man."

"No," the figure corrected, "you are a fiend, stealing the identity and property another! You are not Ho Ling!"

The accused Ho Ling stirred his tea and yawned. "If there is evidence of your assertion, present it."

With that, the figure pulled off the hood and dropped the robe to the floor. Ho Ling lost his composure and gasped at the figure's revelation. "You cannot be Ho Ling, for I am Ho Ling!"

The previously-robed figure matched Ho Ling's features behind the desk, although the costumes were slightly different. The seated Ho Ling regained his posture. "It is quite possible that you are the usurper, and here to steal my position. I happen to know that you are in disguise yourself-Agent X!"

The standing Ho Ling did not flinch at the accusation. "You made many mistakes in your plans. Not the least of which was in impersonating Ho Ling. You knew Ho Ling was out of the country, and used one of Ho Ling's warehouses as a shipping address. That is how you were discovered. You did not know until now that Ho Ling never left the country, but felt it advantageous to have people think he had. Now, your game is at an end. I require the location of Miss Betty Dale."

The false Ho Ling stood to his feet. "So, you know I am not Ho Ling. It avails you nothing. How will you get me to agree to tell you where I have hidden Miss Dale?"

X reached in his pocket and retrieved a perfectly round piece of amber with a number of small, round spots inside it. The imposter's eyes widened as he stood to his feet. "I believe this trinket is of interest to you," X replied. "The Stone of Shiva."

Ho Ling nodded. "You are correct, I am in search of this. I knew you would bring it to me, Agent X, but I have no inclination to trade you anything for it. I already have one exactly like it, and it is rightfully to be possessed by me and my people!" The false Ho Ling tore away his face to reveal another beneath. The tiny, skeletal face seemed disproportioned to the rest of the body.

Similar creatures poured through the door and through hidden panels in the walls. Counting with speed and precision, X found thirty six in the room with him, including the defaced Ho Ling. The creatures surrounded X and held the agent's arms against his sides. One of the skeleton-men held a knife threateningly to the agent's throat.

The fake Ho Ling walked over to X and snatched the amber stone from his hand. "Yes, Agent X, I have taken on the identity of Ho Ling. My true name is Pemerach. I used Ho Ling's identity for the power that it wielded, and discard it now that we are so close to victory!

"My people have worked closely with tyrants and despots in the Orient for centuries, entirely hidden and in secret. We live underground, and are a subterranean tribe of what some would consider subhuman creatures. Far from the truth-we are superior to humans! Our diminutive size makes it easy for us to fit into an artificial body of any size, and our strength is prodigious.

"In times long forgotten, the Earth suffered a plague of proportions devastating to humans. Your black plague is nothing to the destruction that occurred in those days. A small insect spread the disease, but our race remained immune. Our people helped develop a way to destroy the insects, and saved mankind-much to our ultimate chagrin. Mankind turned on each other, and included us as part of their chaos."

Holding the stone to the light, Pemerach continued; "Do you see the tiny dots, X? Those are the few remaining eggs of the devastating insect. We saved them out of scientific curiosity, but humans plundered our dwellings and stole the Stone of Shiva from us. We could no longer trust mankind, and went into hiding where they could not reach us-deep in caverns the most adventurous among them would not dare enter. We dispatched all those who dared.

"Eventually, we put on human suits and appeared on the surface again. We could move about with them freely and struck deals with their leaders. Now that I've recovered the Stone of Shiva and the eggs, we can revive the insect and mankind will have to bow to us! Those few humans that survive, of course…well, they will join the fate that your Miss Dale and the young Gerald Dake will meet within the hour."

X laughed. "You really don't think I'd give you the real McCoy, do you? The stone you're holding is a fake!"

Pemerach's face fell as he held the stone up to the light. "You're lying!"

"No," X replied. "Look closely at the eggs." Pemerach did so and saw slight, nearly invisible x-shaped scratches on the circular areas. "You see, Pemerach? You failed to take me by surprise. One of my agents is an expert jeweler. He wanted to leave the business of creating fakes for jewel thieves, and I helped him get out alive. He created this one in less than an hour. Phenomenal, isn't it? The real stone is with Gerald Dake. I hid it in the heel of his shoe."

"It matters not," Pemerach replied in a low breath. "I have another."

"Yes," X nodded, "but you can't be assured that it carries both female and male eggs, can you? The Ambassador tells me that only one stone has both female and male eggs. It would be essentially useless if there was no way to procreate the insects. There is no way you can take that chance, is there?"

The corners of Pemerach's lips quivered. "Damn you, X! Damn you! Kill him!" he commanded the three figures holding X. He waved the remainder of the skeleton-men to follow. "We must retrieve the stone from Mister Dake before the Navy destroys it forever!"

Followed by the odd parade of skeleton-men, Pemerach boarded a sleek yacht floating next to the pier. He started the engine as his comrades crawled onto the craft. In moments, the craft rushed through the waters at an incredible pace.

Inside the office, the skeleton-man holding a knife to the throat of X pulled the weapon across the agent's neck, cutting deeply. Blood spurted copiously from the wound as X fell to his knees.

***

It took precious time and a good deal of pain, but Gerald managed to chew the ropes around Betty's wrists loose. She instantly went to work untying the rest of her ropes, and then freed Gerald. Gerald rushed triumphantly to the next room to rescue Gina and Professor Fellows. He expected it to be an easy rescue, but his expectations were instantly disappointed on sight of Gina and the professor.

"Stay back!" Gina pleaded as she and Fellows sat tied to a chair in the center of a web of bare wire with pieces of dynamite strapped around their chests. Like Betty, Fellows had his mouth gagged so he couldn't speak. "If you touch the electric wires, the explosives will go off!"

"Damn that X!" Gerald exclaimed.

Coming right behind him, Betty said soothingly, "X is on our side, Gerald! This is not his doing!"

"How do I know that!?" he replied. "He pretended to be Fellows and tricked me!"

Gently pulling his face around, Betty looked in Gerald's eyes. "The man who left us here to die was not X. X fights for justice. Trust me on this. If he wanted to kill you, he would have done so last night."

Looking into those deep blue eyes, Gerald could do no less. "I believe you, but it really doesn't matter unless we can save Gina and the professor and somehow escape this doomed ship!"

Betty nodded. "That's for certain, and X is not here to help us!"

Gerald gritted his teeth. "We don't have time to wait for anyone else's help. We're on our own!" He looked at Gina and Fellows inside the wire net. "Gina, can you move over to the professor and pull off his gag? His knowledge may be very helpful, but please be careful of the wires-especially those attached to your bomb!"

"That's easy for you to say," Gina grumbled. "You're not wearing an explosive necklace." Despite this complaint, she carefully began moving her chair over to Fellows. After a few failed attempts, she managed to pull down his gag.

Fellows spit out the cloth stuffed into his mouth. "Gerald! I am glad to see you, son! A man calling himself Pemerach disguised himself as me. He and some strange little men kidnapped me and Gina while they installed a mummy display in the museum in broad daylight, purportedly so they could search for something after the museum closed. They spoke openly and frankly about it as they constructed this unnecessarily elaborate prison around us! We thought they would kill you!"

"Yes," Gerald agreed thoughtfully. "They didn't plan on X."

"X?" Gina asked.

"We'll explain everything later," Betty broke in. "That is, of course, if there is a later! Professor, do you have any idea how to diffuse the wires?"

"Call me Len," Fellows replied. "We have no time for longer names than necessary. My full name is Leonard Jericho Fellows. My mother named me that because…"

"Professor!" Gerald broke in impatiently.

Professor Fellows looked surprised at the admonishing tone, and then embarrassed. "Oh, yes. I apologize. I will get straight to the point. I do have an idea of how to diffuse the bombs." He twisted his head to indicate a car battery behind them. "There is the power source, but it is behind the wires. If Gina or I can get loose, we will be able to pull off one of the connectors. We will have to reach through the wires to do so, and be careful not to touch them while we are pulling off the connection. All this while ensuring we do not cross the wires connected directly to the bombs on our chests!"

Gina used her teeth to untie the Professor's bonds. Fellows wasted no time reciprocating, but went directly toward unhooking the battery. Careful not to cross the wires running to his chest, he carefully moved his hands in between the wires. "Damn this arthritis!"

"Shouldn't you untie me?" Gina asked.

Shaking his head, Fellows went forward. "We don't have time, and I have a better chance of succeeding here than being able to untie you with these hands." He turned momentarily to Gerald and Betty. "You two should get a safe distance away," he suggested. "There's no need for you to be caught in the blast if this fails." His hands shook as they slipped between the deadly wires.

"Shouldn't you at least take off the bombs?" Gerald suggested.

"No," the professor replied, shaking his head. "They might be wired, and it wouldn't make any difference. We can't get out of this death cage Pemerach has designed for us. This is the only chance. You two go; I will watch out for Gina's life."

"But…" Gerald began.

"Go!" the professor commanded.

Betty motioned Gerald to follow, and he reluctantly went with her down the corridor. "We can't get past the wires to help," Betty said. "We'll just have to trust the professor."

As they spoke, thumping sounds began to carry through the hull of the ship. Gerald looked up. "What is that?"

Following Gerald's gaze, Betty grasped his arm. "I don't know!"

The portholes in the rooms dimly lit the area. Farther down the darkened corridor, they could make out a pair of skeleton-men climbing down the metal stairs. "Quick!" Gerald whispered. "Before they see us!" The pair rushed quietly back down the hallway and into the room where the professor and Gina worked to escape with their lives. The feet pattered outside the door, moving past it. They would not be bothered for the moment, but they were far from safe! The elderly professor still endeavored to disengage the battery without touching a wire. His hands shook horribly, and if they touched the wires even lightly, they would all die!

To make matters worse, the footsteps returned. Gerald used the rusted bar for the purpose of locking the door. The tiny skeleton-men stood outside the door and tried to open it. They started banging on the door, violently seeking ingress. Betty bit her knuckle to stifle a scream.

Chapter Six
THE DEATH STONE

Secret Agent X grabbed his throat. His eyes bulged and he fell forward as the three skeleton-men watched his demise; their eternal grins portrayed their lack of emotion by their constancy. They had defeated their fearsome foe!

If the mirthless, smiling faces thought such a thing, circumstances allowed only a short-lived assumption. X leapt to his feet with amazing quickness and attacked the skeleton-man wielding the knife. He easily removed the knife from the surprised creature's hands and punched it in the face. The weird being slid across the floor, bleeding from its unconscious features. A gruesome wound displayed itself across the neck of agent X, but the artificial putty-skin revealed a metal collar beneath. The collar protected X from having his throat violently cut, and offered a few precious moments of surprise he intended to use to their full extent.

To leave only three skeleton-men to dispose of Agent X proved Pemerach's disbelief in X's abilities. Yet another mistake that X would make Pemerach regret.

The two remaining skeleton-men were momentarily taken aback, but after seeing the results of inaction on their comrade, they rushed X in unison.

Neither creature brandished a weapon, though they struck X with great force, sending him against the wooden wall. The wall, weakened by years of exposure to the salt water, splintered and shattered. The three combatants fell on the dock and continued their struggle.

X picked up one of the skeleton-men by the neck and lifted it into the air. The crushing grip of his fingers caused the figure to cease struggling. Swinging the limp figure's body, he struck the remaining skeleton-man as it rushed at him. The tiny man flew backward under the force and splashed in the ocean water.

Dropping the limp figure on the dock, X rushed to a nearby Chinese junk. The unassuming ship seemed tattered and incapable of ocean travel. It was just as X had desired it in his persona as Ho Ling. He moved to the wheel of the ship and struck a hidden button on the handle. A mighty engine roared to life, and the craft moved away from the pier with a speed outperforming its appearance.

Pemerach had taken the fastest-looking vehicle, but the junk would escape suspicion. Despite the speed of the yacht Pemerach took, the junk plied the water at speeds far in excess of most ships its size. When Pemerach chose to impersonate

Ho Ling, he did it without knowing that X was in fact Ho Ling. X did nothing to discourage Pemerach in the assumption that the agent took up the disguise to fowl the villainy of the skeleton-men. Even if Pemerach were to survive this encounter, nothing would suggest that X was in fact Ho Ling anymore than it would suggest he was actually Ambassador Casavis or Professor Fellows.

Striking another hidden button on the wheel, X caused a red light to blink. All of his craft were linked together with finders. The red light would direct X in his search for Ho Ling's other yacht.

Telling Pemerach that Gerald Dake had the real stone was necessary. He would simply follow the skeleton-men leader's signal and effect a rescue of both Gerald and Betty, if possible. The real stone was in the Ambassador's possession, but there was no way to tell if the stone Pemerach had was the one with both female and male eggs in it. It could be that Pemerach had the death stone that could enslave thousands and murder millions!

Pushing the junk to its amazing limits, X followed Pemerach. Given the superior speed to the yacht, he would soon catch up with the vehicle. Pieces of the junk's façade fell into the water, revealing the true, powerful craft beneath. Any smuggler would be proud to own such a boat, but X used it in the interest of justice. He would soon find where Pemerach had taken Betty and Gerald. There, the archenemies would struggle until one defeated the other.

After some time, Agent X saw Ho Ling's yacht moored to an old battleship. X brought the junk next to the yacht, and found it surprisingly deserted. He moved to the cabin. He retrieved a forty-five automatic from a hidden compartment in the floor. He removed his small makeup kit from inside his robe, and took a few moments for a quick reconstruction of his battle-damaged features.

***

"Come out, Mister Dake," Pemerach droned. "There is little time before the Navy destroys this ship, and you have something I want."

Gerald looked over his shoulder at Professor Fellows, feverishly working at disconnecting the battery leading to the bombs. "How much time do we have?" he asked aloud.

Pemerach laughed. "We? I have all the time in the world, Gerald, but you are out of time unless you relinquish the stone to me!"

Gerald had no idea what Pemerach was talking about. "Look, I'll give you what you want if you'll let my friends go."

"Of course!" came the too-quick reply. "Just give me the stone!"

Gerald looked back once more to see the professor smiling. He had diffused the bombs! Without hesitation, Betty rushed over and pulled down the wires. Nothing exploded. She went instantly to work on untying Gina.

Gerald knew that they must still get past Pemerach and his minions. The villain had no intention of letting them escape alive. Gerald tried to think as the other three gathered around him. "Give me a minute, and I'll come out," he promised dishonestly.

At that moment, the very event they had dreaded for hours came as a promise of salvation. A loud explosion rocked the hull of the ship, as the first experimental torpedo struck the vessel.

"Come on!" Gerald shouted as he pulled the large piece of metal barring the door from its holder. He threw the door open without hesitation and shuttled the others past the skeleton-men, who had fallen and not yet recovered from the violent shock.

Pemerach, his face torn to reveal his true skeletal features, looked up as they stepped past and reached for Gerald. The youth swung the metal bar he still carried and struck Pemerach violently across the face, quickly joining the others in their hastened career down the hallway. Gerald had no idea how they would escape, but he vowed to fight up to his last breath in his efforts to rescue them.

•••

As Agent X climbed the rope ladder, it swayed violently as the torpedo struck the ship. He finished his ascension and climbed over the railing. He saw six skeleton-men holding knives as they themselves rose from the deck after the last shock had knocked them off their feet. They looked at him quizzically, confused to see Pemerach climbing onto the deck after seeing him disappear into the battleship.

X's latest disguise was that of Pemerach himself after the villain tore the face off his Ho Ling disguise to reveal to skull beneath. It was a simple matter for X to retain the trappings of Ho Ling, but add the skullish features and a torn neckline around it. Although his skull was larger than Pemerach's, X hoped the confused skeleton-men wouldn't notice. They didn't.

Without further explanation to the skeletal figures, X pulled the forty-five handgun. The skeleton-men realized the ruse and brandished the knives they carried. X fired as the skeleton-men prepared to throw their knives at him. The knives lost direction as another torpedo exploded against the hull and rocked the ship. X maintained his balance and fired upon his assailants, striking one down.

The skeleton-men recovered quickly and rushed at the agent. X fired at the approaching assassins, careful not to waste a single bullet. Four of his bullets felled four of the creatures, but the fifth rushed at X and grappled with the agent.

The force of the creature brought X to the edge of the railing. The uncanny pair toppled over the side. Slamming to the deck of the yacht far below, X struggled to regain his breath. The skeleton-man recovered quickly, and thrust himself upon X. The creature violently dug his fingers into the agent's chest, drawing blood in an attempt to pull out X's ribs. Fighting past the excruciating pain, X managed to bring his gun to bear. The skeleton-man's chest exploded as the bullet ripped it apart.

Pushing the corpse off of him, X scrambled once again up the rope ladder. Another explosion rocked the ship. Water spurted from the damaged hull. The sea-worn craft began to suffer structural failure as X climbed over the railing for a second time.

As he came on deck, he saw Gerald rush out pulling a young girl with him. Right behind the pair, Betty Dale helped Professor Fellows up the stairs. After the quartet cleared away, skeleton-men poured copiously from the opening.

"Gerald!" X shouted, waving the youth over. Gerald saw X in his Pemerach disguise and nearly turned back before recalling the creatures chasing him with a vengeance. "Come on, Gerald-it's your only chance! I'm Agent X!"

"Trust him, Gerald," Betty whispered into his ear. "X is trying to help."

"Go on!" Gerald shouted to the other three. The others rushed by him as he turned to swing the piece of metal he still carried. He violently smashed a pair of oncoming skeleton-men. He turned and followed the others.

Betty reached Agent X first. "Betty, there's a rope ladder on the side leading to a yacht," X explained quickly. "Take the others, and get the yacht away from the ship!" As if to punctuate the statement, the battleship groaned under another torpedo strike.

While Betty helped Gina and Fellows down the rope ladder, Pemerach rushed after Gerald as the youth ran toward X. The leader of the skeleton-men tackled Gerald. "Where is the stone!?" he demanded. "Give it to me, or I'll kill you!"

Rushing at Pemerach, Agent X struck the villain violently across the face with the handle of his pistol. The blow broke the handle off the forty-five, and X discarded the broken device in favor of his fists. Pemerach sprawled across the deck as more skeleton-men continued to emerge from the portal.

"Run Gerald!" X ordered. Gerald obeyed, and Betty guided him to the rope ladder, following him down as the ship rocked again from another explosion.

Gerald slid down the rope ladder, catching Betty at the bottom. Before they hit the deck, Professor Fellows had the engine started and began to move the craft away from the faltering battleship.

Back on deck, Agent X found himself overwhelmed with skeleton-men. Abandoning their bipedal movement in favor of crawling on their hands and legs, they moved with quick, spider-like motions across the deck. X retreated, kicking them away when he could, as another torpedo rocked the ship and it lurched into a skewed position. This made it hard for X to remain upright. He recovered the piece of metal dropped by Gerald and began to cut a swath through the skeleton-men as he moved toward Pemerach again.

Getting to his feet, Pemerach cursed Agent X. "Damn you X! You have ruined our plan, but only for the now!"

Agent X rushed at Pemerach and wrapped his fingers around the skeleton-man's throat. "You have failed, Pemerach!"

As they struggled against each other, another torpedo struck with uncanny violence. A fireball rose into the air, silhouetting the two combatants. Skeleton-men were thrown about the deck, many over the sides. The deck itself caught fire as the explosion knocked aside pieces of metal; sending them whistling through the air as deadly shrapnel.

X dug his fingers into the fiend's throat. "Give it up, Pemerach. It is finished!"

Shaking his head, Pemerach clutched the agent's head and began to press his

"...they struggled against each other..."

thumbs into the eyes of X. "I will never give up, X! I am not finished until my race grinds your bleached bones under our feet!"

"You will cease, NOW!" Agent X replied. He let go his grip on Pemerach's neck and delivered a powerful blow to his foe's neck, crushing his windpipe. Pemerach fell backwards onto the deck, clutching his throat and gasping for air. Seeing their leader felled, the remaining, battered skeleton-men scattered to the temporary refuge offered below deck.

Standing over Pemerach, Agent X addressed him "You had your chance, Pemerach. You could have approached us peacefully, and we could have come to an agreement with your people. The world is changing. Humans are changing. The old solutions are dissolving. We can come to an understanding, no matter how different we are. Unfortunately for you, that mantle will have to be taken up by another of your race; one far superior to yourself."

Pemerach coughed up blood in response, and closed his eyes for good. X rifled the skeleton-man's clothes, and retrieved the Stone of Death. Placing the stone inside his robe, Agent X stood to his feet. Another torpedo struck the ship, rending another huge hole in the nearly destroyed hull. Agent X was knocked off his feet. His head struck the metal deck hard and he struggled to maintain consciousness. In moments, the USS Swainford sank beneath the waves.

EPILOGUE

"**W**ell?" Detective John Burks demanded as he slammed through the door to the lab. "It's taken you two days to get that damned face!"

Looking up at Burks, Mike Lagwell cleaned his glasses and with the edge of his lab coat and smiled. "It was difficult," he admitted. "The facial makeup wanted to adhere to the plaster, but I finally got the face inside the African mask."

"Well," Burks shrugged his coat up on his shoulders. "Show me the damned thing! Let me see the face of Secret Agent X!"

"What's the hurry? He's dead anyway. He was killed in the Swainford incident."

Burks shook his head. "They said he was on the deck of the Swainford when it sunk. No way! X isn't dead-he's too slippery a character for that!"

Mike shrugged. "Okay. All I have to do is take the plaster out of the mask. You will see the face of X for the first time, at the same time I do."

"I'm not interested in the pomp and circumstance! Just take the blasted plaster out of there so I can get on with tracking down this motherless son of a dog!"

Mike put on a heavy glove and pulled a chunk of dry ice out of a covered bucket on the table very carefully. He began to pull the plaster out of the African mask. The face putty remained with the wooden mask as he used the dry ice to freeze it. He pulled the plaster up and looked at it. "Hmmm," he said simply.

"Hmmm?" Burks repeated as he moved around Lagwell, trying to get a look. "Let me see!"

Lagwell held the plaster face up so Burks could see. "That's…" Burks started. "That's impossible! How the hell did he do that?"

"It looks to me like you are Agent X," Lagwell replied. The cast offered features identical to Burks, except for a tiny X across the left cheek. "Identical, except it's smiling. I don't see you do that too often, inspector. Have you been chasing your own tail this whole time, detective?"

"I'm not X, you idiot! That guy suckered me, and he's poking fun at my investigation!"

Mike Lagwell turned to walk out the door. "I do not know how it was done, John. This Agent X is a smart character. I'm going to get some lunch."

"Wait a minute!" Burks objected as he moved after Mike. "You're not going anywhere-Agent!!!" John's face was red as he pulled at Mike's face.

"Ow!" Mike pulled away from Burk, holding his pinched cheek. "Have you gone crazy?"

The angry red in Burks' skin turned to an embarrassed flush. "Oh geez-it really is you!" The detective sat unceremoniously in a nearby chair. "I'm sorry. This Agent X is driving me nuts! It's like an obsession! I hope you'll forgive me."

Mike did not reply. The search for X obsessed Detective Burks life, and Mike saw that. He shoved his hands into the pockets of his lab coat. "It's okay, John. We all get carried away sometimes."

aaa

Gerald carried his cup of coffee as he walked outside to meet the paperboy delivering the morning edition. Since his adventure with X, life had offered a downturn. He lost his job as guard at the museum. Professor Fellows continued to fight for Gerald, but it seemed to be a losing battle with the museum bureaucrats.

Now, he perused the want ads looking for a new job. All this while he mourned a man he had never seen, but had saved his life several times. After Betty's tearful explanation of Secret Agent X's activities for justice, Gerald began to look upon the man with deep admiration.

"Here's your paper mister," the paperboy said as he got off his bike to hand Gerald the thick pile of pulp. Gerald shook his head, removing himself from deep thought.

"Thanks," Gerald replied as the youth pedaled away. Gerald immediately went to the want ads as he strode up the stairs to his apartment. The balancing act between the coffee cup and the floppy newspaper was tenuous at best, but when Gerald got to the want ads, he lost his grip on the cup. It shattered as it hit the stairs and the coffee splashed all over his legs. Gerald failed to take note of the temporary pain from the hot liquid.

Inside the paper, a clean white sheet with typed letters could not fail to catch Gerald's eye. It said simply, "Job for you if you want it." The message was followed by a phone number and an odd signature consisting of a single letter. A large, handwritten 'X' told Gerald where the message originated from.

Rushing upstairs to the pay phone in the hallway, Gerald dialed Betty's number. He had kept it after she'd interviewed him.

"Hello?" Betty's voice came over the phone after a couple of rings.

"Betty!" he said excitedly. "Agent X is alive!"

"Yes!" she replied, her voice filled with excitement. "He's right here with me!"

Gerald was dumbfounded. A male voice came over the phone, replacing Betty's lilting tone. "Gerald, this is X," it said. "You acted with valor and intelligence in your encounter. I know you have fallen out of favor with the museum. If you seek other employment, I can use a young agent."

Gerald thought of the adventure and danger he had so recently faced. The near death, the heat of the flames, and the abuses he faced at the hands of Pemerach's minions. He thought also of the kiss on the cheek he received from Gina, and the pride her bright eyes showed in him. He smiled. "I'll do it!"

THE END

Kevin Noel Olson

The blinking cursor. It's a bit like the half-typed page our literary forbearers had to stare at trying to think of what to type next. Those to be pitied the most are the quill writers failing to come up with what came next as their inkpots went dry. When they asked me for a bio, I frankly found myself staring at the proverbial ink well drying up. I am proud of what I've written, but I'm not an egotist (I'm fairly certain on this point). There is much better material available than anything I've written, but you'll allow that I've read worse. "Aha!" you might well say. "Here comes Mister Olson's massive ego, like the giant Id creature from that *Forbidden Planet* film with Leslie Nielsen!" Let me qualify by saying I've read worse because I've written worse and went back and read it. I must admit, writing about myself doesn't feel entirely right. The funny thing about it all is that I know how the plotline goes. When I was in elementary school, my teacher asked us to write a short story. Mine was a ghost story. When it came back, the teacher had written on the top something to the effect that I had done a good job and should consider a career in writing. While it's never too late to listen, I waited longer than I would have liked. Sure, I was included in a book of high school poetry and had an article and a story in a middle school paper, but I can't say I pursued writing seriously.

For personal enjoyment in college, I began writing a story about The Shadow's brain being put into a cyborg in the future and posting it to the internet. It was a great deal of fun and not too serious. Ron Hanna approached me about being in a pulp magazine he planned to start. I was excited and of course said 'yes'. This started a long run in Secret Sanctum with numerous original characters. This lead to being published in Thriller UK, Ron Hanna's Strange Worlds, Tabloid Purposes III, New Writers of the Purple Page, and Adventure Mystery Tales. Recently, I've published two children's books; Eerey Tocsin in the Cryptoid Zoo and Entopia. Also, a sci-fi farce entitled Buk Bakus in Darn Near the Fiftieth Century and some comic reviews for Enemi magazine. A screenplay for Eerey Tocsin is in the process of becoming a feature film.

So, you might consider whether or not the cursor should have remained in place with this bio, or at least whether or not the ribbon should have run out sooner. I am not qualified to judge. Remember this; all writing is viewed subjectively, and I hope I have not subjected you to anything painful in writing this.

Secret Agents, Skeleton-Men, and Beautiful Women

When Ron Fortier asked if I would be interested in writing a story for him, I was ecstatic. When I was in elementary school, I would stay up late into the night listening to re-broadcasts of old time radio shows. My favorite, if nobody has guessed, was The Shadow. Equally great was the Green Hornet. This was my introduction to the field of pulps, aside from reading many of my favorite writers like Bradbury and Asimov who started in the pulps and a Doc Savage puzzle I had from the 70s movie I never saw. I also read comic books, and any of the 'mask, suits and guns' characters became my favorites. The Shadow comics by Kaluta in the early 70s were fantastic. Going to college in the early 90s, I fell in love with the Green Hornet series from Now Comics, penned by Mr. Fortier. If you question that love of the comic, I can enter as evidence a beautiful Green Hornet print, a rare hardbound graphic novel by Bonus Books, and all the issues from that series purchased when new. This was my introduction to Ron Fortier, and I take it as a marker that this was around the time I started writing myself. What I would like to suggest here is that the Green Hornet series is at least part of what inspired me to write in the first place.

About the same time, I began to read pulp material. Writing for Secret Sanctum set me off on a course of seeking out stories and novels from the era. Lo and behold, I was already more familiar with it than I thought. Nearly all of the great horror and sci fi writers I had read for years wrote for pulps. What struck me instantly was the high-pacing of pulp writing, while sometimes sublimating meaningful messages. Since then, I have always tried to keep the action high when writing pulp material and the message buried deeply in a shallow grave.

When writing Secret Agent X: The Skeleton Men of Calcutta, I tried to maintain a frenetic pacing throughout. I'd like to say I dreamt the skeleton men, and perhaps I did. When I was around four or five, I dreamt I was in a gondola over a ski run. A man sat across from me with a blanket next to him. He pulled the blanket away to reveal a pair of skeletons. Now, please do not drag Freud into the dreams of a child. I would rather not know. It is simply to point out how deeply the image of a skeleton is ingrained into the human consciousness. That, or children shouldn't be allowed to watch scary movies.

Wherever it came from, I started with the concept of these tiny, corpselike men crawling out of human skins they'd used to disguise themselves. The rest of their story hails back to Lovecraft stories such as The Lurking Fear and The Rats in the Walls. A friend asked me once where I came up with ideas for my stories and I told him it wasn't a new story, just another way of telling an older story. You can't tell a new story, but you can tell an old story in a unique way. That actually helped with my writing a lot. After I got away from the sense that everything I wrote needed to be entirely different from everything else ever written, I was fine.

I was not familiar with Secret Agent X when I agreed to write the story, and quickly asked Ron Hanna if he'd get me some material. Mr. X seems to me a combination of qualities you find in The Shadow, The Saint, and a bit of James Bond and Doc Savage. With all these influences, Secret Agent X remains a unique character. There is one particular section of the story where I play with his Shadow side. During the museum altercation, he displays a mystery that felt befitting of his strange personality.

Another thing to overcome is the limits of possibility. I am surprised that anyone is ever convicted of a crime under the mandates of 'beyond a reasonable doubt'. It is difficult to gauge what someone may define as 'reasonable'. When writing pulp, I've found that you have to go to the limits of what is possible and then step only slightly over the line. There's no real conflict and resolution unless the conflict and resolution seem slightly impossible. I wanted to leave people thinking, "X couldn't possibly do that. Could he?" This seems to be the trick of storytelling from ancient times.

Another requirement in tales is usually a beautiful woman who is strong enough to be with the protagonist (gender roles may switch as in Xena, Warrior Princess, but the equation still applies). X's counterpart is Betty Dale. Miss Dale is not only pretty, but intelligent and strong. Often, X comes to her ultimate rescue, but Betty holds her own in the meantime. X realizes their love can never be consummated while he has enemies, and this is the sacrifice he makes for his beliefs. Despite his hopes, ultimately he will always be alone, although Betty may find happiness and love in another. X is no James Bond where any beautiful woman will do, either. Betty is the love of his life, and he would not betray that love.

A couple other things before I stop taking up white space with my well-intentioned ramblings. In the story, I introduced a new person into Secret Agent X's network. The character of Gerald Dake lives his life so genuinely, it seemed impossible that Secret Agent X couldn't see the value in him despite Gerald's youth. Gerald is based on what I personally admire the most in my friends and what I strive to attain in my personal life, and I hope those friends that read this story recognize themselves in the character of Gerald, Betty, and even in Secret Agent X. Also, Mr. Fortier suggested I write the prologue to this story and offered a possible outline, and I am very glad he did. I sincerely hope you enjoyed my story and do not question that you will enjoy the stories by the other writers. I am proud to be included in this volume and humbled that you, gentle reader, have taken the time to enjoy it.

•••

Kevin Noel Olson started writing pulp-style adventure fiction in college, first published in Secret Sanctum Magazine and such anthologies as Adventure Mystery Tales, Tabloid Purposes, and New Writers of the Purple Page. He has ghost written horror and adventure stories, and now is in his second decade as a writer. Recently, he published two children's novels entitled Eerey Tocsin in the Cryptoid Zoo and Entopia, both published by Cornerstone Publishers. After Buk Bakus in Darn Near the Fiftieth Century, his most recent release, he is working on comic book stories and producing a film based on his Eerey Tocsin book with Cryptic Eightball Productions.

Chapter One

It was after ten P.M. when the man approached the exclusive apartment building in the heart of midtown. He appeared to be late in middle age, defined by his puffy jowls, deeply lined face and white hair. He was dressed in an expensive suit and walked with the aid of a cane, displaying a slight limp. Despite the infirmity, the man carried himself with the dignified air of royalty.

As he reached the building's entrance, the man barely acknowledged the doorman. Once inside, he strolled past the elevator and entered the stairwell. As soon as he was alone, the man's limp disappeared and he quickly climbed three flights of stairs. When he reached the sixth floor landing, his breathing was calm, as was his demeanor. He placed a hand on the door and listened for a few seconds, before stepping through.

A large oaken door marked the entrance to the only apartment on the floor. The man stood silently in front of the door for a few seconds, listening. Then he removed a small padded case from an inner pocket. From this he extracted two thin metal rods. After replacing the case, he inserted the rods into the lock on the door and began to gently manipulate them. In less than two minutes he was rewarded with a small metallic click. He put away the tools and opened the door.

A portrait hung in the foyer of the apartment, its image a duplicate of the man who now silently closed the door. He looked at it briefly and touched his own face, as though seeking imperfections.

Secret Agent "X" was confident his disguise would withstand close inspection. He had only been able to study the banker, Augustus Wellington from a distance and from a few grainy newspaper photographs. His preparations had also been rushed. Only the previous afternoon had K-9, the only man to whom "X" was answerable, told him of the suspicions surrounding Wellington. The banker was being honored at a banquet across town, giving "X" this rare opportunity to search Wellington's home. The Agent deposited his walking stick in the umbrella stand near the door.

As "X" entered the main room of the apartment, he saw that the walls were decorated with an odd assortment of art, including paintings from famous lights of the artistic world. Several tribal masks were prominently displayed, as well as a sword on the back wall of the room, hanging above a large window that highlighted the neon glow of the city. The window was framed by thick drapes.

He studied the sword. It was a Japanese katana, a samurai sword, sheathed in an intricately decorated saya. While an interesting trophy for a New York banker, it had no bearing on "X"'s mission.

A large mahogany desk dominated a corner of the large room. The Agent sat down behind it, turned on a lamp and began to search the contents. Barely taking notice of the items on top of the desk, he opened drawers, quickly examining file folders. He withdrew a single sheet of paper. A brief smile crossed his features, contrasting with the dour, older face. It was the smile of a much younger man, a man who had found what he had been seeking. He folded the paper and slipped it into a pocket of his overcoat. He then checked the desk to make certain everything was left exactly as he had found it, before extinguishing the lamp.

He heard the sound at the same moment he stood. A swish of cloth, so quiet any other man would have convinced himself he had imagined it. Quickly turning, "X" barely avoided the blow that had been aimed at his neck.

Metal claws whizzed past his head. A small man dressed entirely in black held the weapon. "X" took note of this even as he instinctively dropped and kicked out with one leg, sweeping his attacker to the floor. The smaller man rolled into a backwards somersault and regained his feet almost immediately.

Secret Agent "X" pushed off from the carpeted floor and leaped into a jiu-jitsu fighting stance. His opponent's eyes widened in surprise. The eyes identified the black-garbed fighter as Asian, possibly Japanese. "X" had spent some time in that island nation prior to the Great War, studying the fighting arts under the famous Tatsuo Shima, instructor to the emperor's personal bodyguards. He'd had a chance to learn a great deal of Japanese martial history under Master Shima, and now those lessons allowed "X" to identify his opponent as a ninja, one of Japan's legendary warrior sects.

The ninja swung the silver claw device toward the Agent's face. It was merely a feint, and the small knife in the ninja's other hand flashed towards "X"'s stomach.

Forced to make an instant decision, "X" allowed the clawed weapon to brush against his face, where it seemingly ripped away a large patch of skin. He grabbed the wrist that controlled the knife, using the smaller man's forward momentum to propel him into the desk.

With a grunt, the oriental man rolled across the desktop to the opposite side. He stared for an instant at his clawed weapon and the strange glob of putty-like substance that clung to the talons.

The Agent touched his cheek where the face-altering makeup had been torn away. He grabbed an ornate letter opener on the desk just as the ninja reached into his tunic and threw something at The Agent's head. It was a shuriken, a small metal throwing star, tipped with razor sharp blades. "X" used the letter opener to slap away the deadly missile. Even as it clattered against the wooden floor, the man in black pulled the katana from the wall and withdrew the blade from its sheath.

The ninja held the blade in front of him, the polished tip reflecting the lights of the city. "Dare?" he said.

It had been a while since "X" had heard the language, but he immediately knew what the ninjas had asked; Who are you?

"Kisei," "X" replied. *Death.*

With a cry of rage, the ninja launched himself onto the desk. Secret Agent "X" stepped back in time to avoid the thrust of the samurai blade.

The ninja leaped forward, swinging the katana toward the Agent's legs. "X" leaped above the blow, landed on his back and rolled toward the window. He

"Who are you?"
"'**Kisei,**'" "X" replied. "Death."

quickly rose to his feet, even as the black-garbed killer approached. "X" wanted to reach his gas gun, hidden beneath the dinner jacket he was wearing. He would prefer to subdue his opponent with non-lethal means, but the Japanese man was making that prospect very unlikely. "X" suddenly wished he still held the walking stick he had used as part of his Wellington disguise.

With another cry, the ninja charged at "X". The Agent grabbed a handful of the thick curtains and used the heavy material to grab the tip of the katana. For an instant, the ninja froze in surprise, and "X" snapped off a powerful punch, putting his shoulder into it. The blow landed in the center of the ninja's face. "X" heard a crunch and felt the other man's nose flatten beneath his fist. With the hand that still held the blade, "X" jerked the sword from the ninja's grasp. It clattered away along the floor. But as "X" struggled to free his hand from the drapery, the ninja launched a kick into the Agent's solar plexus.

The air was forced out of his lungs in a bright blast of pain, and was propelled back into the window. It was like he was watching from a distance, unable to affect what he was seeing. He felt the glass of the window momentarily slow his momentum before it gave way, shattering into a thousand fragments. "X" fell into the night.

* * *

Somehow he managed to hold on to the end of the curtains. The impact of his fall nearly wrenched his shoulder from its socket, but "X" finally got both hands on the thick fabric and braced his feet against he brick wall of the building. The wind cut his skin like the fine blade of the katana. Five floors below, he could hear the late evening traffic move through the heart of the downtown.

"X" drew in a deep breath to counteract the effect of the ninja's kick. He felt a trickle of blood down the back of his neck and counted himself lucky that he hadn't been sliced to ribbons by the glass.

"X" chuckled. He had been in danger many times in his long career. Only a seasoned veteran of the battle against evil could feel fortunate about his circumstances while dangling from a curtain high above a Manhattan street.

The Agent's eyes never left the window frame. He used the strength of his legs and his grip on the curtains to force his body upward, inch by inch, praying that the expensive fabric and its apparatus held firm. He had almost reached the ledge beneath the window when the ninja peered out.

The Japanese fighter wanted to confirm his kill. Instead, he saw his white adversary mere inches below him, dangling from the drapes. The ninja reached for the curtains, either to cut the fabric or shake "X" loose. Instead, "X" grabbed the man's arm, and, with every bit of strength he still possessed, pulled the ninja through the jagged window frame.

As the Japanese man's body cleared the window frame, "X" released his grip. The ninja grabbed at the Agent as he sailed past him, but he was already too far away. The ninja silently fell to the street below.

"X" slowly pulled himself up and carefully climbed through the broken glass that still edged the now-open space.

By the time he was back in Wellington's apartment, "X" could hear the distant sounds of shouts and screams from the street.

He checked his pocket to make certain the paper from Wellington's desk was still there. The Agent knew he didn't have time to fix his disguise or remove it altogether, so he quickly left the apartment and took the stairs down to a service entrance in the rear of the building. Sirens were approaching, but he ignored them. Keeping to the shadows to cover his ruined cheek, "X" walked several blocks to a large roadster parked on a dark corner. Once inside, he opened a drawer concealed beneath the passenger seat. Inside that drawer were enough makeup and disguise accoutrements to make a theater star envious. There was also a mirror with a battery-powered light atop it.

The Agent removed the mirror and turned on it's small but powerful light. With practiced ease he quickly adjusted the mirror and began removing the face of Augustus Wellington. Gradually the real face of Secret Agent X was revealed, a face that only a few living persons had ever seen.

In the light from the mirror the Agent's face looked so young as to almost be called boyish. The nose was straight, the lips full and clenched in an expression of determination. "X" removed the white wig. His own hair was chestnut brown, thick. He carefully took out contact lenses, exposing eyes that were gray in color.

It was a face The Agent seldom saw. Years ago, with the Department of Justice, after his success infiltrating and bringing down several factions of the Chicago mob during prohibition, he had been asked to fake his own death and become a lone wolf, a anonymous operative for the United States government, an agent who could function outside the restrictions of authority and dispense justice as he saw fit. He was given the title Secret Agent "X", along with an unlimited budget. He was answerable to only one man, the shadowy government official known as K-9.

Since then, "X" lived in a lonely world, full of constant danger and isolation. He longed to one day settle down with the woman he loved, but that could never be, not until his work was done. And "X" knew that day might never come. With death his close companion, he also lived with the knowledge that he might not survive his war against crime.

Still, that woman stood beside him, steadfast and loyal, one of the only people in the world to know who he was and what he did.

The Agent sighed, forcing useless thoughts from his mind. He had to concentrate on his current situation. K-9 had suspected that Wellington was funneling money to a group that was affiliated with foreign spies. The presence of the Japanese assassin made that seem very likely. Still, the ninja had tried to kill the man he thought to be Wellington. Did that mean the banker was not part of the conspiracy? Or had Wellington outlived his usefulness to the foreign group?

"X" ran a comb through his hair and put away his supplies in their concealed space. He pulled the sheet of paper from his inner pocket and examined it closely. It was a record of transactions made to something called OOTEF. The notations appeared to be in Wellington's own hand, indicating a secretive arrangement. Whatever OOTEF was, Wellington supplied them with one hundred thousand dollars each month for the past year.

In Europe and Asia, dictators and imperialists were joining forces to spread their web of horror across the globe. Here in the United States the country was bitterly divided over whether to join in the impending conflict or to isolate themselves from what some considered as someone else's troubles. Already spies and saboteurs from these foreign powers were at work in America, spreading fear and discord. If Wellington was involved in such activities, "X" vowed to stop the man.

The Agent stowed the paper away again within his jacket. For now he had to learn all he could about the recent movements of Augustus Wellington and the identity of the assassin in Wellington's apartment.

"X" started the powerful engine in his roadster. Despite its strength, the automobile hardly made a whisper. He slipped it into gear and pulled away from the curb. As soon as he merged with the light traffic, "X" switched on the car's radio. Once the tubes warmed up, he heard the crackle of static interspersed with steady reports from a police dispatcher. One of the features in the Agent's customized automobile was a radio set capable of monitoring the frequencies used by police agencies, allowing "X" to stay abreast of criminal activity, as well as the sometimes-unwelcome presence of the cops.

After he had driven only a few blocks, one particular police call caught his attention.

"All Units, All Units," the dispatcher said in his clipped tones, "proceed to Klondike Club at 59th and Broadway. Possible homicide. Repeat: possible homicide. Shots have been fired. The victim is reported to be banker Augustus Wellington."

Chapter Two

"**T**he victim was shot approximately 10:28 last evening as he left the Klondike Club," the young officer said. He wasn't very tall, probably just barely cleared the department height requirement. He was nervous, too. His voice frequently cracked and he sweated like he was in a sauna. Several of the reporters giggled. It was apparently his first briefing to the media and the kid had been tossed into the lion's den: the hungry members of the New York press corps.

"Are there any questions?" the officer asked.

"Yeah," a gruff voice from the back of the room said. "When do you get out of high school?"

The remark was met with guffaws. The police officer's face reddened.

"I've got a question," someone said. The voice was rich and deep, carrying over the laughter event though the speaker did not seem to be shouting. "A. J. Martin, Associated Press."

The room quieted. All heads turned to look at the man who had spoken. Martin was a shade over six feet tall, dressed in a rumpled suit that had seen better days. A half-smile marked him as a man who didn't take life too seriously. His press card was stuck in the brim of his worn fedora. He carried a long, thin notebook and pencil.

"What was he shot with?" Martin said.

The anxious officer examined the piece of paper he held in shaking hands. "It says, ah, a .32. The doorman at the club and, ah, Mr. Wellington's chauffeur agree the shots came from a dark sedan that drove by as Mr. Wellington left the club." The rookie officer smiled, proud of the way he'd handled the dissemination of information. Emboldened, he asked, "Any more questions?"

"What time's the next boy scout meeting?" someone shouted. There was more laughter.

"Th-that's all," the young man said. He stepped from behind the podium and exited through a door in the back of the room. The reporters filed out of the small room to the lobby of police headquarters, some still chortling.

The man who called himself A. J. Martin felt bad for the kid, though he knew the experience would serve make him stronger. The rookie would have a better grasp on things next time. If he had the chance, the reporter would seek out the young officer and compliment him.

As he neared the door, a small hand took him by the arm.

"I heard you were the man to give me the real scoop," a soft feminine voice said.

The reporter turned, and his heart beat faster.

The woman could have stepped off the cover of a movie magazine, with her luxurious blonde hair and blue eyes. She was quite petite, yet perfectly proportioned. Though she wore a conservative business dress, every male eye in the building stole a covert glance at her—some less than covert. But Betty Dale's heart belonged to only one man.

Betty Dale was also the only person in police headquarters who knew that reporter A. J. Martin was merely another disguise employed by Secret Agent "X".

"I thought you had your own sources," "X" said. He grinned at the beautiful young woman.

"I'm always open to new avenues of information," she said, returning his smile. Her lips looked wet and inviting. They parted slightly, revealing teeth as white as polished ivory.

Betty's father had been a police captain, working out of this very building. The Agent had known Captain Dale and had respected his character. After he was tragically killed in the line of duty, "X" helped Betty finish her education and aided her in landing a job with The New York Herald, where her natural talents quickly propelled her through the ranks. She was now one of the paper's most honored journalists.

Along the way, the Agent lost his heart to the gorgeous and spunky reporter.

However, they both knew that a conventional romance and marriage were not possible while Secret Agent "X" still waged his war against the underworld. Betty was willing to wait, and for that, the Agent would be eternally grateful.

When the room had emptied, Betty stepped closer to "X" and whispered, "Were you there when Wellington bought it?"

The Agent shook his head. "I was cross town, in Wellington's home, where I met another of the banker's uninvited guests."

Betty's eyes widened. "I saw something this morning about a dead man who fell from that building. Was that – ?"

"X" nodded.

"What's going on?" Betty said.

"Wellington was mixed up in something, that's for sure," "X" said. "But it's not what I originally thought it was. I have to find out more."

"How?"

The Agent raised his eyebrows, the cocky half-smile back on his face. He was once again A. J. Martin. "Let's go upstairs and see what shakes out."

"Oh, no," Betty said. "You know how much he hates reporters to drop in."

"The commissioner may not think much of A. J. Martin, but he loves the daughter of his old friend Captain Dale," "X" said.

Before Betty could reply, a young man burst into the room, as breathless as if he had run the ten blocks from the Herald building. Which he probably had. "X" recognized the lad as one of the interns at Betty's paper.

"Miss Dale, Mr. Dent wants you to call him immediately," the kid said, between gasps.

Betty sighed. "My editor is so dramatic. You go on up. I'll join you as soon as I can."

She left to find a pay phone and the young intern followed her like a love-struck puppy.

"X" made his way to the staircase and climbed the three floors to the office of Police Commissioner Charlie Foster.

When he stepped out of the third floor stairwell, he saw that the hallway outside Foster's office was crowded.

Two men in uniform stood against the wall next to the office. An older cop who was assigned as chauffeur for the mayor stood by the door. He nodded to the man he thought of as reporter A. J. Martin. "How's it goin'?" he said.

"Fine, Sgt. Murphy," "X" said. "You threw a party and nobody told me?"

"This is a high level meeting, Martin," the other uniformed man said. "No press allowed."

Lieutenant McAllister was one of the commissioner's top aides, a shameless political opportunist. Most of the other members of the New York Police Department believed McAllister would sell out his own mother, not to mention other cops, if it would advance his career.

Murphy rolled his eyes at his colleague's comment. "X" noticed that Murphy was careful to do this when McAllister was looking the other way.

"The mayor asked me to drop by," The Agent said. "He wants to consult with me."

"I didn't tell you Mayor Grauman was here," McAllister said. "How did you find out?"

"X" smiled and nodded in the direction of the mayor's chauffeur. Sgt. Murphy put a hand over his mouth to stifle his laughter.

McAllister grimaced. He turned to the older cop and said, "Sergeant, is there anything you would like to say to me?"

Murphy cleared his throat. His face and neck were crimson from the effort required to keep his face expressionless. "No sir, Lieutenant. I have nothing to say that you'd care to hear, sir."

"Nothing that I'd 'care' to hear? Listen, you grizzled –"

"Mac! Get in here!" a voice bellowed from within the office.

McAllister took a second to glare at Murphy, then the Agent, before he turned and stormed into the commissioner's office.

"A charming fellow," "X" said.

"I'd like to catch him down at my neighborhood bar on a Saturday night," the grizzled veteran replied. "I'd show him some charm."

"X" chuckled.

"You're going in there, ain't you?" Murphy said.

"The people have a right to know, Sarge."

"Yeah, I know," Murphy said. "Say, when Hizzoner orders me to beat the stuffing out of you and haul you away, you won't hold it against me, will you?"

"Are you kidding? I'd consider it a privilege," the Agent said.

Murphy shook his head. "You kill me, Martin. You oughta have your own comedy show on the radio."

"Thanks, Sarge," "X" said. He stepped into the office.

It was a pretty spare office for such a high ranking official, but Charlie Foster was a no-nonsense man who had worked his way up from patrolman to the most powerful police office in the country. He'd made it his goal to eliminate corruption on the force and had said many times that there was no room for frills while he was on the job. The desk was not large. The surface of it was clean, save for a few family photographs, a testament to its owner's penchant for organization.

Foster was tall, a handsome man with a well-manicured gray mustache and a ruddy complexion that bespoke of health and a vigorous life spent outdoors.

Seated across from Foster's desk was the mayor. Grauman was a short, stout man. At first, he gave the impression of softness, fat. But the mayor was built like a fireplug, with the thick arms and shoulders of a wrestler, which he had been in college. Lieutenant McAllister stood next to the commissioner. Another man leaned against the wall, someone "X" would have preferred to avoid.

Inspector John Burks was the top detective on the force, a powerhouse when it came to crime solving. He was also a man dedicated to the capture of Secret Agent "X", whom he believed to be the vilest of criminal masterminds. Burks was a force of nature, a tall, tireless dynamo whose unflagging energy contrasted sharply with his full head of white hair.

"What I need, Charlie, is your word that this will be your top priority," the mayor said as "X" walked into the room.

"Of course, sir," Foster said.

"Hey, who let the rat in?" Burks said. He stood ramrod straight, fists clenched at his sides.

"What?" Foster said. "Oh. Martin. What the hell do you want?"

"An exclusive," "X" said. "The word from the inside. My readers want to know."

"The hell they do," Foster said. He stood up.

"Allow me, Charlie," Burks said. He stepped toward the Agent.

Inwardly, "X" sighed. If Burks tried to throw him out, the Agent would have to play along. It wouldn't do for the ace New York detective to get licked by a mere reporter.

"Hold on," Mayor Grauman said. He had turned in his chair to look at "X" "You're that newspaperman from the Associated Press."

"That's right, Your Honor. We've met a few times." "X" flashed his best Martin smile.

"What do you know about this Wellington mess?"

"Mr. Mayor, please…" the commissioner said.

Grauman held up a hand. "I want to hear what he says. These people have their sources. And Wellington was a friend of mine."

"Then you won't like this," the Agent said. "There's a rumor that Wellington was involved in some way with foreign governments."

"Rubbish," the mayor said.

"Where did you hear that?" Foster asked.

"I can't say," "X" replied.

"Mr. Mayor, if that was the case, I would know that, I assure you," Foster said.

"Really?" "X" said.

Grauman swore. His face was flushed with anger. He wanted to take a swing at "X", that was certain. Finally, he sputtered out, "You're trying to besmirch the reputation of a fine man who cannot defend himself."

"X" shook his head. "I wish it was that simple. Chief, you know Gibson at the FBI office?"

"Of course," Foster said impatiently.

"Get him on the phone and run this by him." "X" nodded at Burks, who glared back. "I'll wait outside."

The Agent strolled into the hallway, where Sergeant Murphy stood smoking a cigarette.

"You have a way with people, don't you?" Murphy said.

"People love me," "X" said. "It's a gift."

"Want a smoke?"

"Nah," the Agent said. "I'll be back in there in a minute."

Sure enough, sixty seconds later the white-haired detective leaned out of the office long enough to say, "Get in here, you hack."

"X" winked at Sergeant Murphy, and returned to the commissioner's sanctum.

All the men were now standing. Commissioner Foster scowled at "X".

"The regional director of the FBI in New York wants me to ask how you obtained secret information about Augustus Wellington."

The Agent smiled. His information had been confirmed. "First, let me ask you something."

"What?" Foster said. "You're in no position to—"

The mayor interrupted. "Let him speak, Charlie. I want to hear it."

"Who benefits from Wellington's death?" the Agent asked.

Mayor Grauman pressed his lips together for a few seconds. At last, he said, "I spoke to Gus's lawyer this morning. He had a revised will hand delivered to the attorney by messenger yesterday evening. He's leaving his fortune to some organization called The Order of the Eternal Flame."

The Order of the Eternal Flame. "X" remembered the ledger entries from Wellington's office. One hundred thousand dollars each month had been given to something called OOTEF.

"Was it legitimate?" "X" said.

"The will? Yes, the lawyer said it was in Gus's own handwriting. I can't believe he would leave everything to some lunatic group."

Burks spoke up. "The Order of the Eternal Flame is a crazy religious group headed up by some Jap."

Now it was the Agent's turn to frown.

"What is it?" Grauman said.

"There was a Japanese guy who fell from Wellington's apartment last night," "X" said.

"How do you know that?" Commissioner Foster demanded.

"Chief, when a guy dressed in black falls in the middle of a New York street people are going to talk."

The mayor shook his head. "I can't believe this mess. These accusations against Gus and that statement from the door man…"

"What's this?" "X" said.

"Tell him," Grauman said.

Burks made a noise of displeasure. "The same time Wellington got popped at the Klondike Club, the doorman at his building says Wellington had just come home."

"The man must have been drinking," the commissioner said.

"I don't think so," Burks said.

Commissioner Foster said, "Here we go."

"Listen, sir, you know I'm right."

"What is it?" Grauman asked.

"X" spoke up. "The inspector believes every unexplained occurrence in the city is the fault of a mystery man."

"Secret Agent "X" isn't make believe, you two-bit ink slinger," Burks said. "He's as real as you or me."

"Speak for yourself," the Agent said.

Burks ignored him. "He can make him self up to look like anybody. If the door man saw Wellington last night, I'd bet my next paycheck it was really "X"."

Grauman turned to Foster. "This man – this "X" – really exists?"

Foster sighed. "It's possible, sir. Though there's no evidence he's a murderer."

"We just haven't found it yet," Burks said. "But if the G-men think Wellington was some kind of spy or something, then Secret Agent "X" is behind it. I guarantee that."

Normally, the rambling of Burks would amuse the Agent, but at the moment he was puzzled by Wellington's behavior. Why would the wealthy banker leave everything to a fringe cult?

A flash of activity at the door broke the Agent's train of thought.

Lovely Betty Dale ran into the room. She stood with her hand on her chest, trying to catch her breath.

"Betty?" Foster said. "By god, you're a sight." But he had an affectionate, if bewildered, expression on his face.

When she could finally speak, she said, "Hi, Uncle Charlie." She turned to "X". "A note was just delivered to the Herald offices. Some group calling itself The Order of the Eternal Flame is holding a special meeting tonight."

"For what purpose?" "X" said.

"Don't think I'm crazy," Betty said. "I'm just reporting the news."

"Get on with it, young lady," the mayor said.

"The Order of the Eternal Flame has invited the public to witness the resurrection of the dead body of Augustus Wellington."

"Holy Hannah!" Burks exclaimed.

For a moment no one spoke.

Secret Agent "X" broke the silence. "Did anyone examine the body of Wellington?"

"I saw it myself," Foster said. "There's no doubt he was dead."

"What a crock," Burks said. "This has "X"'s fingerprints all over it."

"That again?" Betty Dale scoffed. "Please."

Burks narrowed his eyes. He had long suspected a link between the gorgeous young reporter and "X", though he could never prove it.

'Well, this has been fun," the Agent said, "but I have a story to file."

"Hold on," he commissioner demanded. "You never told us where you heard the rumor about Wellington."

"Oh, that," "X" said. He pointed at Inspector Burks. "He told me."

Betty laughed.

"That's a goddamned lie," Burks said.

"Come on, toots," "X" said. He took Betty by the hand and made a hasty exit.

In the stairwell, the jaunty demeanor of A. J. Martin was replaced by the serious bearing of Secret Agent "X". "I have to find out more about The Order of the Eternal Flame," he said.

"Darling, how can I help?" Betty squeezed his arm affectionately.

"Call on the FBI. Ask about the rumor tying Wellington to unfriendly foreign powers. Maybe we can slow this thing by shining a little sunlight on it."

"What will you do?" Betty said.

"I have to make a call, then make plans to go to the big show tonight."

"You don't think this group can actually raise the dead, do you?" "X" felt the girl shiver against him. They had faced many odd and usual events together, and the Agent knew that all of it served to only make their bond closer.

"Of course not," "X" said. "It will be some sort of trickery. Still, I have to find out who these people are and what ties they may have to any group that may do harm to this country."

"Will you go tonight as Martin?" Betty said.

The Agent offered her a grim smile. "No, I think I should go as our wealthy friend."

aaa

Moments later, reporter A. J. Martin strolled into a diner near police headquarters. The place was frequented mainly by reporters. He waved to a few he recognized, then he went to the phone booth, placed a call and spoke quietly for a couple of minutes. Afterward, he took a seat at the counter and ordered a slice of pie and a glass of milk. Martin ate and chatted jovially with other patrons for nearly forty minutes until the pay phone rang.

A large fellow who covered sports for the Post answered it. "Hey Martin, it's for you." Martin smiled and waved his thanks. He slid into the booth and closed the door behind him.

"Bates?" "X" said. His natural voice was deep and resonant. It could issue commands men would follow without question.

"It's me, boss. I've got something for you."

Harvey Bates was one of the Agent's most dependable and trusted operative. Bates ran an efficient organization with worldwide connections, dedicated solely to the collection of information, information that might one day be needed by Secret Agent "X". The Agent solely and handsomely funded Bates' efforts.

"Go ahead," "X" said.

"The Order of the Eternal Flame first showed up about a year ago in Los Angeles. They next spread to Chicago. About three months ago they hit New York. They rented the old Gibson Theater downtown. The head guy is Japanese. Name of Professor Sato. It doesn't look like a Jap outfit, though. The board of directors is made of mostly Americans. Rich guys."

Bates read the names to "X". All were well known businessmen in the country. Many were personal acquaintances of one of the Agent's other identities.

"What do you have on Sato?" "X" said.

Bates hesitated. He was a man who was proud of his work and he hated to disappoint his employer. "Nothing yet. I'm waiting on my contacts in Japan. Sorry, boss."

The Agent chuckled. "Don't be so hard on yourself, Harvey. That's an excellent job for 45 minutes' work. Keep at it. I'll be in touch."

"X" hung up the phone and stepped from the booth. As he did, he was facing the front window of the diner.

A tall man stood on the street. There was nothing remarkable about him, but something triggered an alarm in the Agent's mind. The man was middle-aged, with thinning hair and a goatee. The only thing unusual about the fellow was the way he studied "X".

The man abruptly turned and walked quickly away.

"X" stared after him. It was something about the man's posture or his walk that tugged at the Agent's memories. Though the man was completely unfamiliar, "X" was sure he had seen him before.

Chapter Three

The line of limousines in front of the Gibson Theater stretched around the block, a sign that the rich and famous were anxious to witness New York's latest entertainment: the resurrection of a dead man.

When it was time to disembark from his vehicle, a valet opened the large car's door and Elisha Pond stepped to the sidewalk.

Almost immediately, he noticed a number of young, well-dressed men and women of Asiatic origin circulating through the crowd, smiling and speaking to the white arrivals. One of the Asians stepped up to Pond. The wealthy man caught a glimpse of his own face in a newspaper photograph before the young man casually hid it behind his back.

"Mr. Pond?" the man said, in an accent that hardly bore a trace of its Japanese ancestry.

Pond nodded.

"Ah, I wish to welcome you to tonight's ceremony, on behalf of Professor Sato and The Order of the Eternal Flame."

"Thank you," Pond said. "I hope it proves to be as intriguing as it promises to be."

"I don't think you shall be disappointed," the young man said.

"Will I get an opportunity to meet Professor Sato?"

"I'm certain that can be arranged," he said.

"Mr. Pond?" a voice said. "Do you have a moment for the press?"

The lithe, radiant form of Betty Dale stepped between the Asian man and the millionaire. The young man looked disgusted.

"Please excuse me. I have details to see to," he said. He walked away and was quickly lost in the growing crowd outside the theater.

Betty Dale removed a notebook and pen from her purse. She smiled at Pond, as she began to scribble on the paper.

"Just act as if you are interviewing me," Pond said.

"Imagine the story I could write if I really wanted to spill the beans," Betty whispered.

Pond smiled, for he knew without an instant's doubt that Betty Dale would give her own life rather than reveal that Elisa Pond was merely another disguise employed by Secret Agent "X".

"I won't be the story tonight," "X" said. He nodded toward the busy curb, where a cab disgorged a harried-looking middle-aged man carrying a battered valise.

"That's Dr. Adams," Betty said. "From Mercy Hospital."

The doctor stared nervously around for a moment, then spotted someone he seemed to recognize. He moved into the crowd. The Agent saw the same young Asian man who had spoken to him earlier greet Dr. Adams and escort him inside.

"He's here to verify," "X" said.

"Verify what?"

The Agent smiled. "The resurrection."

A siren, growing in volume, drew the attention of the crowd. A white ambulance rounded the corner and turned down the alley next to the theater.

"The guest of honor arrives," Betty said.

"It's time to see the miracle," The Agent said.

* *

The interior of the Gibson Theater was impressive, if a bit worn. Finely detailed artwork and gold light fixtures on the wall, along with an elegant red velvet curtain across the stage, spoke of an earlier age of opulence. The seats were solid, though the fabric covering them was threadbare in places. No one seemed to mind. There was an air of excitement in the place, a mood of barely-contained exhilaration, as though the attendees were children waiting for the opening of a new amusement park. The crowd seemed to be evenly divided between the rich and famous and a large contingent of press. "X" saw many reporters he recognized from his time as A. J. Martin. Betty Dale stood to the side of the stage speaking with a few other newspaper people. Several newsreel cameras were set up along the back wall of theater and in the balcony.

There were no traditional ushers working the Gibson that night. Instead, more of the smartly dressed young Asian men – likely Japanese – escorted the guests to their seats. One such fellow directed "X" to a seat in the second row, all the while telling "X" how honored Professor Sato was to have Elisa Pond in attendance. He was seated between a well-known munitions manufacturer and a famous radio newsreader.

A murmur passed through the crowd as the lights were rapidly switched off and on three times. The show was about to begin. Those who were still making their way to seats hurried, and the crowd grew quiet. The lights dimmed for a final time, and then a spotlight came to life, shining upon the scarlet curtain in front of the stage. With the lights down, and the only illumination from the single spot, the curtain seemed grander somehow, as if the Gibson Theater had suddenly shrugged off the years. "X" could feel the anticipation of those seated nearest him. Though he did not believe in the supernatural, even The Agent found he was very interested to see what unfolded upon that stage.

The curtains parted and a small Asian man stepped through the opening. He stood silently until the curtain rustled closed behind hum. He was dressed in a simple black tuxedo and wore a cloak around his shoulders. His hair was black and his face unlined, making it hard for "X" to determine his age.

"Greetings," he said in perfect English. He didn't appear to raise his voice, yet the word carried easily and clearly to all corners of the auditorium. "I am Professor Sato. On behalf of The Order of the Eternal Flame, I welcome you."

A few members of the audience clapped politely.

Once the applause died down, Sato continued.

"We are part of an ancient group, founded centuries ago in Japan, to study the mysteries of life and death. It is only recently that we decided to share our knowledge with the rest of the world, in the hope of bringing the nations of Earth closer together. We hope that tonight's demonstration of our methods will convince you of our sincerity."

Sato paused for a few seconds.

"The fear of death," he continued, "cripples our society. Holds us back from greater accomplishments. The world could be a utopia if we could leave the fear behind us. Tonight The Order of the Eternal Flame will demonstrate that death no longer must be feared."

He bowed slightly and slipped back through the curtain. The spotlight went out. A few members of the audience clapped again. Others whispered to those next to them. "X" even heard a few peals of skeptical laughter.

The radio man next to the Agent said, "I've heard these Orientals know a lot about mysticism. They have secrets they've never shared with the Western world."

"X" made a non-committal grunt. The radio man sniffed indignantly and turned back to his companion.

The spotlight came to life again, just in time to illuminate the opening of the curtain. As the stage was revealed, the crowd could see a long table in the center of the stage, draped with the rising sun design of the Japanese flag. At each end of the table stood a golden brazier in which some substance produced tendrils of gray smoke. From somewhere offstage, the music from a flute-like instrument wafted across the now-silent crowd.

For perhaps three minutes, nothing happened. Then, accompanied by a gasp from the audience two Japanese men, dressed in black robes, carried a simple wooden box across the stage and placed next to the table. The box was long enough to hold a human body. Indeed, second later the two men opened the lid of the odd casket and removed a figure covered by a white sheet, placing it on the table. The two Japanese then moved to opposite sides of the table and stood in silence.

The strange music grew louder and, at the same time, the smoke produced from the two braziers thickened and covered the stage like a fog.

After a moment the smoke thinned out. Most of the audience gasped again as it became apparent that another man was on the stage, standing in front of the table that held the body.

Professor Sato was now dressed in a flamboyant robe. It was scarlet and had intricate golden line work running through it. Atop Sato's head was some sort of golden headpiece that covered the top of his skull. In the center of the piece was a ruby.

Another ovation swept through the crowd. Sato acknowledged it with a slight bow, but otherwise showed no expression. With a dramatic sweep of the arm, Sato directed the attention of the audience to the shrouded form upon the table. The professor walked around the table is a motion so smooth it seemed as if he were floating.

When he stood behind the table, he took the top corner of the sheet and pulled it away from the shape beneath it.

The body of a man was unveiled to the crowd.

It was Augustus Wellington.

The sheet had only been pulled down as far as the corpse's stomach. That was enough. Three bullet holes were visible on the pale torso. "X" heard sobs coming from several of the women in attendance. It was certainly a gruesome display, and the Agent wondered what Sato's game might be.

With a gesture from the professor, a man entered from the wings of the stage. It was the doctor "X" had seen earlier outside the theater. The man glanced nervously in the direction of the audience then stared straight ahead as he made his way to the center of the stage.

Sato pointed to the corpse with another theatrical gesture. The gold thread in the Japanese man's robe caught the light and reflected back in a way that was almost mesmerizing. "X" wondered if hypnosis was one of the tricks in Sato's repertoire.

The doctor sat his scuffed bag on the floor, opened it and removed a stethoscope. The Agent noted that the doctor's hands were shaking as he pressed the bell of the stethoscope against the dead man's chest. After listening for a few seconds, the doctor smiled and shook his head in the direction of Professor Sato. The doctor proceeded to lift the dead man's eyelids and peer intently into the eyes of the corpse. Finally, the examination was finished. The doctor said something that "X" could not hear. Sato leaned toward the doctor, whispered something and then led the man to the front of the stage. Sato nodded to the audience.

The doctor cleared his throat and said, "This, uh, this man is, uh, dead."

A few of the audience members clapped briefly, then stopped, as if realizing what an odd thing it was for which they applauded.

Sato nodded solemnly, allowing the doctor to dart for the wings of the stage.

When the doctor was gone, the lights went off again. The weird music resumed, accompanied by chanting in a language unfamiliar to "X". In fact, it seemed to be random syllables and noise, nonsense speech designed to impress the audience. It sounded like the voice of Sato.

The music and chanting continued for three or four more minutes. "X" could sense restlessness from the crowd, perhaps mixed with nervous anticipation. Finally, the stage was illuminated again.

A wall of smoke – as crimson as the curtain on the stage – wafted across the proceedings like a nightmarish fog, covering everything up to the waist level of Sato and his two assistants.

The body, shrouded once more by the sheet, remained visible on the table.

Professor Sato rubbed his hands briskly together while chanting in that imaginary language of his. He stretched out his arms until his hands were palms down over what would have been the dead man's chest.

A murmur of excitement went through the crowd.

"Please," Professor Sato said in a strained voice. "I must have...total silence...for what I must do. The...concentration required is...tremendous."

The audience hushed.

Sato stood like that, with his hands over the corpse, chanting again. His voice rose in volume until Sato cried out a single syllable. It sounded like a martial arts shout, the kind of release the Agent had learned during his time in Japan before The Great War.

Simultaneous with the shout, Sato slapped his hands down on the chest of the dead body. There was a flash of light as the hand made contact with the dead, a spark between living flesh and cold dead skin.

The lights went out again.

A moan could be heard coming from the stage, distant and first, then gaining in volume as though the person who made the sound was frightened or angry.

After only a few seconds, the stage lights came on again. Sato and his two assistants had taken several steps away from the table, which they stared at in amazement.

On the table, the shrouded form moved.

It became instantly apparent that the moaning sound came from the body on the table.

The figure under the sheet thrashed its limbs about. Professor Sato said something to his assistants and the two men rushed to the table, attempting to restrain the thing under the sheet. It was a wasted effort. The crowd watched in amazement as the figure under the shroud threw off the two young men. One pale hand emerged from beneath the sheet. It grabbed a corner of the fabric and pulled it down.

The formerly deceased man known as Augustus Wellington sat up and glared at the crowd.

Several audience members cried out. "X" heard a woman scream somewhere behind him.

The resurrected man on the stage tilted back his head and wailed. It was a cry that had more animal than man in it.

Professor Sato stepped over to the screaming man and grabbed the fellow's head in his hand. The formerly dead man's scream ended. He stared at Sato.

"Do you know who you are?" Sato said.

Wellington did not answer.

"You are Augustus Wellington," Sato said. "Do you remember?"

The man tilted his head slightly, like a dog or a small child, as though he were trying to understand words that did not make sense to him. But he had calmed down. Sato spoke softly to him, too softly for the words to carry to the audience. Wellington nodded a couple of times, an indication the he now understood what

"The resurrected man...tilted back his head and wailed."

Sato was saying to him.

At a signal from Sato, the two assistants helped Wellington stand. The sheet was wrapped around the man's waist. Before they left the stage, Sato spoke a single word. The two assistants turned Wellington around and led him back to face the audience at the edge of the stage.

Sato gestured to the man's exposed chest.

The chest was unblemished. There was no sign of the gunshot wounds that had been visible only minutes earlier.

At a signal from the professor, the two assistants led the revived man off the stage. Watching the revived Wellington walk away, "X" was struck again with the idea he was watching someone he had previously met.

"My friends," Sato said, "you have witnessed the power of The Order of the Eternal Flame. Let us remove your feat of death. Forever."

The theater exploded in applause. The audience rose to the feet, shouts and whistles joining the ovation. The Agent stood and joined in, even while he found it amusing that many of these sophisticated men and women, who would never dream or expressing themselves in an undignified manner, were now behaving like school kids at a sporting event.

On the stage Professor Sato staggered as though he had lost his balance. He grabbed the now-vacant table for support. The professor waved away shouts of concern. He wiped a hand across his brow. The jewel in the center of his headpiece glittered in the spotlight.

Two different young men walked quickly from offstage and assisted Sato's exit.

The curtain closed and the house light's came on.

The radio newsman next to the Agent was smiling like a little boy on Christmas Day.

"Boy, that was something," he said. "Really something. I have to get back and write my script. The world needs to know about this. Wasn't that something?"

"It was…something," the Agent said.

The crowd was slow to leave. "X" thought they were reluctant to let go of what they truly believed to be a mystical experience. Audience members stopped in the aisles to discuss the phenomenal event that had just witnessed. No one seemed impatient to leave, save for the Agent.

After an interminable wait, he made it to the crowded lobby of the building, where more of the young Japanese men and women were circulating among the wealthier members of the audience, no doubt seeking donations. As if reading his mind, the young man who had met "X" outside the theater appeared by the Agent's side.

"Mr. Pond, did you enjoy the demonstration?"

"It was quite a spectacle," the Agent said.

His comment appeared to offend the young man. "It was more than a spectacle, sir. It was a display of the secret arts of The Order of the Eternal Flame, revealed to the world for the first time. This will change the fate of mankind."

"So it wasn't a trick?"

The man sniffed. "Certainly not. Professor Sato has trained for years in the hidden ways of the Order. He has dedicated his life to the Order's teachings."

"Fascinating," the Agent said.

"Yes," the acolyte of Sato said. The smile had returned to his face. "We have much work ahead of us to spread the word. We need the help of generous individuals such as yourself."

"Certainly," "X" said. "Have someone call at my house tomorrow afternoon."

"Thank you, Mr. Pond." The acolyte bowed before he hurried off.

Seconds later someone touched the Agent's arm.

It was Betty Dale. She appeared worried.

"I'll admit it," she said. "That spooked me."

"X" led her outside. At the corner of the theater, "X" spoke softly to her.

"You're a rational, intelligent girl. You know what you saw in there was some sort of fakery," he said.

"But it seemed so real," Betty said.

"Trust me. It was a trick."

"How did they do it?"

"X" smiled. "I can think of a dozen ways."

Buoyed by his confidence, Betty returned the Agent's smile. "Okay. It was trick. Why did they go to such elaborate lengths?"

"I plan to come back later tonight to discover the answer to that question," he said.

Betty squeezed his hand discreetly. It wouldn't do for anyone to investigate a connection between the reporter and wealthy Elisha Pond.

"We'll talk later," she said.

The Agent had his driver drop him off a few blocks away. "X" stepped into a phone booth and dialed the number of Harvey Bates.

"It's me," the Agent said.

"Listen, boss, I got a line on that Sato. I should know something soon," Bates said. "I know a guy who knows a guy, you know?"

"Fine," "X" said. "But right now I have something else for you. Can you send a couple of men to watch Elisha Pond's house?"

"Sure," Bates said. "You okay?" He sounded puzzled. Bates, like Betty Dale, was aware that Elisha Pond was merely another disguise "X" wore.

"Never better," the Agent said. "I'm just being cautious. I'll check in later."

"X" disconnected. He exited the telephone and headed for one of the apartments he kept downtown.

* * **

Later, after most of the city's residents had retired for the evening, a shadowy figure stumbled through the alley that ran next to the Gibson Theater. The instant he was lost in the darkness, the man's stride became sure and confident. "X" was certain that any observer would think he was a drunk looking for a quiet spot to sleep it off.

He made his way to the rear entrance of the theater, where his lock pick tools provided easy access. Once inside, he utilized his battery-powered light to search the backstage area. The silence convinced the Agent that he was alone.

Among the boxes, sandbags, costumes and other detritus of the theater life that was stored behind the stage, "X" found several trunks that were cleaner than the rest.

Inside the cases, "X" discovered the robes Sato and his assistants had worn, along with the professor's fancy headdress.

Another trunk contained flash powder, smoke bombs and other tools of the magician's trade.

Behind his shabby disguise, "X" smiled. His suspicions had been confirmed. Now if he could only find "Wellington" snoozing away back here, his night would be complete. But it didn't look like things were going to be that easy.

"X" found an office just off the stage, probably set aside for the theater manager. It was locked, a situation he quickly changed.

The room looked as if it hadn't been used for years. Old yellowed posters for obscure productions dotted the walls. The drawers contained little more than ancient playbills and financial records that dated back to the last war. If The Order of the Eternal Flame kept financial records, they were stored somewhere else.

The Agent's search was punctuated by a scream. A female scream.

"X" bounded through the office door and up across the stage. His eyes had adjusted to the darkness. In the aisle in front of the orchestra pit a struggle was taking place.

A figure dressed in black was grappling with a smaller from.

"Let of go of me, you creep!"

The smaller person was Betty Dale.

"X" leaped from the stage. He hadn't been noticed yet, but that changed when he slammed into the man who restrained Betty. With a whoosh of breath, the attacker fell back into the front row of seats.

It was another ninja.

Betty screamed again. "X" grabbed her wrist and pulled her close to him.

"It's me," he whispered.

"Oh!"

"What are you doing here?"

"I was worried about you. I – "

Something struck the Agent from behind, propelling him into Betty. They both fell to the floor. He landed on top of her. He quickly rolled off Betty and struck out with his legs. He made contacted with a second ninja, who fell to the floor.

"X" leaped to his feet. The ninja was scrambling to stand, as well.

A soft rustling of cloth gave the Agent enough warning to duck. A small sword whizzed over his head. He reached up, grabbed the arm that held the sword, and used the first ninja's momentum to throw the attacker to the floor.

The second ninja grabbed the Agent around the neck. "X" tried to break the man's grip, but he couldn't force the choking arm to move. Red and yellow spots flared in the corners of the Agent's vision. His temples throbbed. "X" released the ninja's arm and drove an elbow into his assailant's stomach. The ninja double over, releasing the Agent's neck. "X" drove his forehead into the ninja's face. The man cried out and dropped to the floor.

A flash somewhere in front of him caused the Agent to drop to the floor. The first ninja struck again with the knife. His enemies were incredibly difficult to see in the gloom.

After he dodged the latest attack, "X" reached beneath his coat and withdrew his favorite weapon.

It was a gas gun, loaded with pellets of the Agent's own design. "X" preferred to use non-lethal force against his enemies when he could.

As the ninja advanced on him again, "X" triggered the gun.

The pellet struck the ninja's chest and exploded, releasing a cloud of anesthetic gas. In less than two seconds, the black-garbed attacker was unconscious on the floor.

The Agent released the breath he had been holding. The gas dissipated within seconds. He could breathe safely.

He aimed the gas gun in the direction of the second ninja.

There was no one there.

"X" trigged his flashlight, sweeping it around the theater.

There was no sign of the other ninja.

Even worse, Betty Dale was missing, too.

Chapter Four

After a rapid, efficient search of the theater, "X" knew that Betty and the second ninja were gone.

Throughout his long career, Secret Agent "X" had learned to function in the face of crisis by setting aside his emotions.

In the case of Betty Dale, that was going to be difficult. His feelings for the young reporter were strong indeed. But how could his enemies know this? Had it just been coincidence that they had snatched away the one person who meant the most to him?

"X" cursed under his breath. He should have known that Betty's reporter instincts, along with her concern for him, would have insured that she showed up at the theater.

Now he had to get to work.

He returned to the unconscious body of the first ninja. After checking to make sure the man was still under the effects of the gas, the Agent used rope found backstage to securely tie his attacker. He removed the ninja's mask. The young face belonged to one of the ushers from Professor Sato's performance earlier that evening.

"X" checked the man's bonds again before he slipped out the stage door of the Gibson Theater. He had to work fast.

His custom roadster was parked several blocks away on a quiet corner. Once he was safely inside, "X" opened a hidden drawer beneath the passenger seat. Inside the compartment were the tricks of his trade, a collection of makeup and wigs that would make the most veteran of theatrical performers seethe with envy. The Agent removed his present disguise with practiced ease. He then applied a putty-like compound to his face. "X" himself had devised the substance after years of experimentation. It was soft and pliable, yet it retained its shape remarkably well and for a long time. His fingers worked to shape the stuff into familiar features. He covered the putty with makeup and added a wig and a false mustache he had used often. When he was finished, "X" examined his work in the mirror he carried in the concealed compartment. The face that stared back belonged to Police Commissioner Charlie Foster.

"X" had employed the disguise in the past when he felt it was expedient to secure certain information, or when the police needed to be pointed in a certain direction. And that was what the Agent now intended to do.

He started the automobile's quiet, powerful engine and pulled away from the curb. Traffic was light, making the trip a short one.

He found a parking spot one block away from the imposing building. When he alighted from the car, he walked with the determined military bearing of the police commissioner.

Though the hour was late, "X" found Inspector John Burks at his desk, as expected. The detective lived for his job. The Agent respected Burk's dedication, even if the man was resolved to bring "X" to justice.

"Burks," the Agent said.

"Commissioner?" The detective stood up. "What are you doing back at this hour?"

"Someone called my house anonymously. Said there had been a dust up at the Gibson Theater. And Betty Dale is missing."

"Did you—" Burks began.

"I called, then went by her apartment. She wasn't there. My wife is frantic. That girl is like a daughter to us."

"What can I do?"

"Good man," the Agent said. "I want you to get down to the theater and see what you can find. Take as many men as you need. We have to find that girl."

"I'll get right on it," Burks said.

"X" noticed an open folder on the detective's desk. "Is this the file on The Order of the Eternal Flame?"

"Yeah," Burks said. "I keep thinking that if I stare at it long enough, I'll figure out how Secret Agent "X" is involved."

"Maybe you're off base on this one," the phony commissioner said. He picked up the file.

"No, I can smell him all over this thing," Burks said.

The file contained very little on Sato, other than his address. He had a suite at the Stanford Hotel. "X" placed the file back on the detective's desk.

"Get to work," the Agent said. "I'm going to look up a few of Betty's friends."

"X" made his way back to his car, confident that Burks and his men would discover whatever there was to find at the Gibson Theater.

The Stanford Hotel was only a few miles from police headquarters. In the lobby, "X" flashed a badge and asked for Sato's room number.

"Don't call ahead," "X" warned the desk clerk.

Sato's suite was on the third floor of the hotel. The Agent knocked on the door. It was answered quickly by one of the young ushers from the theater.

"Yes?" the Japanese man said.

"X" showed his badge again. "Let me see your boss. Now."

The man started to speak, but "X" shoved him back into the room and followed him in.

Professor Sato sat on the couch in shirtsleeves and slacks, before a table that bore a number of papers covered with small, careful Japanese script. Behind the couch, a man stood near the window. He had been gazing out at the city until the Agent's abrupt appearance. He was Caucasian. His face and clothing were unremarkable, yet "X' was struck again by how familiar another stranger seemed to him.

With the shield still in his hand, the Agent nodded at Sato. "We need to talk," he said.

"Certainly," Sato said. "And who are you?"

"He's the police chief," the white man said.

"Ah," Sato said. "Welcome, Chief…"

"Actually, it's Commissioner," the Agent said. He turned his gaze to the stranger. "And you are…"

"Mr. Smith is a supporter of our cause," Sato said.

"Smith?"

"Joe Smith," the man said. "From Des Moines."

"Right," "X" said. He smiled. "If you give me a moment alone with Augustus Wellington, I won't trouble you any longer."

"I can't do that," Sato said.

"Why?"

"Because Mr. Wellington is not here." Sato took a careful sip from a cup of tea. He placed the saucer and cup on the table, then stood. "I offered him the use of my suite. He declined."

"Where did he go?" the Agent said.

The Japanese man shrugged. "He was not a prisoner, Commissioner. He left us funds to continue our work. He then left us to discover his new life, free from fear of death."

"Do you mind if I look around for a moment?" the Agent said. "I'm the skeptical type."

Sato bowed. "Please consider this your home for as long as you would like to stay."

"X' quickly searched the suite of rooms. There was no sign of any other occupants. He was certain Betty wasn't hidden there.

He returned to the front room. "Do you have other rooms here?" he asked Sato.

"Of course," the diminutive man said. "For my staff."

"Do you mind if I have them searched?"

A flash of irritation flicked across Sato's face for so brief an instant, "X' thought he could have imagined it.

"I am pleased to accommodate you any way I can," Sato said, fixing a large smile to his features.

"Good," the Agent said. He strode to the telephone on the table in the entryway and dialed police headquarters. "It's Foster," he said. "Find Burks. Tell him to get some men over to the Stanford. Search every room registered to the order of the Eternal Flame." He hung up the phone.

"Don't you have criminals to capture?" the white man asked. His voice was flat, with no trace of an accent, foreign or domestic.

"X' smiled again. He strolled over top the stranger, stopping only a few feet from the man.

"You remind me of someone," "X" said. "Have we met?"

"Funny," the man said. "I was about to ask you the same thing."

They stared at each other in silence. The stranger's eyes were gray, as was his hair. "X" had the feeling the man was wearing a disguise, just as the Agent did.

If only he had time to deal with this man. If only Betty was safe.

"It's been a real pleasure, Joe Smith from Des Moines," he said. "I'll be sure to look you up when I'm through capturing, ah, criminals."

"X" turned on his heel and left the room. The same young Asian who had tried to stop him from entering now held open the door for his departure.

When he reached the sidewalk, "X" made good time to the spot where he parked his car. Once in the vehicle, he warmed up his radio and dialed in a certain frequency.

"Bates, are you there?"

Static crackled from the speakers for a few seconds. Then the voice of Harvey Bates filled the car.

"Boss? Is that you?"

"I need you to find any other property that Sato and his organization may have rented or purchased within the last few years."

"Got it," Bates said. "I've got something for you."

"Yes?" the Agent said, hoping for word of Betty Dale.

"The guys I have outside Pond's place just checked in. Someone's been watching the joint. A car has been parked near the place for a couple of hours. Two guys inside. Want us to brace 'em?"

"X" thought a moment. "No," he said into the microphone. "Pull your men off the surveillance. I've got it now."

"If you're sure," Bates said. "I'll get started on this other thing."

"X' switched off the microphone. Working fast, he opened the compartment under the front seat and removed the Foster disguise. He then applied the necessary touches to transform his appearance into millionaire Elisha Pond.

Once he was satisfied with his appearance, he dialed another frequency on the radio and contacted the garage that remained on call for his needs.

In minutes, Elisha Pond's limousine pulled to the curb a block away from "X". As the Agent approached, a chauffeur jumped out to hold the door for him. "X" slipped into the back seat and gave the address to the driver.

Fifteen minutes later the car came to a stop in front of the large brownstone owned by Pond.

"X" spotted a dark sedan parked two blocks away, just as Bates had described. He stepped out of the limousine, dismissing the driver before he headed up the walk to the front door. He pretended to fumble with his house key as he surreptitiously watched the parked sedan. He could see the two figures that Bates had mentioned, but if they were planning to make a move against Elisha Pond, they must have been waiting for him to enter the house.

"X" obliged them by opening the door.

He slipped into the foyer and stopped for a moment, listening. The house was silent. It seemed empty.

"X" doubted that it was. He thought he had a pretty good idea of what The Order of the Eternal Flame was planning. And he had dangled Pond above them as bait. Now he was going to see if they would bite.

He stripped off the topcoat and suit jacket he wore, and dropped them to the foyer's floor. He next removed the gas gun from its shoulder holster.

Secret Agent "X" switched on the lights in the front room of the house as he stepped around the corner.

It was only his battle-hardened instincts that forced him back into the hall just far enough to avoid the blade of the sword. The metal whizzed by his neck, nicking him along the jaw line as it did. "X" felt his blood run hot and wet down his neck. He dove through the doorway, keeping close to the floor.

Someone stomped on his wrist, sending the gas gun flying.

The Agent rolled to his right at the same instant a sword crashed into the highly polished wood of the floor. He leaped to his feet and jumped onto the couch. The heavy piece of furniture tipped over, taking "X" with it. The Agent used his temporary shelter to survey the situation. He risked a glance around the side of the couch and was rewarded with the visual confirmation of three foes – ninjas, all wielding short, thin swords.

The Agent's only weapon was lost somewhere on the other side of the room.

He knew he couldn't afford to wait for his enemies to attack, "X" pushed away from the couch, scooping up a small area rug as slid across the floor. He wrapped the rug around both hands before he stood.

As soon as he was visible, the ninjas attacked.

The one closest to "X' ran toward him with sword extended. "X" raised his arms, sheathed by the rug, and brought them down on the sword, driving the point into the floor. The ninja wasted a precious few seconds trying to tug the blade free.

"X" struck upward, his hands still enclosed by the rug. The impact of both fists, muffled, as they were, still drove the ninja's head back. The black-clad man fell and did not move again.

"X" released the rug and freed the ninja's sword from the floor.

The remaining two ninjas attacked in unison.

The Agent moved, as he had been taught. The attackers were prepared to battle a soft old man, so they weren't prepared for the speed their opponent displayed. In a few steps, "X" had maneuvered his opponents so they faced him in a line. The man in the rear hissed in frustration, as the lead ninja parried the Agent's attack.

As the ninja counterattacked, "X" shifted away from the blade and managed to bring his left arm down over the sword, pulling it against his ribcage. His suit vest and shirt protected him from damage. As the shocked ninja tried to pull the sword back, "X" slammed the hilt of his own weapon into the man's chin. The ninja slumped forward, trying to steady himself. The Agent drove a knee into the man's face, and the second attacker fell silent.

"X" took a quick step backward to prepare for the assault from his final opponent.

The final ninja screamed, likely out of frustration at the way this old man had fought against them. The masked man dove at the Agent, swinging the sword in wide, powerful arcs.

But the sword movement was just a distraction. With his left hand, the Japanese warrior threw one of the razor sharp shurikens at "X". The Agent's attempted dodge wasn't quick enough. The throwing star dug into the bicep of his right arm. The pain was incredible, sending white-hot lances of agony through his body. His vision blurred and filled with tiny red explosions of light.

He couldn't afford to give into to the pain. He knew the ninja was even now closing in with a killing blow. "X" had been wounded before, and he knew that if he hesitated, he would soon be in a place where he could feel nothing ever again. He sucked in a great lungful of air and did the one thing his attacker would not expect.

"X" ran at the ninja.

His attacker held the sword over his head, ready to bring it down on "X"s head. The tactic left the ninja's midsection vulnerable, so "X" took the only shot he had.

He drove the sword deep into the belly of the Japanese man.

The ninja moaned quietly before collapsing on the floor. "X" let the sword fall along with the dead man. The Agent avoided killing whenever possible. However, in his line of work, the death of an opponent was sometimes unavoidable.

In the quiet of the house, the sound of the blood dripping from his arm seemed very loud. "X" placed a hand over the shuriken still lodged in his flesh, carefully avoiding the exposed blades.

"You fight well for a soft man."

"X" whirled. A figure stood in the doorway.

It was the resurrected Augustus Wellington, and he held a gun pointed at the Agent.

"Who are you?" "X" said. Once again, he experienced that eerie sense of familiarity.

"I could ask the same of you," the man who looked like Wellington said. "Why don't you step over here and we'll discuss it."

"Before or after you shoot me?" the Agent said.

The other man pulled back the hammer on the revolver in his hand. "Step over here, please."

"X" took a step forward and staggered to one knee, as though his wound had weakened him. "X" pulled the shuriken from his arm and in one movement threw it at Wellington. The whirling blades grazed the man's cheek.

"Mein Gott!" he screamed. He fired the gun.

The round struck "X" in the center of his chest, driving him backward. The Agent skidded across the polished floor, then lay still.

Chapter Five

He never truly lost consciousness, but his senses swam and the sounds around him were strangely distorted. When "X" finally opened his eyes and sat up, he didn't believe much time had passed. Wellington – or, more accurately, the man who looked like him – had fled, probably due to the sirens "X' heard in the distance. The two unconscious ninjas were gone, too. Only the dead man remained.

The Agent opened his shirt. The bulletproof vest had done its job. He was sore, though, and wouldn't be shocked to find he had a broken rib.

But he was alive. And now he knew the identity of his enemy.

He now realized that the men who had seemed so familiar to him were all the same man wearing a series of disguises, the latest of which was the persona of Augustus Wellington. "X" hadn't been sure until he had grazed Wellington with the throwing star. His shouted oath, in the man's true voice, had confirmed the Agent's suspicion.

How "X" would use the information was something he would have to figure out later. He had very little time before the police arrived in response to the gunfire.

From the inner pocket of his vest, "X" removed a compact makeup kit he always carried. It contained a small quantity of the putty he favored, along with other useful component. He quickly stripped the black fighting togs from the dead ninja. He then removed his own wig and placed it on the head of the corpse. Using all the skill he had mastered over the past decades, "X" applied his cosmetic to skill to altering the dead man's face until the cadaver resembled Elisha Pond.

With the sirens growing closer, "X" stripped off his clothing and dressed the dead man as Pond. He folded the ninja's outfit into a compressed ball, used it to wipe up his own blood from the floor, and carried it up to the master bedroom, where the Agent hurriedly bandaged his wound and dressed in casual clothes. Exiting down the back stairs, "X' left the house through a back entrance, crossing several blocks at a pace that was quick but not fast enough to draw undue attention.

When the police arrived at Pond's house, the Agent was safely away, plotting the end of the Order of the Eternal Flame.

By the time morning arrived, "X" wore the face of A. J. Martin and was seated at the counter of the reporter's favorite diner near police headquarters.

As he finished up a cup of coffee and a plate of eggs and bacon, the radio news began with a startling announcement.

"Millionaire philanthropist Elisha Pond was murdered in his Manhattan home late last night, according to police reports," the excited announcer said. "X" thought he sounded like the same man who sat next to him at the theater the night before. The Japanese organization known as The Order of the Eternal Flame now claims that Pond left his entire fortune to them, and their leader, Professor Sato has announced that Pond will be resurrected tonight, in a repeat of the miraculous ceremony that recently revived the corpse of banker Augustus Wellington."

"X" finished his coffee and considered the plans of The Order of the Eternal Flame. The money from the estates of Wellington and Pond would provide a nice war chest. "X" couldn't be sure of the plans the group had for the money, but the involvement of the man who had played Wellington gave him a pretty good idea of the Order's true motives. Now he had to find Betty. He prayed she was still alive.

"Bringing back the dead. Ain't that some crazy stuff, Martin?" Maggie, the waitress smiled at him.

"Don't you believe it, toots," the Agent said.

"But a lot of people saw it happen."

"X" laughed. "A lot of folks saw King Kong climb the Empire State Building a few years back, too. The only difference was they knew upfront that was a trick."

She shook her head and cleared away his plate.

The Agent stepped into the phone booth and called Harvey Bates. The private investigator sounded tired, but happy.

"It took all night and I had to call in a few favors and make a few threats, but I got something, boss."

"Let's have it," "X" said.

"Ever hear of the Chaney Group?"

"No."

"That's because it's a dummy corporation. It's really those Eternal Flame guys. They used the Chaney name to buy the old Vanderpool Shoelace factory."

"That's right next to the Stanford Hotel," the Agent said.

"Right."

"Good work."

"I've got something else," Bates said. "It's the dope on Professor Sato. His real name is Dai Yamamoto. He was a two-bit hustler and street magician before the war. Later, he was nabbed for cheating at cards in a ritzy casino. He escaped and since then he's knocked around most of Europe doing magic under the Sato name."

"X" considered this new information.

"Boss? You there?"

"Harvey, did he spend much time in Germany?" the Agent asked.

"As a matter of fact he did. Mostly Berlin. He even has an apartment there."

"X' smiled. "You've earned a bonus, Harvey. I'll be in touch."

He hung up the telephone, but stayed seated in the booth for another moment. The threads of the plot had begun to come together. What had seemed like a scam, albeit a murderous one, was now revealed as something much greater. Something that "X' vowed to end, even at the cost of his own life.

He waved at the crowd of reporters and made his way to the door. A few blocks later, he was seated in the backseat of his car. The back of the driver's seat pulled away to reveal a cache of weapons. The Agent made sure his gas gun was loaded with fresh cartridges, though he had a feeling this confrontation was destined to be lethal. He also took a silver-plated .45 automatic from its hiding place. He stored both weapons under his jacket before he climb out of the backseat seat and settled in behind the wheel.

The early morning traffic was heavy, which made the trip to the old factory tortuously slow. "X" hoped that he was heading for Betty Dale. He wouldn't allow himself to consider that he might be too late. He had long ago come to grips with the knowledge that his life could be forfeit at any moment in service to the citizens of this country. But he couldn't bear the thought of harm coming to the young woman who owned his heart.

The Agent gripped the wheel tighter and fought the urge to scream at his fellow motorists.

Finally, after what seemed an eternity, "X" saw the massive sign for the Stanford Hotel. He parked in a spot down the block. The former Vanderpool Shoelace factory was set back from the street, presumably to accommodate what must have been some sort of courtyard. All that remained today was a patch of bare earth littered with trash. "X" spotted evidence that people had once camped here, likely some unfortunates who had been displaced when the nation's economy had collapsed.

From his position across the street he spotted two sentries atop the building. If he were to gain entrance to the building, he would need a distraction.

He returned to the backseat of his car and to the concealed weapons compartment, where he removed a few objects and stuffed them into his pockets.

"X" strolled down to the next block. A group of kids were playing stickball on a side street. Two other boys were sitting against a wall reading comic books.

"Hey," the Agent said. "Want to make some quick money?"

The taller of the two boys looked at "X" suspiciously. The Agent removed a five-dollar bill from his pocket. The eyes of both youths grew wide. They set aside their comics.

"What do we have to do?" the tall one said.

"You know that abandoned building next to the hotel?"

"Sure," the smaller boy said.

"Ever light a firecracker?" the Agent asked.

"You bet," the tall boy said. He stood up and dusted off the seat of his pants.

"X' showed the boys a handful of firecrackers. "Run over to the building, light these and toss 'em as close to the front door of the place as you can, then beat feet. You do that, and this fiver is yours."

"How do I know you'll pay me?" the tall kid said.

"X" handed the firecrackers and a pack of matches to the boy. He then held up the bill and carefully tore it in half. He gave one piece to the tall boy. "One half is no good to either of us. When you get back, you get the other half. Get over there, count to a hundred before you strike that match. Okay?"

The tall boy didn't answer. He took off running.

"X' handed the other half of the five spot to the smaller boy. He then removed another fiver and a nickel from his pants.

"This is for you," he said, handing the bill to the boy. "X" held up the nickel. "I just need you to do me a small favor."

Second later, the Agent walked briskly away from the stickball game. He crossed the street and circled behind the old factory. He hid behind a row of shrubs where he had a good vantage point to observe the building. He noticed a Japanese man standing at a door in the back of the factory. "X" could also see a sentry pace back and forth on the roof.

The pop-pop-pop of the firecrackers sounded like gunfire. The guard at the door pulled a gun from beneath his coat and ran to the front of the factory. The man on the roof likewise disappeared.

"X" leaped from concealment, rushing toward the unguarded door. He had no time for finesse. He kicked at the lock once, twice, then wood splintered and he was in. His eyes needed a few seconds to adjust to the darkness. He felt around until he discovered a railing, which he held to as he climbed down a flight of stairs. Near the bottom, he found he could see a little better, and he became aware of a light in the distance.

He was in a cavernous room. Dark skeletons of ancient machinery haunted the corners of the vast space. Beyond the great room was another door, and from this opening the Agent could hear voices.

He closed the distance as quietly as possible, knowing his time was short. Soon the guard would return and notice the damaged exterior door.

"Is everything ready?" "X" recognized the accented voice of the man who had played the part of Wellington, the man who had shot the Agent.

"Yes," the voice of Sato replied. "Preparations at the theater are complete."

"Good. Our men will retrieve the body of Pond and I will take his place at the ceremony."

"What about this woman?" Sato said.

Betty. They were talking about Betty.

"She was insurance against the man called "X"," the other said. "Now that he is gone, we can dispose of her."

A burning rage overwhelmed the Agent's thoughts. He ran through the open doorway, his .45 held in front of him.

Sato and the man who was still disguised as Wellington were seated at a bare table. In the corner of the small room, Betty Dale was bound to a chair. She was gagged, and ugly purple bruises marred her beautiful face.

The Agent's breath caught in his throat.

Sato ducked under the table. "X' saw the other man draw a gun from beneath his coat.

"X' leveled his own weapon and squeezed the trigger. At the same instant something slammed into his back, knocking him off his feet. "X" rolled with the impact, turning the fall into a somersault. He came to his feet just as "Wellington" fired. The bullet whizzed past his ear and slammed into the table. "X" fired a shot at the other man, then rolled to the side and faced the doorway.

It was the guard from the back door who had attacked him. The Japanese man had a revolver in his hand and was trying to get a bead on "X". The Agent fired first and a red spot blossomed over the heart of the guard.

The Agent didn't wait to see his enemy fall. He threw himself to the floor just in time to avoid another shot from "Wellington".

The man cursed in German and fired again. "X" dived under the table and discovered the body of Sato. "Wellington's" first shot had gone through the table into the Japanese man's skull.

"X" fired through the table until his .45 was empty. He heard a gasp, then felt something slump against the table. He crawled out from under cover. "Wellington" was slumped over the table. His blood was pooling around him. "X' removed the gun from the man's unmoving hand.

"Herr Kruger," "X" said.

"Ah, you remembered," the man whispered. A trickle of blood ran from the corner of his mouth. "I'm...flattered, Captain Read."

It had been a long time since the Agent had used that name. Captain James Read of the 81st Infantry had been dead for a long time. He had thought Carl Kruger dead as well. The German master of espionage had clashed with the Agent many times in the last war, culminating in a hard fought battle in France. Captain Read had left Krueger for dead in 1918. Today, twenty years later, he had finally finished the job.

Krueger exhaled one last rattling breath. "X' turned away from the corpse and rushed to Betty's side. He quickly freed her and removed the gag. She slumped against his chest. Neither spoke as "X' gently touched her bruised face.

Finally, she straightened and looked him in the eye. "It was all a con," she said. "I heard them talk. They were crossing the country, raising money to fund their spy organization here in the States. That Doctor Adams was on the payroll, too, to swear the dead bodies came to life. The Germans and the Japs together. Can you believe that? We're not even involved in all that fighting in Europe."

He held her close. "We will be," he said. "Even though we want peace, we can't continue to turn a blind eye to the suffering and destruction caused by madmen."

Betty pulled away from his embrace. "Wait a minute. This place was crawling with guards. What happened to them?"

Almost instantly, the pair could hear the distant sounds of gunfire. "X" took Betty's hand and led her through the basement and up the stairs. They exited the back of the building just in time to see Inspector Burks round the corner of the factory with a dozen cops in tow.

"X removed the gun from the man's unmoving hand."

"What the hell?" Burks said. He took in the sight of the two of them. "Martin? What are you doing here?"

"I could ask you the same thing," the Agent said.

"I got a call from some kid," Burks said. "He told me Secret Agent X was here at this place." Burks narrowed his eyes. "Say, what is going on here? We shot a bunch of foreign guys."

"There was a man down there," Betty said, nodding toward the factory's back door. "He fought off Sato and his spies, then freed me. He just ran out of the door and around the block. Didn't you see him?" She batted her eyes at the detective.

"Spies? And "X" was here, huh? I knew it." Burks stood with his fists on his hips, chewing his lip. "And how'd you show up here, Martin?"

"X" shrugged. "I was having lunch at the hotel when I heard shots. Then I saw a damsel in distress."

Betty flashed a bright smile, despite the bruises on her face.

"Yeah?" Burks said. "And how do I know you're not Secret Agent X?"

The Agent laughed. "Really, Inspector. I think you need a nice vacation. Somewhere warm. Maybe a quiet island."

Burks stared at "X' for a few seconds.

"I've got my eye on you, pal," he said. To the other cops, Burks said, "Come on. Let's see what kind of mess we have to clean up."

Burks and his men went through the door and out of sight.

"X" took Betty's hand and walked her away from the decrepit building.

As they approached his car, she said, "This is only the beginning isn't it?"

He tried to think of words that would comfort her, but nothing came to mind. At last, he simply said, "Yes."

She squeezed his hand tightly. Secret Agent "X" knew that he and the rest of the country would have to be even more vigilant against the forces of darkness that would seek to destroy the American way of life.

He glanced again at the beautiful woman who walked beside him.

Dark times were coming.

But he knew he wouldn't have to face them alone.

THE END

ON WRITING PULPS: MARK JUSTICE

I was blessed that I grew up in a family of voracious readers. Seeing everybody around me reading was the greatest motivation possible to discover what those little squiggles on the paper meant. So learned to read at about age four. My Uncle Paul gave me my first comic books around 1965, an early Daredevil and an action-packed copy of Fantastic Four (I wore out both books, but I still have the replacement copies I tracked down many years ago). For a few years, I was content with the four-color world.

Then came the day Uncle Bud handed over the gift that would transform me.

It was three Doc Savage paperbacks. The Dust of Death. The Other World. The Flaming Falcons. For a couple of days, I just stared at those gorgeous James Bama cover paintings, so dynamic and full of possibilities. I just knew that within these pages were the greatest adventures anyone could imagine.

I was hooked.

Later, through a letter column in Marvel's Doc Savage comic book, I discovered pulp fandom, and was soon reading G-8, Secret Agent X, The Phantom Detective, The Black Bat and the blood-soaked, nearly hallucinogenic novels of my favorite pulp hero, The Spider.

While in high school I teamed up with another fan to publish a Doc Savage fanzine, which included the first chapter of my original Doc novel. For the never-to-be-published second issue, I interviewed Philip Jose Farmer via telephone. I wish I could find that cassette now.

Though my literary tastes grew, leading me to many other types of fiction, I still come back to the pulps on a regular basis. The pulp stories are always dependable, like a fondly remembered childhood snack. They cleanse my mental palette and offer an escape from the grim world I see on the news.

Because in the pulps, the good guys always win.

•••

MARK JUSTICE: Writer, DJ, Podcaster September 23, 1959—February 10, 2016. Author of *The Dead Sheriff: Zombie Damnation,Looking at the World with Broken Glass in My Eye*, co-author of *Dead Earth: Sanctuary*. He lived in Kentucky with his wife, Norma Kay, and their cats. Airship 27 has published other author's stories featuring the "Weird Western" character Dead Seriff chreated by Mark in a series of novels. (airship27hangar.com).

Chapter One
COBBLESTONES AND BLOOD

William Galvin stumbled through the late evening fog, which seemed to cling to his legs and arms as he passed through it, giving him an almost spectral appearance. He struggled through a myriad of dark and dirty alleyways, smack dab in the heart of downtown Seattle, leaving a sickly trail of blood behind him.

He watched with trepidation as thick droplets of his blood tapped their way into the cobblestones, mixing with the rainwater collected in the grooves. He couldn't help it, though. Even with his left hand holding his wound shut, Galvin was slowly bleeding to death and it was all he could do to keep his mind focused on the task at hand: To escape certain doom and contact Secret Agent X before it was too late.

Galvin continued to lumber through the winding alleyways, trying to find his way home or to help, but the loss of blood made concentrating difficult. As the night's dire events kept flashing before his eyes, he found it harder and harder to stay centered on the here and now. The images popped into his head, one after another, replaying all of the details at random. They were scratchy and larger than life, as if he was watching an eroded movie reel skipping slightly in the projector. It seemed like a lifetime ago when he received the wound to his stomach, yet only an hour or two had passed since Galvin's life took a serious turn for the worse.

Distracted and betrayed by his own thoughts, Galvin stumbled on a loose cobblestone, causing him to fall face first into a fairly large and muddy puddle of water. Of course, the poor lighting in the alley did not help matters, either. He rolled over to his side, coughing and spitting out the dirty water he just took in.

Exhaustion and the extent of his wound were taking its toll on him, that much was clear, but Galvin was a strong man. He gave it a few seconds, maybe ten, before he managed to slowly roll over and sit up. He was not about to give up, but he knew well enough that he needed to pause for a few moments before continuing on. He needed to get out of sight and rest up; otherwise, he was not going to make it.

Galvin noticed an empty spot between a pair of old trash cans, drenched in shadow. It seemed like the perfect position to hold up. Scooting over to this spot, Galvin rested between the garbage cans, his back against the cold yet comforting brick wall for support.

All of a sudden, a sharp twinge hit him from his wound. He looked down to his stomach, where his once white shirt was now completely stained red with blood. He shoved his left fist back into the wound again, hoping to buy just a little more time. He only had a few more blocks to go, and then he would be safe. At least, he hoped, anyway.

As he sat there, catching his breath and preparing to muster up his remaining strength, Galvin allowed his mind to race back to earlier in the evening, when he first received the strange phone call that spurred on the rest of the night's horrid events…

Chapter Two
THE PHONE CALL

The old, battered phone rattled out its ring; a sickly sound, one denoting the end of its days. It sat on the far end of the large and poorly-stained oak desk, just out of hitting range of Galvin's fist. He placed it there on purpose, to keep from breaking it, yet again.

Like the phone and the desk, the rest of his office had a worn look to it. It was hard to tell if the room was just well-used, or just a complete dump. Either way, Galvin called it home.

Ever since his private eye business took a severe turn for the worse, he could no longer afford the rent on both his apartment and his office. Since the office was cheaper, he now slept on his small couch or at his desk. Well, mostly at his desk, usually after a few drinks of Scotch. Such as this evening, for instance.

The phone continued to ring, showing no sign of stopping. Whoever was on the other end was quite determined to talk to him.

Galvin knew that he should answer it, especially since it might actually be a paying job, something he needed. After all, even a man with Galvin's steel stomach needs more than shots of booze to survive. Regular meals would be a good start.

He raised his head off of the desk and out of the small puddle of drool he was sleeping in. Rubbing his stubbly cheek in an effort to wake himself up, he reluctantly pulled the phone's receiver off of its cradle.

"Galvin Investigations," muttered Galvin, allowing his lack of interest to show through, just slightly. He may need a job, but that doesn't mean he wanted one.

"Mr. William Galvin?" said the man on the other end of the line. His voice sounded odd, slightly muffled, as if the connection was bad or he was covering the phone with a cloth.

"Yeah, that's me. What can I do for you?" asked Galvin. He was fully awake now, his catnap on the desk a thing of the past. Still, his attention was drifting elsewhere; most likely to one of the other bottles of Scotch that he kept in the metal filing cabinet next to the window.

"I have some important information for you, sir, vital to the future of this great nation of yours. It is imperative you act on this knowledge right away, this evening, before it is too late to stop him."

"Uh huh…stop who?"

"My Master…He's truly insane…I see that now." The man's voice was still muffled, but it was clear to Galvin that fear laced it. "He will bring your country to its knees with his cold touch, leaving death and confusion in his wake…"

The tone in the man's voice certainly sounded quite sincere in its underlying terror, but Galvin was not quite convinced. Being a smalltime sleuth in Seattle, he's heard his fair share of craziness from all types. Still, there was something about the way he said it that made Galvin listen in a little longer, instead of just hanging up on him. After all, he's also seen his fair share of craziness.

That drink of Scotch he's been craving for the last couple of minutes will have to wait a little bit longer.

"That's great, pal. Now, you gonna tell me who you are and what exactly you want, or do I hang up? Telling me that your master is about to lay waste to the country is not what I call specific."

"I am nobody of consequence, one who has seen the error of his ways. I am just another servant of the cold Touch of Death, Note des Todes. What I want…I want redemption for the part I have played in all of this."

For a moment, Galvin sat there silently, unsure of what to say. On one hand, it sounded ridiculous; on the other hand, he's heard far worse. Then, a thought occurred to him. Why was this man asking for him, by name?

"Why did you call me?" asked Galvin. "You knew my name, my number. Why did you bring this to me?"

The man on the line must have known this question would come up, as there was no hesitation in his answer.

"My Master keeps extensive records on all of those who would oppose him. In those records, the one he considers the greatest threat is a mysterious emissary of justice, an operative with a thousand faces and names, who has a network of acolytes who serve him loyally.

"You are one of those acolytes, a servant of X, are you not?"

Galvin was speechless. No one knew of his connection to Secret Agent X except for X himself and his operative network coordinator, Harvey Bates. Hell, there were times that Galvin was not too sure of his own connection to Secret Agent X. He's only met X about a dozen times, and each time he looked completely different. If it weren't for the steely, intense eyes of the man, Galvin would have been certain he was dealing with multiple people.

"My Master is certain the Secret Agent is in Seattle at this time, and fears his involvement. I wish to see his fears come true." The man stopped for a second, then continued in his raspy voice. "Only the Secret Agent can stop my Master, and only you can contact X."

Realizing there was no point in denying the fact he knew Secret Agent X, Galvin figured his best choice was to figure out what the hell was going on with this strange man on the phone and his so-called "Master".

"Listen…before I contact anybody, I need proof of what you're talking about. I need names. Real names, not this Death's Touch crap. Let's start with yours."

"There's no time! You must contact the Secret Agent immediately! He must be at the warehouse tonight to stop my Master!" said the man, whose muffled voice was beginning to strain. Whether it was from fear or stress, it was unclear.

Galvin was unsure of what to make of this. Either this guy was truly afraid of what his boss was going to do, or this was one huge set-up. And if this was a set-up, then the trap being set was for X, not Galvin. This meant he was being used as a pawn, one way or another.

Galvin did not like being used, period.

"Fine, fine, I'll call him right away, okay? Where do I send him?" asked Galvin, seemingly giving in to the man's request. Actually, though, Galvin had just lied through his teeth. He had no intention of calling Secret Agent X, at least, not yet. Not until he checked things out for himself.

The strange man on the phone quickly gave over the address of a warehouse down by the docks and the time in which this mysterious event was taking place. Galvin quickly scribbled it down on a nearby notepad. Before he could ask anything more, the man on the line said he had to go and hung up.

Galvin sat in his chair for a few minutes, thinking about all that has just occurred. He looked at the time on the paper, then at the clock on the wall.

Galvin sighed. He had no time for that drink of Scotch.

Chapter Three
THE WAREHOUSE

A little later in evening, Galvin approached the warehouse at the address given by the mysterious man on the phone. He kept to the shadows and moved cautiously. He had no idea what was going on, but just the fact that this guy knew of Galvin's connection to X was cause enough to take things nice and slow.

Galvin eventually made it to the building without being seen, or so he assumed. The night was quiet, and there was no one to be seen out on the streets. Not too unusual for the docks, but it did seem a little too quiet.

Galvin knew it was best to ignore to the main entrances, so he crept along the wall until he found a large window. The window was partially seeped in shadows, thanks to an oddly placed street lamp, and there was a section of the window broken away, allowing access to the lock inside.

Reaching his hand through the broken window, Galvin caught his reflection in the glass. He looked like shit. His usually short brown hair was in need of a trim, and he was certainly in need of a good shave. After another day or so of growth, it would officially be a beard. His eyes were the worst, with dark circles carved underneath. The long nights of drinking his troubles away were starting to take their toll.

Galvin unlocked the window and slowly pulled it out and up, swinging it open, making sure as he did that it did not squeak. With the window now open, he slid through and gained entrance to the warehouse.

Silently dropping to the floor, Galvin reached into his cheap brown overcoat and pulled out his Colt .45 automatic, a souvenir from the war.

As his eyes adjusted to the darkness, Galvin's ears picked up the faint chattering of voices, coming from the center of the facility, where there was also a small glow of light. He carefully made his way toward the voices, zigzagging between the myriad piles of crates and boxes and barrels.

The closer he got, the louder the voices. Unfortunately, Galvin could not make out anything they were saying, except for the fact that they were speaking German. Well, that was not entirely true. He could make out a few words, thanks to his time in the war, but nothing that made any sense.

He was nearing the center of the warehouse. The voices were clear; he could tell that there were at least five or six people waiting on the other side of a large and irregularly stacked pile of crates.

Deciding it was best to get a better view, Galvin climbed up the stack of crates, nestling in at the top. From this point of view, he could see everything that was going on below.

What he saw, that was something he would never forget.

Chapter Four
THE ORDER OF
THE HAND OF DEATH

The middle of the warehouse had been cleared into an open circle, with many of the crates and barrels piled up and encircling the area. Strange designs were painted on the floor, a star within a circle surrounded by bizarre symbols. In was unclear to Galvin if these were ancient glyphs or just some weird language, but the coppery smell emanating throughout the large area seemed to indicate that the paint was actually blood.

All of this was nicely highlighted by the various candles aligned carefully throughout the painted designs, which let off a pleasant aroma and partially masked the smell of the blood. Without them, the stench might have been overpowering.

The candles also served to bring an eerie light to the entire area, since the rest of the warehouse was pitch black. The flickering shadows caused by the disturbing candlelight only added weight to the creepiness of the scene Galvin was now watching.

There were six men, dressed in black and blue robes with large hoods that covered their faces completely. Embroidered on the robes were many of the strange symbols that were inscribed on the concrete floor. They each held what looked to be daggers with wavy blades. It was hard to tell, what with such low light, but they seemed to be made out of glass.

As Galvin watched intently, the six robed men moved about the floor and into specific positions, facing one another in a circle. They began to chant in yet another language, heads cast down and holding their daggers toward the center of the circle. All except one, that is.

One of the six men kept raising his head and looking to the sides. His attention seemed slightly distracted, even bordering on frantic, as his eyes seemingly darted about the room. His movements were subtle, though, not drawing the attention of the others, but Galvin could tell that this man was looking for something or, more specifically, someone. This was the man who called Galvin.

But, before Galvin could make any move, a voice boomed firmly from the darkness. It sounded as if bone was being crunched underneath the heel of a leathery boot, and it made Galvin's skin crawl.

"It is time!"

All chanting stopped. The robed men raised their heads and daggers up in unison, with just one of them lagging slightly behind.

Then, after a moment of silence, they chanted something short and loud, inviting the mysterious stranger from the darkness to approach.

Stepping into the amber light of the circle, the man from the shadows appeared, but he was different than the others. Well above six feet in height, the man wore a solid black cloak, not an actual robe, but still embossed with many of the same strange glyphs as the others. Yet, this cloak barely disguised his stocky physique. It was clear by the way he held himself that he was a confident man, physically and mentally.

As he stepped into the middle of the circle, the cloaked man reached up and pulled back the hood, revealing a horrible sight. Deep scars ran throughout his entire head, which was void of all hair. Although it looked as if he had suffered from serious burns, his skin color was quite fair, pale even, almost ghostly.

His eyes were the worst, though. As grisly as his face was, the eyes were hellish. Black as coal, they burned with a barely contained animosity for something indefinable. Whatever fueled this man's hatred, it had been burning within for a long time.

Galvin was sure this was who the man on the phone referred to as Note des Todes, Death's Touch.

"The time has come, my acolytes!" announced Death's Touch. Spreading his arms outward, he continued. "Soon, we will strike at our target, exposing this country's weakness and driving it to the ground! The Order of the Hand of Death will soon leave its mark on this depraved and unworthy nation!"

The acolytes of Death's Touch yelled out in praise of their master, even if one of them seemed slightly less than enthusiastic. This did not go unnoticed by Galvin, who had been keeping a close eye on his would-be informant. Unfortunately, it did not go unnoticed by Death's Touch, as well.

"But first, before the evening's sacrifice that I have arranged," said Death's Touch, almost softly, "we have other business to attend to. A serious matter must be dealt with."

Throwing back his cloak, Death's Touch revealed the rest of his outfit. He wore a strange mix of the old and the new. Prominently displayed across his chest and abdomen was a dark brown leather breastplate, along with leather bands slapped across his wrists. Strips of brown leather with small rivets of metal hung from a matching thick belt, which contained a short sword and a large holster. Underneath the leather armor, black military fatigues covered the rest of his body, finishing off with a pair of large leather boots. If the Roman Legion still existed today, this is what they would have looked like.

Death's Touch reached into the holster and extracted a strange looking gun, something that Galvin had never quite seen the like of before. It looked somewhat like the German DWM Luger pistol, only twice the size and with strange canisters and hoses attached to the sides and top. Perhaps it was a trick of the light, but it even seemed to be letting off an unusual vapor while in his hands.

"It seems as if we have a non-believer in our midst," announced Death's Touch. "One of our very own has betrayed us."

Outrage emitted from the acolytes, and they all started looking at one another, trying to determine who was the snake in their midst. Even Galvin's contact did this, hoping to divert any attention away from him. Too little, too late, it would seem.

Death's Touch quickly swung his arm around and aimed the strange gun at the acolyte-traitor.

"You have deceived us, and you have abandoned the teachings of the Order," said Death's Touch, his voice mired with hatred. "You are disavowed."

"No, please, have mercy," whispered the acolyte, fear dripping off of his voice, but there was no mercy to be had.

Death's Touch pulled the trigger of his gun. Immediately, it recoiled and let loose its bullet, but there was no noise, not like a real gun. Instead, it hissed and shot out chilled vapors of air from the attached canisters, as well as leaving a trail of the mist from the barrel.

The bullet found its mark, hitting the acolyte square in the chest. The impact of the shot threw him back several feet, crashing him into a large pile of crates. He sunk to the ground, unmoving, and vapor emitted from the wound like steam.

Having watched this entire ordeal unfold in a matter of seconds, Galvin had no time to act, not from where he was perched. But, the acolyte did not die entirely in vain, as the all too real danger of Death's Touch was exposed.

This crazed man had religious zealots at his beck and call, and he was armed with a dangerous pistol that could fire ice. It was the only thing that made sense to Galvin.

Somehow, this man had a gun that created and shot bullets of ice. It was the perfect weapon for murder. The bullet would melt after the deed was done, leaving be no evidence to be found.

It was falling into place for Galvin. This cult leader was an assassin, and he was here to kill someone that was so important to America, it would throw the country into chaos.

"Oh, no," muttered Galvin under his breath, as it dawned on him as to whom the target would be.

It was the President of the United States, who was in town while on the campaign trail for the upcoming election.

"No, please have mercy..."

Chapter Five
THE SHOWDOWN

Galvin knew he had to get out of there, right away. This was far above his head. He needed to contact Secret Agent X.

Galvin carefully crept backwards, making his way down from the perch he made on top of the crates, but he stopped as soon as he heard Death's Touch call him out.

"Don't go just yet, Mr. Galvin," said Death's Touch, "We're not quite through with our evening's rituals."

Galvin stopped cold. How did he know Galvin's name?

"Did you really think I would not know you were here?" asked Death's Touch. "I am the Touch of Death itself. Nothing is beyond my ken."

Knowing he was basically screwed, Galvin figured it was time to go on the offensive. Standing up, Galvin revealed himself to the acolytes and their master.

"Really? Then, you must have known I've got a gun of my own," said Galvin, aiming his pistol at them. "Drop your weapons and grab a little air, all of you."

Death's Touch grinned slyly at Galvin's request, as if it was just a joke, nothing to be taken seriously. The grin made his appearance all that more hideous. "Please, Mr. Galvin, don't make this any harder on you. We still need our proper sacrifice for this evening. If you come on down with no fuss, I'll make your death quick and painless."

"You have got to be kidding me," said Galvin, his aim focusing on Death's Touch. "You make it sound like…"

"As if I arranged this?" asked Death's Touch, rhetorically. "Of course I did. The Order of the Hand of Death requires a proper sacrifice for our upcoming mission. And what better choice than one of the pawns of X…?"

All of the blood rushed from Galvin's face, leaving him pale as a ghost. More pieces of the puzzle fell into place.

"You set me up, didn't you?" whispered Galvin.

Stepping closer to the pile of crates on which Galvin stood upon, the grin worn by Death's Touch grew even more ghastly.

"I knew I had a deserter among my ranks, so I allowed him to contact you, Mr. Galvin," whispered Death's Touch in return. "I figured you would not believe him outright–who would, really?–so you would investigate this matter yourself, giving me what I need for tonight's event: a human sacrifice.

"And even if you had believed him, you would have sent for X. I would have gotten what I wanted, either way."

Anger brought the color back to Galvin's cheeks. "Screw you, you bastard," said Galvin, "You're not getting a thing from me." Tensing his finger, Galvin squeezed the trigger on his Colt.

He knew this bastard was too dangerous to let live, he could fill it deep in his gut. He had to take him out before it was too late.

Unfortunately, it already was.

For as large a man as he was, Death's Touch was fast. He easily dodged Galvin's shot and returned fire. His aim was perfect. Another bullet of ice cannoned out of the unique gun, slamming into Galvin's right side of his lower torso, near one of his kidneys.

The impact of the shot knocked Galvin right off the top of the crates, and his gun went flying out of his hand. He crashed into several other boxes on the floor. Luckily, those boxes were only made of cardboard, cushioning his fall a slight bit.

Groaning, Galvin picked himself up. Regardless of the pain from the shot and the fall, he had to get out of there, as he could hear Death's Touch ordering his acolytes to retrieve him. Covering his gunshot wound with his left hand, Galvin took off running, heading towards the back of the building.

One of the acolytes managed to catch up to Galvin quickly, grabbing the tail of his coat and trying to pull him down. That didn't work too well, though, as Galvin swung back wildly with his fist, knocking the acolyte aside.

Just ahead of him was the back entrance to the warehouse. Hitting it with all he had, Galvin smashed through the door, lucky the old lock snapped easily under the pressure. He was free of the building, but still had the acolytes and their master behind him. Now, he had to run for his life.

Chapter Six
THE LAST STAND

A sharp but subtle noise, like a pebble being kicked aside by accident, snapped Galvin back to the present. Adrenaline shot through him, shaking the grogginess from his head.

He darted his head down the alley, hoping to discover the source of the noise before the source discovered him. Yet, with the darkness of the night, the poor lighting and all of the surrounding fog, there was nothing to see. There was nothing more to hear, as well.

At least, at first. Soon, Galvin heard the slight sound of shoes rapping on stone. Then, it became louder. Someone was out there, and that someone was getting closer.

As quietly as possible, Galvin pushed his body up the wall, slowly scraping against it as he used it for support. His left hand was still placed over his wound, keeping it tightly closed as best he could. This made it hard to get up from the ground, but he managed to do so without giving away his position.

The rapping of the shoes slowly turned into a thumping sound.

His body flat against the wall, Galvin reached with his free hand for his pistol, finding his shoulder holster empty. Unfortunately, he forgot he lost it at the warehouse, which now left him defenseless.

Silently, he cursed himself for leaving his gun behind as his eyes darted around, looking for anything that would work as a weapon. All he saw was a small brick being used to hold down the lid of one of the trash cans. He picked it up, palming it in his right hand.

The thumping sound now turned into the loud thudding sound of a man who did not care that he was announcing his presence. In fact, the sound had an aloof quality, almost regal. Galvin knew this man approaching him was someone who held himself above all others, whose mere comportment commanded people to obey. Galvin knew who this man was, even before he stepped through the eerie fog and into the dim light of the alley.

It was the man he saw murder one of his own followers earlier in the evening, and the man who shot him. It was the monster they called Note des Todes and he was ready to finish the job he started earlier.

"You may come out now, Mr. Galvin," said Death's Touch. "I know you are here. You've left quite the trail of blood."

Realizing he could not hide for long or even outrun this man in his condition, Galvin steeled himself for the upcoming confrontation and stepped into the middle of the alley, cupping the brick in his right hand and tucking it out of sight. If he was going to die this evening, he was going to do it like a man.

"I'm here," said Galvin, daring the cold-blooded murderer to make the first move. "Let's get this over with. I ain't got all day."

"Don't worry, Mr. Galvin, this won't take any time at all," replied Death's Touch, pointing the ice gun straight at Galvin.

As Death's Touch began to squeeze the trigger, Galvin made his move. Hoping that Death's Touch would be caught off guard by such a last ditch effort, Galvin threw the brick at Death's Touch. Luck was on Galvin's side, as the brick nailed the ice gun and knocked it out of his hand as it fired, missing Galvin by mere inches.

Taking the offensive, Galvin pushed his surprise attack further. Using the last of his strength, he landed a solid right hook across the jaw of Death's Touch, causing him to reel back. Galvin pushed onward, landing blow after blow after blow. It was like hitting a bag of rocks, but Galvin kept pushing onward, until Death's Touch fell to one of his knees.

For a brief second, it looked as if Death's Touch was going to fall down, but instead, he turned and let loose that ghoulish grin of his.

"Nice try, Mr. Galvin. Now, it is my turn."

Death's Touch struck out with his huge, muscular arm, causing Galvin to be tossed aside like a rag doll. He smashed into the very same garbage cans he was hiding behind just moments ago.

Galvin couldn't get up. He was spent, used up. Hell, he could barely keep his eyes open. He knew his time was up.

"It was a valiant effort on your part, Mr. Galvin," said Death's Touch, as he retrieved the ice gun from the alley floor. "Of course, I'd expect nothing less from one of X's operatives."

"He'll stop you, you know that. It won't matter that I wasn't able to warn him. He'll find out and he'll stop you," said Galvin, defiant to the end, regretting nothing, except that he didn't get that last drink of Scotch.

"Don't worry, Mr. Galvin, Secret Agent X will get your message," said Death's Touch, once again pointing the ice gun straight at Galvin. "It just won't be delivered the way you were hoping."

Death's Touch fired the weapon one last time.

Chapter Seven
THE MORNING AFTER

The body of Mr. William Galvin was discovered the next morning by a pair of beat cops walking the Pioneer Square area. At first, they assumed he was just another bum sleeping off a night's bender, but when they tried to roust him, they uncovered what must have been a ghastly death. Within an hour of calling it in, the crime scene had been cordoned off and was under investigation by Detective Michael Mayborn.

Mayborn was atypical for the Seattle Police department, not being a local and having a generally positive attitude and demeanor. He was taller than most, just over 6'3" tall and weighed in at 195 pounds of lean muscle, all thanks to a youth spent on the beaches of Hawaii. His platinum white hair also set him apart from the wash of brown and black hair that most everyone else had in the Pacific Northwest. Still, even with the differences that set him apart from the rest of the police force, he was well-liked and respected as a fine police detective.

While the Deputy Coroner performed a cursory inspection of the body, Mayborn set about reconstructing what had happened the night before. At first glance, it seemed to be a simple case of assault; a robbery gone wrong, except… there was no robbery.

Mr. Galvin's wallet was still inside his jacket, completely untouched, which is how they were able to identify the body so quickly. This also led to the discovery of Mr. Galvin's PI license. And since gum-shoes are usually a tough breed, no normal thug could have taken one down so easily on his own. Yet, there was no evidence of there being two assailants. Only two sets of footprints were found in the semi-dirty alleyway; the victim's and the assailant's. This was no case of a couple of goons trying to rob some rube.

Then, on top off all that, there was the matter of an empty shoulder holster on Mr. Galvin. Mayborn looked all over the crime scene and found no gun, not even a spent shell. This suggested that whoever attacked Mr. Galvin took his gun and cleaned up afterwards, indicating a professional hatchet man.

After a closer inspection of the evidence at hand, including the trail of blood, Mayborn surmised an already injured Mr. Galvin, most likely on the job, stumbled into the alley and rested against the wall of the building. He stayed there until an unknown assailant attacked. There was a struggle, blows were exchanged, and then the unknown assailant shot him, possibly with his own weapon.

"Detective Mayborn!"

Slightly startled, Mayborn turned around to see the Deputy Coroner calling him over to the body.

"What do you have, Johnson?" asked Mayborn, kneeling down across from the body and the Deputy Coroner.

"It's what I don't have, Detective," said Deputy Coroner Johnson, pointing out the gunshot wounds on Galvin's body. "This man has injuries consistent with two gunshots, but there are no bullets in him, nor are there any signs of the bullets being dug out."

"What? How can that be?" asked Mayborn.

"I'm not sure what to tell you, Detective," he replied. "The entry wounds are large enough to see into, indicating a large caliber bullet, but they are not large enough for someone to just pull out the bullet without any effort. Honestly, I've never seen anything like this before."

"Okay, thanks," said Mayborn, standing up.

While Mayborn wrote down his notes and theory of what happened to Mr. Galvin in his small leather-bound notepad, another police detective arrived on the scene. He flashed his badge at a flatfoot at the edge of the crime scene, who allowed him to pass through. He headed straight for Mayborn.

This new detective was tall, with a powerful build. Not quite Mayborn's height, but stockier. He had neatly combed black hair with a well-trimmed beard, and wore a finely tailored black suit. It was his eyes that caught Mayborn's attention, though. His eyes had an intense driving force burning through them.

"Detective Mayborn?" the detective asked, showing his badge to Mayborn. "I'm Detective Joe Haueter, from the North Precinct. I was told you're in charge here?"

"That I am," replied Mayborn, as he shook hands with Haueter. "It's a pleasure to meet you, Detective. What can I do for you?"

"I heard about what happened to Mr. Galvin. I was hoping you could fill me in on the details," said Haueter, who turned his gaze towards the lifeless body of Galvin nearby, just as the Deputy Coroner was covering him up.

Mayborn noticed that those steely eyes softened for a brief second, and then the extreme fury behind them was back as Haueter returned his attention to Mayborn.

"Well…news certainly travels fast," commented Mayborn, "Why do you want to know, Detective? This is out of your jurisdiction, after all."

"I know, but he was…a friend. We worked on a few cases together. I want—no, I need—to know what happened to him."

Unlike most detectives, Mayborn never prescribed to the notion of 'not sharing' a case with another detective. He didn't care who got the collar, as long as the case was solved, so sharing any information he had was not a problem.

Still, Mayborn had a funny feeling about Haueter. There was something not quite right about him, something he just couldn't put his finger on. Could he trust him?

Should he? Ah, what the hell. He was a fellow officer of the law, who he just lost a friend.

Mayborn nodded in understanding. "Okay, here's what I got…"

Mayborn handed over his notebook to Haueter and walked him through his initial investigation, including his theory of Mr. Galvin being killed by a professional killer and the mystery of the missing bullets. Making a few notes of his own, Detective Haueter thanked Mayborn and walked away, leaving Mayborn to wonder about that intangible feeling at the back of his head, the one put there by this strange and brusque detective.

Chapter Eight
A NOTE FROM THE DEAD

Soon after his impromptu meeting with Detective Mayborn, Detective Joe Haueter found himself staring at the office door of Galvin Investigations, idly fingering a large crack in the opaque glass window inset within the door. He briefly wondered to himself how Galvin came to be at such a low point in his life; no home, no family, barely surviving at a job he excelled at.

Putting those thoughts aside, Haueter reached into one of his pockets and pulled out a set of master keys, designed to open just about any lock imaginable. With them, he easily gained entrance into the abode of the late William Galvin.

Stepping inside, Haueter shut the door quietly behind him. He left the lights off, since the morning sun was streaking through the large window behind Galvin's desk, offering plenty of light to work with. What he saw did not impress, nor did it surprise. The interior of the office was small and worn, with old furniture and a slight musty smell permeating the room. The fabric on the couch was threadbare, and the oak desk was unimpressive.

Again, Haueter's thoughts were drawn to the sad state of Galvin's former life, but he had to shake free of these thoughts and concentrate on the task at hand. If Haueter hoped to find any clue as to the identity of Galvin's murderer, it was going to be within this office.

After all, he had good reason to be so invested in this case, because Detective Joe Haueter was but the latest identity of Secret Agent X, the man of a thousand faces, and William Galvin served as one of his operatives. He would not rest until he found who was responsible for killing him.

It didn't take long for Secret Agent X to search the small office, including the adjoining bathroom and closet. Unfortunately, he found nothing but a few bottles of Scotch tucked away in cabinets and files of cases that have been closed for a while. It was pretty clear that Galvin had not been working in a while, and was spending a lot of his free time on the sauce.

Despondent and trying to decide his next move, X sat at Galvin's desk until he noticed a blank pad of paper and a pencil next to the phone. Following a hunch, he picked up the pencil and ran it across the entirety of the top sheet of the pad, making a negative impression of the last thing written.

The sheet of paper revealed the following note:

GALLOWAY IMPORTS WAREHOUSE
PIER 48 AT MIDNIGHT
DEATH'S TOUCH?
CONTACT X?

Secret Agent X was honestly surprised by the last part of the note. Why did Galvin include him in the note? Why contact him, and what was Death's Touch? Could it possibly have anything to do with X's visit to Seattle?

Just the other day, X received a tip from another one of his operatives about a possible assassination attempt on the President while in Seattle. So, X flew out to Seattle just to make sure the President's visit on the campaign trail went smoothly. In fact, Secret Agent X was going to look up Galvin for assistance, since he was not that familiar with Seattle.

Was it possible Galvin already stumbled across whatever plot was in the works? Was he killed by some assassin? After all, according to Detective Mayborn's theory, it was some sort of professional hit man who killed Galvin.

The note left behind raised a few more questions for X to answer, but at least they were questions pointing in the right direction. It also gave him his next move.

Secret Agent X had a warehouse to check out.

Chapter Nine
THE WAREHOUSE REVISITED

Sitting impatiently inside his rented Chevrolet Coupe, Secret Agent X waited across the street from the Galloway Imports warehouse off of 1st Avenue, right on Pier 48, just where the note said. He wanted to rush in and find those responsible for Galvin's death, but he knew from experience that could be a dire mistake with deadly consequences. He knew he had to case out the joint first, especially during the middle of the afternoon.

After spending the better part of an hour watching the building, X finally assumed that no one was there, which was unusual. Since the morning was creeping up on the afternoon fairly quickly, the warehouse should have had at least a few employees working, if not a full staff. Instead, there was no sign of anyone working there all. That gave X reason to believe that this warehouse was most likely being used as a front.

With that in mind, there was still a slim chance that those Galvin was investigating were still inside, laying low, but they were most likely gone, especially if they were responsible for Galvin's death. Either way, any evidence left behind should still be there.

One thing was certain, though. He wasn't going to find anything sitting in his car. It was time to go inside.

Secret Agent X exited his Coupe and walked across the street, passing the front of the warehouse as casually as he could. He slyly kept an eye on the windows as he passed, looking for any sign of movement. He saw nothing.

Slipping into the alley next to the building, Agent X made his way to the rear of the warehouse. The loading docks were empty and locked up, but the back entrance seemed to be slightly ajar. Upon closer inspection, X noticed the back door had been broken, the handle hanging loosely. Someone had kicked the door open from the inside.

Pulling out his gas pistol, Secret Agent X carefully opened the door and entered the warehouse. Although the interior of the warehouse was somewhat gloomy, there was plenty of light streaking through all of the windows to easily navigate between the many piles of crates and barrels.

As he treaded lightly through the warehouse, he noticed several boxes knocked over. Following the trail of overturned crates, X found a pile of smashed cardboard boxes. But, before he could investigate, his foot kicked something, which screeched across the floor as it slid.

Flinching at the sound, Secret Agent X stopped in his tracks and listened carefully. Not hearing anything, he decided to continue his legwork. Putting his gas pistol away, he reached for the mysterious object he just kicked and picked it up, revealing it to be a gun.

Turning it over in his hands, X recognized it as a Colt .45, the same exact gun that he knew Galvin owned. Agent X was positive that Galvin had been here.

Slipping the gun into a coat pocket, X pulled out his gas pistol once again and continued on. He moved through the maze of crates and barrels, careful to keep an eye out for more clues. He found one; a really big one.

Secret Agent X stumbled onto what could only be described as a scene of satanic ritual sacrifice. A large inverted pentagram encircled an open area, with many ancient glyphs inscribed within. Although ancient languages were not his specialty, X was pretty sure the glyphs were Sumerian. Regardless of the language, though, this was not a site to take lightly, especially with the smell of blood heavy in the air.

All of a sudden, before Secret Agent X could make his next move, a pair of voices from behind him broke the silence.

"Drop the gun!"

"Don't make any sudden moves!"

Although alarmed, Agent X was more embarrassed than shocked. He was allowing himself to be far too distracted on this case, allowing simple goons such as these to sneak up on him.

X slowly lowered his gas pistol, but did not drop it. It was time to get back into character, and get back into the game.

"Relax…I'm a police officer," said X, slowly turning his head around, trying to get a look at who was behind him. "My name is Detective Joe Haueter. I'm investigating a murder."

"That's too bad, because you've already seen too much," said one of the voices, "We have standing orders to kill any more intruders."

"I think you'd better reconsider that statement, pal. You don't want to go bumping off a copper. That's real bad news," replied X, buying a little more time.

"Yeah, that's real bad news for you, but real good news for us," said the other voice, parroting his partner's barely disguised glee for bloodlust.

The first one spoke up again, this time directing his statement to his partner. "Oh, yeah…the Master will most assuredly praise us for our unflinching loyalty and hard work."

While these two jabbered on, Secret Agent X took advantage of the spare moments he bought. Through his peripheral vision, he saw the owners of the two voices. They were strangely dressed, with the very same Sumerian glyphs embroidered in cloaks of black and red. Each one of them held a long wavy dagger, which seemed to be made of glass, at first glance. Unknown to him at that time, he was face to face with acolytes of the Order of the Hand of Death.

The most important detail, though, was where they were standing. They were both about six feet away from him. This gave Secret Agent X the advantage. Armed with only daggers, they did not have the reach to do instant harm to X, whereas his gas pistol would reach them easily once fired.

X moved like lightning. He quickly spun around and shot the gas pistol straight at the two acolytes. The shot worked instantly on the first acolyte, who unfortunately took the brunt of the shot, allowing for the second acolyte to move out of the way. As his partner fell to the ground, the second acolyte shot forward, his dagger pointed straight at X's heart.

Secret Agent X dodged out of the way and lined up his gas pistol for another shot, but it was too late. The acolyte slashed with the dagger, connecting with the gas pistol. The tip of the dagger shattered upon contact, but it hit with enough force to knock the gun out of Agent X's hand. As the gun fled from his grasp, he noticed the rest of the dagger was evaporating rapidly. It was not made of glass, after all, but of some sort of special ice.

Now, they were both unarmed, leaving this contest to skill and strength. Secret Agent X immediately grabbed the outstretched arm of the acolyte and pulled hard, throwing him off-balance. He followed with a solid left hook to the jaw, knocking the acolyte down.

Although dazed from the punch, the acolyte got to his feet quickly, just not in time to dodge the right cross that Secret Agent X delivered to the side of his temple. The acolyte went down like a sack of potatoes.

Catching his breath, Secret Agent X stood victorious over the acolyte when, all of a sudden, another mysterious voice rumbled from out of nowhere. Unlike the others, this voice was like gravel scraping together and put a chill down X's spine.

"Bravo, X! Well done!" scraped the horrible voice, "Had your friend Galvin fought as well as you, he might still be alive."

X twisted around and found himself face to face with a large cloaked man, as yet unknown to him as the man called Death's Touch, flanked by three more of the acolytes. X was at a major disadvantage. This mountain of a man knew who he was, even though he was wearing a brand new face. Yet, X did not know who this man and his allies were, except for the sudden confession that he had something to do with Galvin's death.

"Surprised, Secret Agent X?" asked Death's Touch. "Well, you shouldn't be. You took to the bait I laid out for you like a bee to honey. Galvin's death has led you right to me. Faster, in fact, than I had planned for."

"Let's skip the games," said Secret Agent X, straightening up and preparing to fight further, if need be. "Who are you? How do you know who I am? What do you want?"

Death's Touch chuckled slightly, making an even worse sound. "Listen to you, wanting all of the answers right away. I don't think you've earned them yet."

Death's Touch paused for a few seconds. His acolytes waited patiently next to him, although they did seem curious as to what he would do next, as they all turned their attentions off of X and onto Death's Touch.

Grasping the sides of his hood, Death's Touch pulled it back, revealing his dreadful visage to X. As unlikely as it seemed, he seemed even more horrific. Whatever deep-seated fury and hatred fueled his fires, they appeared to be rising.

"I will tell you this…I am the Note des Todes, Death's Touch, the Master of the Order of the Hand of Death, whom these acolytes serve unwaveringly. I am the instrument of William Galvin's death, as I will be the instrument of yours and your precious leader! The answers to the rest of your questions, you will have to earn with your pain and blood!"

With this exclamation announced, Death's Touch moved closer, followed by his acolytes. Had they been paying attention to their surroundings, they might have noticed the man stepping out between the crates, gun in hand.

"I don't think so, dingus! Freeze!" exclaimed Detective Michael Mayborn, who had his .38 revolver aimed straight at the head of Death's Touch.

Chapter Ten
OUT OF THE FRYING PAN

A strange look spread across the face of Death's Touch as he stared at the gun in his face. The sudden appearance of the police detective would have startled, if not scared, any other villain, but not Death's Touch. An unusual calm washed over his features, softening his horrible mug. He seemed genuinely surprised by Mayborn's action, as if the detective really thought he had a chance at stopping him.

Detective Mayborn was standing in between Death's Touch and Secret Agent X, who was still poised to jump into action. The acolytes all had their ice daggers at the ready.

"And you are…?" asked Death's Touch.

"Detective Michael Mayborn," announced Mayborn, his gun unwavering from its target. "You are all under arrest. Drop your weapons and place your hands above your head."

Death's Touch softly shook his head, still amazed by the audacity of Detective Mayborn. "I don't think so, Detective," said Death's Touch. "As much as I admire your tenacity and spirit, you have stepped into the middle of a situation not of your making.

"It's a shame, really. You see, in order to continue on our appointed task, your death is now required."

Realizing what was about to happen, Secret Agent X broke his silence and yelled out a warning.

"Move, Mayborn! Now!" screamed Agent X, but it was too late.

Mayborn's eyes went wide as they registered Death's Touch lightning fast move. In less than a second, Death's Touch shot his arm out and backhanded Mayborn across the cheek, hitting him with enough force to knock him clean off of his feet. Mayborn hit the ground with a thump.

Secret Agent X was unarmed, his gas pistol missing somewhere within the crates of the warehouse, but he was not about to back away from this fight. X immediately launched into Death's Touch and pushed him into a stack of crates. Unfortunately, the crates were full and heavy and barely moved under the massive weight of Death's Touch.

"That's putting your back into it, X," said Death's Touch, as he cracked his hideous grin. He pushed forward, knocking Secret Agent X back several feet. X barely managed to keep his balance and avoided hitting the ground like Mayborn.

The acolytes moved in for the attack, daggers poised to strike. Secret Agent X wasted no time, throwing several punches and kicks in rapid succession. The fight was taken out of them immediately, but only briefly. They would regain their composure within seconds, but that time gave X an opening to bring the fight back to Death's Touch, who was waiting for him to make his move.

Secret Agent X threw a right hook, which was instantly blocked by Death's Touch. He followed that punch with a left jab, but that was also stopped. X threw another punch, then another, all of them blocked. Death's Touch was just too fast.

"Frustrating, isn't it, not being the better man?" asked Death's Touch, who was clearly enjoying this small bout, blocking punch after punch with little effort.

"Not really," replied Secret Agent X, who suddenly changed tactics mid-swing and kicked him hard in the knee instead. Death's Touch buckled underneath his own weight and fell. X quickly landed some sweet chin music to follow up the kick.

"Ahh!" yelled out Death's Touch, letting a bit of pain squeak past his pale lips.

Secret Agent X was about to push his advantage further, but noticed the acolytes were recovered out of the corner of his eye. It was time to wrap them up before he could be seriously outnumbered.

"Watch out, Haueter!" yelled Mayborn, out of the blue, "Behind you!"

X turned around quickly and saw that the first two acolytes he fought earlier were charging him. He easily jumped out of the way, thanks to the timely warning from Detective Mayborn. The two acolytes crashed into the other group.

X moved over to where Mayborn was still lying on the ground. Grasping his hand, Secret Agent X readily pulled Mayborn to his feet. Still armed with his revolver, Mayborn gave them a good chance of ending this fight.

"Thanks for the save, Mayborn," said Agent X.

"My pleasure, 'Secret Agent X'," replied Mayborn, revealing that he heard enough earlier to know that X was more than he appeared. "Shall we finish this?"

Before X could reply, Death's Touch made his presence known once again.

"The only one finishing this scuffle will be me!" growled Death's Touch, bringing his deadly ice gun to bear, squeezing out a bullet of cold death.

Both X and Mayborn reacted immediately, but differently. X dodged out of the way, but Mayborn opted to return fire instead. That proved to be the wrong move.

The ice bullet ripped through Mayborn's right shoulder just as he fired his own revolver, throwing his aim completely off and tossing him back like a rag doll.

Mayborn's shot screamed through the air and slammed into an unmarked barrel nearby. The barrel, which was apparently filled with some sort of flammable liquid, exploded into flames and set fire to several more barrels nearby. Within seconds, the resulting explosions engulfed the warehouse in flames.

The fire grew so fast that all were caught unaware. The acolytes swarmed to their master, as X rushed to aid the wounded Mayborn.

Death's Touch moved towards X, unfazed by the fire licking at his heels. Then, without notice, a pile of flaming crates collapsed in front of him, effectively blocking him from reaching Agent X and Detective Mayborn.

Death's Touch glared through the flames, his eyes making contact with Secret Agent X. He stared intensely back at his monstrous opponent, revealing his own driving force that blazed within, showing Death's Touch that he was not the only one with such an intimidating look.

"I had truly hoped to kill you with my bare hands, X," snarled Death's Touch, "But I will make due with the knowledge that you suffered horribly, burned as I was once burned, before dying in an inescapable fire.

"Secret Agent X, you are disavowed."

With that, Death's Touch and his acolytes turned away and disappeared into the surrounding smoke, making their escape and leaving Secret Agent X and Detective Michael Mayborn trapped within a circle of blazing fire.

Chapter Eleven
INTO THE FIRE

X watched as Death's Touch and his acolytes took flight, leaving him and Mayborn to burn to death within the warehouse. Although not fueled by the same fire as Death's Touch, Secret Agent X was starting to feel a strange burning hatred for this monster.

"Disavowed…" muttered Secret Agent X, finding that specific term unsettling. Why would Death's Touch use such a word, instead of doomed or dead? This was important, but X just didn't know why.

Ignoring the fire for the moment, Secret Agent X left his thoughts behind and turned his attention back to Detective Mayborn. Mayborn was hurt badly, his shoulder soaked in blood.

X slipped Mayborn's light-colored jacket away from his shoulder, then tore open Mayborn's shirt, peeling it away to get a good look at the bullet hole. It was a clean wound, with a small trail of vapor leaking away from it. Upon closer inspection, X could see that no bullet was lodged in the flesh.

Between the lack of a bullet, the vapor, and the acolyte's ice dagger, X quickly put the clues together. He reasoned that the bullet was made of a special ice, one that did not shatter when fired but evaporated into thin air afterwards. It was the perfect bullet.

"Mayborn? You awake?" asked Secret Agent X, gently shaking the detective.

Mayborn groaned as he regained consciousness.

"Can you move?" asked X.

"I…uh, I think so," muttered Mayborn. "Yeah, I can."

"Good," stated Secret Agent X, as he looked around. The fire was everywhere, devastating all of the stored goods in the warehouse, but it also supplied X with something he needed. "Stay put for a second."

X moved back towards the collapsed and shattered crates that currently trapped them inside the pentagram circle. Carefully, he reached into the flames and snagged a small piece of wood that was partially on fire. X returned to Mayborn, who was now sitting up, cradling his right arm.

Curiously, Mayborn watched as X pulled the shirt and jacket away from his wound. Then, X lightly smothered the small flame on the shard of wood with Mayborn's jacket, leaving the hot embers intact at the rounded point.

"This is going to hurt," said Secret Agent X, as he shoved the tip of the wooden stick onto the top of the bullet wound.

"Aaaaahhh!" screamed Mayborn. The pain was bad, but the smell and sound of his flesh sizzling was even worse. After a couple of seconds, X pulled the stick away and tossed it aside.

"Are you okay, Mayborn?" asked X, concerned about his newfound ally.

Sweat trickling down his forehead, Mayborn replied with a weak nod.

"Sorry about that, but you were losing too much blood and I can't afford to have you pass out on me while we escape," said Secret Agent X.

"You must know something I don't know, Haueter," said Mayborn, straightening what was left of his shirt and jacket, "as it looks as if we're trapped here."

"So it seems. Look up."

Mayborn raised his head up and saw several ropes and chains from the various girders in the ceiling; most of them connected to a series of pulleys. One chain in particular was actually quite close to them, only about twelve feet above them.

Mayborn turned to X. "Are you kidding? That's too high to jump."

"We're not going to jump," replied X, "I'm going to stand on your shoulders."

"Now I know you're kidding," said Mayborn, shaking his head. "There's no way I can support your weight, not with this bum shoulder."

"Look around you, Mayborn. It's our only way out. The fire's getting too close," stated X. "If I stand on your shoulders, I can reach the chain. All you'll have to do is hold onto my ankles while I pull us up."

"There's no way you can pull both of us all the way up that chain."

"I don't have to. I just have to get us a few feet up, just enough so we can swing over that pile of burning rubbish," said X, pointing to the collapsed crates that blocked their path out. "Look, you won't be able to pull yourself up with that shoulder, let alone me, but I can."

Mayborn shook his head is slight disbelief, but then a smile appeared.

"What the hell, let's try it," said Mayborn optimistically, as he patted X on the back. "After all, we can't stay here, right?"

"Right," replied Secret Agent X, returning Mayborn's smile. "You ready to do this?"

"Oh, I'm as ready as I'm going to be."

Mayborn got down to one knee and cupped his hands together in front of him, as a makeshift step. X stepped into his hands and Mayborn launched X upwards, groaning as sharp twinges of pain shot through his wounded shoulder.

X used the upward thrust to step onto Mayborn's shoulders, staying there only briefly, as he snagged the low-hung chain immediately. He quickly wrapped one of his arms around the chain for extra support.

"I'm good!" yelled X. "Grab my legs!"

Mayborn steeled himself for more pain and gripped Secret Agent X's ankles with as much strength as he could muster. Another groan escaped his clenched teeth.

"Are you okay?" asked X.

"I'll be fine," strained Mayborn, "as soon as we get this over with."

"Understood."

Secret Agent X pulled him and Detective Mayborn up the old, rusted chain, hand over hand. Within seconds, they were about five feet off of the ground, plenty of height to swing over the burning crates.

Swaying his body back and forth, X started to swing towards his objective, gaining momentum with each swing. Soon, the bottoms of Mayborn's legs were passing over the pile of burning debris.

"Jump!" yelled "X". "Now!"

"Jump!" yelled X. "Now!"

Mayborn let go of X's legs and flew over the flaming crates, landing roughly on his feet and tumbling down to the ground. X followed suit on the next swing over, landing a couple of feet before Mayborn.

Helping him off the ground, X threw Mayborn's good arm around his own shoulders for support and led the way through the smoke. X followed the path Death's Touch used, which was clear of debris, if not the occasional shot of flames. Moments later, Mayborn noticed a break of light cutting through the smoke. It was the back door.

"That way!" exclaimed Mayborn, pointing weakly with his bad arm at their way out.

Saying nothing, X pushed them through the encroaching flames and into freedom. They were met by glorious daylight, and they both took several gulps of fresh air, clearing their lungs of the smoke that was beginning to take its toll on them.

They were free!

Chapter Twelve
THE RIDE

After their narrow escape from the fiery deathtrap, Secret Agent X helped Mayborn across the street to his car, sitting him in the passenger seat to rest. So far, at least as Agent X could tell, no alarm had been set off and the Fire Department had yet to be dispatched to the scene. In fact, with the exception of a few trails of black smoke pouring out, the warehouse seemed fine from the outside.

Still, this would not last long. It was the middle of the day and there were already a few people coming and going throughout the street, giving them strange looks, as well as the occasional car driving by. X needed to get away, and fast. But first, he needed to deal with Detective Mayborn.

"Mayborn?" asked Secret Agent X. "How do you feel?"

"I've been better," said Mayborn, smiling weakly, "thanks for asking."

"Look…I need to be on my way, but I need to be sure you're going to be okay," said X. "That maniac and his goons have escaped without a trace, and my only chance of stopping him is heading him off before he reaches his objective."

Mayborn straightened up in his seat. "Then let's go."

"No," said X, "You need to stay here, wait for help. You need a doctor."

"I can help, Haueter. You did a good job stopping the bleeding," stated Mayborn, "Besides, that bastard shot me. I'm not letting this go."

Although leaving Mayborn out here in the street seemed to be his best chance at getting medical help at this point, as this place would soon be crawling with cops and firemen, X knew there was the matter of Mayborn knowing too much about just happened. The last thing X needed was to have the local police getting involved. Perhaps it was best if they stayed together.

"Fine...you'll stay with me, for the moment," replied X, who closed the passenger door on Mayborn. X quickly jumped into the driver's seat and gunned his Coupe down the street, looking to put a little distance between the them and the warehouse, which was currently shooting flames out of the front door and windows.

As they drove through the Industrial District, Mayborn looked carefully at X. They had just been through an incredible ordeal, yet the man he knew as Haueter was calm and collected, almost calculating. It was clear to Mayborn that X was working on his next move.

"It's the President, isn't it?" asked Mayborn. "That's who that monster is after, right?"

X turned and stared at Mayborn with those dark, intense eyes, but he wasn't glaring at him. He was impressed.

"You're a pretty good detective, Mayborn," said Secret Agent X. "How did you figure that out?"

Mayborn shrugged. "It was what he said in the warehouse, before I announced my presence. He called you 'Secret Agent X', so I have to assume you're some sort of top level agent or spy. He also said that he was going to be the cause of your death and that of your 'precious leader'. Toss in the fact that the President is in town today only for his campaign trail visit, and that leaves me with a very big coincidence, one just a little too hard to ignore."

X smiled at the explanation. Some of the details were a little murky, but Mayborn got to the bottom of the mystery in no time and with few clues to go on.

"Not quite right, but pretty close," said X. "You seem to do well with little information."

"It's a gift," replied Mayborn. "I've always been good with puzzles and problems, since I was a just a small kid. When you get down to it, most crimes are just that... puzzles needing to be solved."

This sparked a thought in X's head, one that had been bothering him since Mayborn confronted Death's Touch. "Speaking of puzzles, I have one for you to solve for me."

"Okay, sure."

"How did you know to go to the warehouse?"

Mayborn smiled again, that warm smile that seemed to be infectious, as X immediately cracked a small grin.

"Well...after you left the crime scene, I started thinking about what you had said, about being Galvin's friend and working together," said Mayborn. "That got me thinking about him as a shamus. So, I decided to check out his place. I figured if I was going to find any more clues to his death that would be the place to start.

"As I got there, I saw you driving away. It was too late for me to follow you, so I went up to his apartment. Since you left in a hurry, I decided to bet on you leaving whatever evidence you found out in the open."

"Which I did," stated Secret Agent X.

"Right," agreed Mayborn. "I found the highlighted note about the warehouse, and I figured that was where you were headed. I checked the rest of the office, to be sure, and then I followed after you. Once I got there, I saw your car parked across the street, empty, so I cased the building,"

Mayborn reached into one of his pants pocket and pulled out a rumpled sheet of paper. "I found the original note by an open window on the side of the building. Galvin must have dropped it when crawling through it."

"Hmm…I can't believe I missed that…," muttered X, slightly disappointed with himself.

"Don't be," said Mayborn, as he carefully rubbed his wounded shoulder. "I only noticed the note because it was dry, and since it rained the night before, it had to be new.

"Anyway, I crawled through the window, as well, and I heard the sounds of fighting."

"That was me fighting a couple of those damn acolytes," stated X.

"By the time I made my way there, that freak calling himself Death's Touch was giving his big speech about how great he is and was about to make short work of you with the help of his goons. That's when I jumped in."

"Thanks for that, by the way," said Secret Agent X. "I'm sorry you got shot because of me. All I wanted was to avenge my friend's death. You should never have gotten involved with this."

Mayborn sat quietly for a second, looking out the window as they drove through Seattle, before he answered.

"Perhaps not, but I am involved now," said Mayborn. "Perhaps it's time you filled me in on what our next move is."

"Our first move is simple. We're heading to my hotel to get cleaned up. We're not going to get very far looking like we do, bloody and sweaty, all covered in dirt and soot. Plus, we need to clean out your wound and get it bandaged up."

"And then?" asked Mayborn.

"Then, we need to find a way past security at the President's speech later today," said Secret Agent X.

"Oh, that's easy," said Mayborn, his usual smile turning into a mischievous grin. "I can get us in there."

"How?" asked X, not quite believing what he was hearing.

"Deputy Chief Monroe, my boss, is one of the men in charge of security for the President's visit."

"Perfect," said X, returning Mayborn's grin with one of his own.

Chapter Thirteen
THE INSTRUMENT OF DEATH

D eath's Touch was angry, brimming not with the same hatred as before, but with resentment over the fact that Secret Agent X escaped his clutches. It was supposed to be his hands around X's throat, wringing the life out of him. It was supposed to be his victory, proving to him and everyone else that betrayed him so long ago, once and for all, who the better man was.

"Master?" inquired one of the acolytes, breaking Death's Touch from his train of thought.

"What is it?!" snapped Death's Touch, annoyed by the interruption.

"We are here," he said, pointing to their destination.

They arrived at the University of Washington campus, the very same campus in which the President of the United States would soon be speaking to a large crowd of constituents as he vied for their votes in the upcoming election. They were in a large work truck labeled as being part of a construction company. A simple but perfect disguise, this ruse allowed them to pass through the police security and enter the campus.

The truck came to a stop at a semi-secluded part of a parking lot. Death's Touch took a moment and looked out of the window, surveying all of the activity surrounding them, as preparations for the upcoming speech were well underway.

Although the President would be speaking at a podium assembled in the west side of the Liberal Arts Quadrangle, a beautiful courtyard affectionately called the Quad by the students and was located not too far away from Red Square, security was spread throughout the entire area. Due to the upcoming presence of the President, security was heavy and made up of officers from several organizations. The Seattle Police, along with the University's own police force, were handling most of the security around and throughout the grounds, while the Secret Service was in charge of all safeguards concerning the President.

At first glance, one would think that there was no chance in hell of Death's Touch and his acolytes getting inside that secured area, but that was where the construction company cover came into play.

Death's Touch and the acolytes exited the truck, all decked out in denim jeans and overalls, flannel shirts, and other work attire. They grabbed some equipment, cases, and bags from the back of the truck and made their way over to the Suzzallo Library, undisturbed. They easily mixed in with various other construction workers, who were either working on the podium or doing construction on the south face of the library.

They passed through the construction area and entered the building. Being careful not to draw undue attention to themselves, they made their way through the library, going all the way to the top floor and entering the stairwell to the attic.

"Let us prepare," said Death's Touch, as they entered the room.

At his command, the acolytes shed their disguises and donned their robes out of the bags they were carrying. One of the acolytes opened what looked to be a toolbox, but in reality, was a weapons cache. With a click of the latch, the cache hissed open, releasing a familiar vapor. He pulled out multiple daggers and throwing knives, all made of their special ice, and passed them to his fellow servants. As he did this, another acolyte opened a different case and started assembling another sort of weapon, but it was unclear yet as to what it was.

As they prepared for the upcoming mission, Death's Touch stared out of the small window overlooking the roof of the building and, most importantly, the west side of the Liberal Arts Quadrangle. The site they chose was perfect. They had a straight view to the podium.

An acolyte moved over to Death's Touch, standing at a respectful distance.

"Master, the Instrument is ready," he announced.

Death's Touch turned around. His loyal acolytes were standing in a semi-circle, armed with their daggers at the ready. Sitting before them was a large rifle with several metal canisters and hoses attached to it. Ice vapors were pouring off of it. It was a large-scale version of the ice gun.

It was the Instrument of the Hand of Death; capable of allowing his deadly Touch to reach out to those who would think they are safe.

Death's Touch shed his overalls with a simple pull, practically ripping it off with ease, revealing his leather armor. The acolyte at his side handed Death's Touch his cloak, which he threw on in a swooping motion as he walked over the large weapon.

Picking up the ice rifle, Death's Touch felt its weight in his hand, comforted by the cold metal. It was brutal and unforgiving, just like him.

"We are ready, my acolytes," said Death's Touch. "Soon, the President of this false nation will be no longer.

Chapter Fourteen
CHANGES

They reached Secret Agent X's hotel in little time after deciding their course of action. To avoid unwanted questions concerning their appearance, especially Mayborn's, they entered the building through the service entrance in the back. This allowed them to move silently through the service corridors, unfettered by nosy guests.

Once they entered his room, X quickly set about cleaning out Mayborn's bullet wound as best as he could. He still needed to see a doctor, but the wound looked pretty good. Agent X's quick thinking back at the warehouse stopped the blood loss and hopefully prevented any infections from setting in. X bandaged the wound tightly with strips of linen he tore from the sheets of his bed.

As Mayborn left for the bathroom to clean up, X took stock of what assets he had left. If they had been in New York City instead of Seattle, X could have taken them to any one of many safe houses, apartments, or garages, filled with all of the supplies they would ever need. Of course, this was not his hometown, his regular base of operations, so all he had with him was what he had packed for this trip.

X emptied his two suitcases. He had several suits and assorted clothing, which was good, as they both needed a change of outfits. Fortunately, X was nearly as tall as Mayborn, so his extra suits would fit him just fine. What he did not have, though, was an extra gas pistol to replace the one he lost in the fire. All he had left was a portion of his array of specialty items: his portable make-up kit, to change his appearance when needed; a set of master keys, to allow him entry into just about any place; his bulletproof vest, which he would need shortly; his leather case of drugs such as truth serums, which might come in handy later, but he doubted he would get the chance to use them; and his trusty penlight.

As he scanned his meager supplies, Secret Agent X remembered what he had in his coat pocket, an item he picked up at the warehouse and promptly forgot all about, due to the day's frenzied events. After all, he was so used to having his various pockets weighed down from all of his tools that he did not take notice until now. X reached into his pocket and pulled out the Colt .45 pistol that once belonged to his operative, William Galvin.

"Good, you do have a gun," said Mayborn, appearing out of the bathroom. "We're going to need it against those goons of Death's Touch."

X looked at the gun for a moment. Was he at that point? Was he going to be forced to use a real gun once again? Without his gas pistol, he was completely unarmed against a monster like Death's Touch. X needed an edge, something to take him out quick. After that fight in the warehouse, Agent X knew he might not be able to beat him again, especially with all of those acolytes at his beck and call. He was lucky earlier, and he could not count on that same luck again.

X couldn't do it. Not yet, anyway. He would find a way to stop Death's Touch without having to resort to that he had sworn off.

Secret Agent X tossed to the gun to Mayborn. "You use it, Mayborn. You lost your gun in the fire, as well, and I may need you to take care of the acolytes while I deal with Death's Touch."

"Thanks," said Mayborn, checking out the piece. "This is a nice gun, it looks like Government Issue. From the war?"

"Yes. It was Galvin's," replied X, whose otherwise strong voice softened for a second as he thought back on his friend, "He didn't know it, but we served together several times during the war. It was one of the reason why I chose him to be one of my operatives."

"How was that possible?" asked Mayborn.

"The same way that you are about to find out that Detective Joe Haueter is nothing more that one of a thousand faces," said Agent X, as he tossed a suit to Mayborn before he could inquire further. "Here, put this on while I change into something more useful."

Leaving Mayborn in the main room to get dressed, Secret Agent X entered the bathroom with a new suit, bulletproof vest, make-up kit, and a small manila folder. Once he cleaned up, X changed into his fresh clothes and laid out the contents of his make-up kit, preparing for yet another amazing transformation.

X opened the folder to reveal several files on high-ranking police officers throughout the Seattle area. He assembled these files earlier on this trip, in preparation for the creation of 'Detective Joe Haueter', the latest of his legion of identities. As luck would have it, one of those files pertained to Deputy Chief Carl Monroe.

Agent X removed his fake beard and the last remnants of his Haueter identity. Afterwards, X molded the special plastic over the contours of his true features, shaping his appearance to resemble that of Monroe. With the proper use of pigments, he easily matched the same coloring of the fair skinned Deputy Chief in a matter of moments. His luck held out further, as X had to do little with his current hair color and style, other than changing the style of the cut. With the transformation complete, Secret Agent X exited the bathroom.

Mayborn was finishing getting dressed into his new blue suit when X entered the room. He was shocked at seeing his superior officer. The resemblance to Monroe was more than uncanny. It was perfect.

"Amazing," muttered Mayborn. "How did you…do this?"

Secret Agent X decided it was time to come clean with Mayborn and let him know the whole truth. It was time to bring Mayborn into the fold.

"I am a master of disguise, Mayborn. I can alter my appearance and voice to match anyone," said Secret Agent X. "I am like a shadow, I blend into the darkness, becoming one with the background. I am like a spider, I fight for justice with fangs to incapacitate my enemies, weaving webs to catch them and delivering them to the authorities. I am like a phantom, a ghost that can slip in and out of anywhere at anytime, unhindered by the world around me.

"I am Secret Agent X. I was appointed by a very high-ranking government official to be a free agent with carte blanche to mete out justice and I answer to no one."

X paused for a moment, to allow what he just said to sink in, before continuing.

"Still, I can't be everywhere," said Agent X. "That is why I have operatives of my own. Men and women who keep their ears to the ground and eyes on the road, letting me know where I am needed most and to back me up when things get too hairy. Now, with Galvin gone, I need a new operative for Seattle.

"Are you up for it?"

Mayborn stood still for a second, a contemplative look etched in his face. He reached down and snagged Galvin's pistol from a small table next to him. Mayborn double-checked the safety and slipped the gun into his belt holster before speaking up.

"Count me in," said Mayborn, smiling like the cat that got the canary.

Chapter Fifteen
THE CALM BEFORE

Detective Michael Mayborn was once again in Agent X's car, but this time he was the one behind the wheel. As they shot through the streets on their way to the University of Washington, his thoughts turned back to the events of the last hour, their narrow escape from the fiery warehouse and his indoctrination as an operative of Secret Agent X.

"We're not going to be able to call on help from the other cops, are we?" asked

Mayborn, his mind still mired on the possibilities and repercussions of what laid ahead.

"No," replied Agent X. "In fact, if we are not careful, they will most likely think we are involved and will try to stop us. What I do is generally considered to be outside of the law, as you know it. My invisible status often marks me as a criminal by those I aid and protect."

"Well, that will make this a lot more difficult," said Mayborn, "but I imagine you have a plan."

"I do. Well, most of one. An idea of one, really."

They spent the rest of the short drive in silence. For Secret Agent X, it was time for formulation. He had only a few minutes left in which to cook up a plan to locate and stop Death's Touch before it was too late. For Mayborn, it was a time of contemplation, to adjust to his new role and the idea of working on a scale of justice far larger than he had ever known.

As they approached the University, Mayborn brought them to an entrance close to the President's speech, which was guarded by the local police. The guard at the gate was a simple flatfoot by the name of Sweeney, who was from the same Precinct as Detective Mayborn and 'Deputy Chief Monroe'.

They were about to find out if X's disguise would get them behind the secured area.

Although he had the physical features of the Deputy Chief down perfectly, X had never met or heard Monroe before. All he had to work with was a crash course on mannerisms and a sound check supplied by Mayborn back at the hotel.

"Detective Mayborn!" exclaimed Sweeney, as he noticed who was driving the car. "What are you doing here? I though you were working a murd—Oh! Deputy Chief! Sorry, sir, I didn't see you there!"

"You're damn right you're sorry, son!" harrumphed X, doing his best to come of as the surly commanding officer. "Now, move out of our way and get back to your job!"

"Yes, sir! Sorry, Sir!" Sweeney snapped, practically jumping out of his skin. He waved through them. "Go on ahead!"

"Not bad," said Mayborn, as they passed out of earshot, "The voice wasn't quite right, but you scared him enough that he didn't notice, not that he would. Most beat cops at our precinct go out of their way to avoid him, so I doubt he's all too familiar with the exact sound of his voice."

"Well, hopefully, we won't be put to the test again," said Secret Agent X.

After parking away from the entrance, Mayborn and Secret Agent X moved through the open-aired area called Red Square on their way to the Quad. They moved with purpose, as if they belonged, and as far as any of the other cops or agents knew, they did. As long as they did not run into the real Deputy Chief Monroe, they were fairly safe to move about behind the scenes.

"Are you sure we should looking back here, Haueter?" asked Mayborn, still calling X by the only name he knew him by. "Wouldn't it be easier for them to attack from the other side, where the access is open to the public?"

"No," said X. "The Secret Service would be expecting any problems to come from the crowd, not from the back area filled with cops and assistants and other such people. In their minds this section is secured, so they are going to be looking outward."

"Good point," agreed Mayborn. "So, where do we start? What's your plan?"

X stopped and faced his ally. Even with a completely different face, Mayborn was amazed that X's eyes still burned with the same intensity.

"Here's my plan…We don't have time to search every nook and cranny, and we can't be overt about what we do," said Secret Agent X. "So, we need to deduce where he is from what we know. I've already said you were a good detective, Mayborn. Now, it's time to put your skills to work."

Mayborn was a bit stunned, but also a bit embarrassed, by X's faith in his abilities, as was shown by his sheepish grin. "That's your plan? You're going to have me just figure it out?"

"You can do this, Mayborn," said X. "This is just another one of your puzzles, remember?"

The confidence Secret Agent X showed in Mayborn's abilities was impressive, to say the least. Mayborn not only felt he had to do this just to show X that his faith was not misplaced, but he wanted to.

"Okay, let's give it a try."

"Good. I want you to focus on what I'm about to say," said Agent X, pausing for a few seconds before continuing on. "You are a 7-foot tall scarred maniac in leathers with a gun that shoots ice and an entourage of bootlicking minions at your beck and call. You obviously do not blend into a crowd.

"How are you going to get in, then? Where are you going to hide? How are you going to strike?

"These are the questions you need to answer."

Mayborn closed his eyes and worked the details in his head. He stood silent for a few moments, and then started to whisper his thoughts for Agent X's sake.

"Death's Touch and his cronies had to come in here to complete their mission. The President is here. He is well-guarded. They had to wade through all of the police and Secret Service to get in…

"He's a monster, and he knows it. He can't just blend in with a crowd…and besides, the crowd is out there. It's not in here. There are only cops and agents in here…

"Oh! Staff and service members…I almost forgot them!

"Yeah, the workers…they are the ones keeping this event running. They are invisible to the people they are serving. They could disguise themselves as them."

X shook his head. "Close, but not quite. Maybe his goons could sneak in that way, but he's just too big and burly. Keep thinking."

"Right…they're too—what's the word?—pretty," said Mayborn, his eyes still closed. "Servants have to be presentable. Who else back here is invisible to everyone else…?

"I got it! The construction workers!"

X nodded in agreement, slyly looking around and getting a bearing on the construction taking place at the library. "Yes. A big man like him would easily fit in with the construction workers, and no one would look too hard anyway since the workers are cordoned off from the main event, yet are still behind the stage."

"That answers your second question, as well," replied Mayborn, eyes open once more, his brainteaser done. "If they are disguised as workers, then that places them inside the library."

"Okay, good…Then, if you're Death's Touch and you are stuck inside the library, how are you going to strike out and kill the President?" asked Agent X.

Mayborn thought for but a second before the answer jumped out of him.

"Simple…the roof," said Mayborn. "He's an assassin, right? He'll go to the roof to get his shot!"

With Mayborn's revelation, they turned their attention to the Suzzallo Library. A quick glance at the building gave them all they needed to know where to go. With the layout of the podium set at the west end of the Quad and its surrounding buildings, the only viable spot for an assassin to get a clear shot was the northwest corner of the library, which was closed off due to the construction on the southwest end of the building. At that exact spot, they noticed a small attic window embedded within a stone spire that was cracked open.

That was where they had to go.

With Agent X leading the way, the two of them moved back towards the library. They were careful not to move too quickly; otherwise, they would catch the attention of nearly every law enforcement officer in the area.

Unfortunately, they caught the attention of someone far more sinister, as a pair of dark and malicious eyes watched them from the very same attic window.

Chapter Sixteen
THE STORM

Entering the construction site of the library was easy enough. Mayborn and X flashed their badges at the foreman of the job, who nodded and let them pass without question, as he had done for a couple dozen other cops that day. From there, Mayborn led the way inside, as X followed.

They moved through the maze of rooms and halls, making their way up towards the attic as best they could, what with not being all too familiar with the layout.

After a few minutes, Agent X and Mayborn entered a huge cathedral-style room with tall stained glass windows and rows of upon rows of beautiful oak tables intermixed between aisles of books. With the library closed to the public, the room felt even larger than it normally was, due to the emptiness. In fact, it was so empty, every move they made in this room echoed throughout, giving them immediate pause.

As X stepped into the room, he immediately noticed something was amiss, that the room just didn't feel right. He grabbed Mayborn lightly by the shoulder, the wounded one, careful not to put any undue pressure on it.

"Wait…," whispered Secret Agent X. "Something's wrong here."

Detective Mayborn stopped in his tracks. "What?"

"Have you ever been all alone in a house that was empty?" asked X. "It has that…feeling. You just know that there is no one there."

"Sure."

"That feeling just went away. We're not alone."

At that very moment, a sliver of razor sharp ice flew by Mayborn's head, missing it by mere inches. It stuck into the wall behind them, surprising both of them that it did not shatter upon impact. But, a second later, the small throwing knife evaporated into a fine mist, leaving no trace.

That shard of ice was quickly followed by several more.

"Move!" said X, pushing Mayborn away as he jumped for cover from a nearby bookshelf.

Mayborn ducked under one of the oak tables and flipped it over to its side, giving him protection from the flying ice knives. His eyes darting slightly above the top of the table, Mayborn looked for any sign of the ones throwing the ice shards. Of course, he already knew they were there, but he just could not get a bead on where they were hiding.

"The acolytes are on the other side of the room, Haueter," said Mayborn, pulling out his gun, "but I can't get a clean shot at them."

"Hold your fire!" yelled Agent X. "We don't want to announce our presence to anyone else. A gunshot will bring the Secret Service and the rest of the police."

"Great…what should I do then?" asked Mayborn as he put the gun away.

"Wait there for my signal," said X, as he launched into the air and landed on one of the tables.

Wasting no time, X jumped from table to table with lightning speed. More ice shards flew through the air, sticking into the tables less than a second after he was there, leaving a trail of them evaporating behind him.

Secret Agent X was taking a dangerous but necessary risk. He needed to remove the acolytes from the fight, leaving only Death's Touch to deal with, and every second out in the open left him exposed to an icy death.

Originally, X was hoping they could take them by surprise, but this ambush had changed his game plan. Now, He needed to take them out fast and hard, and what he had planned was going to hurt.

In the mere seconds he had as he charged across the library tables, Agent X followed the flying slivers of ices to their points of origin, thereby discovering exactly how many acolytes were there and exactly where they were. He was in luck; all five of the acolytes were downstairs. He may yet preserve the element of surprise for his final confrontation with Death's Touch's.

There was a little bad luck, though; only three of the acolytes were together. The final two were positioned separately. Still, his plan would eliminate the majority of them in one simple yet painful move.

Hitting the last table, Secret Agent X launched right into the top of a very large bookshelf, the very same one that three of the acolytes were hiding behind.

"Now!" yelled X to Mayborn, as his body hit the bookshelf with enough force to knock it over, crushing the acolytes under its heavy weight. The pain was intense, shooting straight through his left arm and shoulder, the point of contact. It traveled down his spine, knocking the wind right out of him. He knew it was going to take a few seconds to recover from this downright stupid move, but he had full faith in his new operative to take out the remaining acolytes.

Mayborn shot from his cover behind the overturned table, rushing towards X as fast as possible. Ahead of him, Mayborn saw one of the other acolytes appear from his hiding spot, a large ice dagger in hand. The acolyte was moving straight for the dazed Secret Agent X.

Still running, Mayborn deftly snagged a wooden chair and in one smooth action, he clubbed the acolyte over the head just as he was turning his attention to Mayborn. The chair splintered into dozens of pieces, knocking the acolyte out cold.

With his opponent out of the way, Mayborn turned to check on X, who was moaning lightly and trying to sit up.

All of a sudden, the final acolyte jumped from his position and sliced Mayborn in his right arm. It wasn't a deep cut, but it was right next to the bullet wound from earlier.

"Bastard!" screamed Mayborn through clenched teeth, as he turned to face the final lackey of Death's touch.

The acolyte slashed with his dagger in several short strokes, trying to connect with Mayborn's torso. Mayborn stepped back from each slash of the knife, avoiding it at all costs.

"You will die!" screeched the last acolyte, enraged at them for taking out his fellow brothers in the Order of the Hand of Death. He pressed his attack, swinging his blade faster and with more force.

Mayborn noticed a stack of books on the oak table next to him. With his left arm, he swept them off the table and straight at the acolyte. The acolyte was not fast enough to avoid them, as the books hit him in the chest. They did not really hurt him, but they did leave him open for Mayborn to tackle him.

Mayborn rushed in with his good shoulder, his left arm blocking the dagger. He smashed into the acolyte, throwing them both down to the ground. Pinning the acolyte down with his legs and keeping the dagger away, Mayborn landed several good left jabs, one after another. The acolyte's nose cracked loudly, now broken, and blood spilled out.

The acolyte struggled, but did not have the proper leverage to remove Mayborn. His dagger was useless, as his right arm was pinned. He had only one chance.

Reaching into his robe, the acolyte pulled out one of the small throwing knives. He slammed it into Mayborn's side, just below the ribs.

"Ahh!" yelled Mayborn, his control lost, as the acolyte pushed him aside. The knife in his side vaporized into a mist almost immediately, which was a minor blessing, as he did not have to worry about removing it.

The acolyte saw he had only seconds to finish off Mayborn, as Secret Agent X was about to get up. He pulled out another throwing shard and jumped Mayborn, intent on driving it into his heart.

Mayborn had other plan. Time for screwing around had long since passed.

Mayborn pulled out the Colt from his holster and pistol-whipped the acolyte. Snagging the padding from the broken chair, Mayborn shoved it into the dazed acolyte's chest. He jabbed the gun dead-center of the pillow and pulled the trigger, twice. The padding muffled the sound of the shots, but it was quite clear that they hit home. The acolyte's eyes went wide with disbelief, then slowly closed as he died.

"Mayborn," called Secret Agent X, trying to get his friend's attention. "Are you okay?"

Mayborn slid his gun back into its holster as he stood up. "I got stuck with one of those throwing knives, my bad arm's been cut, and I think the bullet wound is bleeding again. Yeah, I'm okay. You?"

"I'm fine. A little dazed, but it will pass in a minute," replied X.

Mayborn helped Secret Agent X off of the overturned bookshelf. "Good. We should go."

"I agree, but only I'm going any further."

"What? Haueter, I thought we were in this together?" asked Mayborn.

"We are, but you're in no shape to face Death's Touch," replied X. "You'll be a liability. I'm sorry, but I have to finish this myself."

For the first time since X met him, Mayborn almost looked mad. His usual casual demeanor faded away, to be replaced with what could only be anger, albeit barely. But, as soon as it appeared, it disappeared.

Mayborn sighed. "You're right. I don't like it, but you're right. I'll stay here and make sure these goons don't go anywhere. If any are still alive, that is."

X put his hand out to Mayborn. "Thanks, Mayborn, for all of your help today."

"Why am I getting the feeling I'm not going to see you again?" asked Mayborn, grinning slyly as they shook hands.

"If all goes well, you'll see me again," replied Agent X, as he turned to leave. He headed for the back entrance, the one the acolytes were guarding.

As X disappeared from the room, an exhausted Mayborn pulled out a nearby chair and sat down, wondering how he was going to explain all of this to the real Deputy Chief Monroe without giving away the truth of Secret Agent X.

Grinning, he looked down at the acolytes.

"You mugs got off easy," commented Mayborn.

Chapter Seventeen
THE FINALE

Secret Agent X found the door to the attic a few minutes after leaving Mayborn. Although locked, X quickly popped it open, thanks to his set of master keys.

Opening the door as quietly as possible, X entered the dark and narrow stairway.

He climbed the stairs slowly, careful not to put too much pressure down on the steps. The last thing he needed to do after all he and Mayborn just went through was to alert Death's Touch with a squeaky step. X reached the top of the stairs, which opened to the fairly spacious but dusty attic. Standing in front of the window, straight ahead, was Death's Touch.

His back to the room, Death's Touch stared intently out of the window, watching the President's men prepare for the upcoming speech. Resting against the wall next to him was the Instrument of Death. Although Secret Agent X did not know it by that name, he knew by a simple glance that it was the rifle version of the ice gun. Taking into consideration the killing power behind that gun, one could imagine the devastating effects of the rifle if used.

X's approach seemed to have gone unnoticed by Death's Touch, giving him one chance to end this quickly. Unarmed, his best chance at subduing the monster was to slam into him, as he did with the bookshelf. Although there were other objects strewn about that could be used as weapons, such as cases and equipment, X could not afford to take the chance of grabbing one. He had to take out Death's Touch now, before the element of surprise was lost.

Agent X vaulted from his position. He sped as quickly as possible for Death's Touch, who was standing about thirty feet away. He almost reached him.

Spinning about in the blink of an eye, Death's Touch reached out with his large, meaty arm and backhanded Agent X with ease, throwing him across the room.

"I do not know how you survived the fire, X," said Death's Touch, his gravelly voice laced with a perverse glee. "But I am so glad that you did. Now, I get the pleasure of killing you myself."

X stood up, brushing off some dust from his jacket. "You can certainly try, but we both know how this fight is going to end. I beat you back at the warehouse, and I'm going to beat you here."

His face flushed with anger, as Death's Touch spat at his opponent. "You did no such thing, X! A couple of lucky hits did not make you the victor!"

"I took you down easily," said X, goading him further. "Had you been alone, I would have finished you off."

"I'm all alone now, X" said Death's Touch, taking his cloak off and letting it drop to the floor. "Care to try again?"

"Gladly," replied Agent X.

Wasting no more time, Death's Touch moved in for the attack. His huge fists pounded through the air, as X dodged the punches.

For all of his previous bravado, X knew he could not afford to let Death's Touch land any punches. All it would take would be a few shots to the head or stomach, and it would be over.

Death's Touch was too fast, as well. X could barely stay ahead of each swing, so it was nearly impossible to get in a shot of his own.

It was time to change tactics.

Suddenly, X dropped down and kicked out, sweeping both of the monster's legs out from under him. Death's Touch fell to the ground with a sharp thud, shaking the floor upon contact.

Pressing his advantage, Agent X jumped into the air and came down hard with his elbow, striking Death's Touch in the sternum. This move would have knocked the wind out of any other man, perhaps even cracked the bone, but not Death's Touch. All he did was let out a grunt before grabbing X by the throat.

"I'll choke the life out of you, X!" yelled Death's Touch, tightening his grip with his massive hand.

X slammed his elbow once, twice, three times into that horrific face. A loud cracking occurred, as a nose that had been broken so many times before snapped once more. It didn't hurt Death's Touch too much, though, as his pain threshold was fairly high.

Cracking a small and nasty grin, Death's Touch released his hold on X's throat, followed by a solid punch to the side of X's head. Agent X went reeling to the floor. A trickle of blood trailed away from a gash in his scalp.

"Did you like that, X?" inquired Death's Touch as he got up from the floor. "I'll bet you did. Here's some more for you."

Death's Touch kicked Secret Agent X hard enough to toss him into the air and move him several feet, cracking a couple of ribs in the process. X had never been kicked like that before. The pain was so intense, he nearly blacked out.

Agent X slid up against the various cases that the acolytes brought in earlier, knocking one of them over. A couple of ice daggers spilled out of the case. This was fortunate, as X needed an edge. Now, he had two.

Picking up the daggers, a dazed Secret Agent X carefully got to his feet. Holding both knives in front of him while in a defensive stance, X squared off against Death's Touch. Woozy from the punch and kick, X needed to buy a few moments to clear his head. What better way than to get this maniac talking, find out who he really was?

"Who are you, really?" asked Secret Agent X. "Don't give me any of this Note des Todes crap, either."

Death's Touch slid his short sword out of its scabbard, revealing the gladius-style blade to be constructed of the same special ice as the daggers. He eyed the edge of the icy blade, turning it in his hand, hoping it would soon taste the blood of his enemy.

"I've told you who I am, X," said Death's Touch. "Who I was and what this is all about, however, that is what you really want to know, isn't it?"

"You know it is," said X. "You knew who I was from the start. You were gunning for me. Why?"

"It's not that easy, X," said Death's Touch. "I told you back at the warehouse, you'd have to earn those answers with pain and blood."

"I think I just did," replied Agent X.

"Not nearly enough."

Death's Touch charged forward and sliced his sword through the air. X blocked the sword with one of his daggers. Chips of ice flew off both blades, but they held together. As X pushed the sword aside with his dagger, he thought it was odd that these strange blades of ice evaporated upon contact with other things, yet held together when touching one another.

With the sword out of the way, an opening was made for X to attack. X stabbed Death's Touch with his other dagger, jabbing it into the center of his breastplate. A perfect hit, but the blade did not go through the thick leather. Instead, it shattered upon impact.

"Too bad, X" taunted Death's Touch. "Nice try."

Death's Touch brought his blade back down again, only to be blocked once more by X's final dagger. He tried again, this time using his incredible strength to push X back against the wall.

As Death's Touch brought his blade down for the fourth time, Secret Agent X dropped down and shot to the side. Death's Touch missed X completely, as his sword smashed into the wall. As it shattered into hundreds of little shards of ice, X stabbed the ice dagger into the monster's unprotected left bicep, penetrating through the entire muscle.

Death's Touch screamed as he twisted away, stumbling. The dagger stuck in his arm vaporized, the chilling mist streaming from the bloody wound.

"Enough of this!" yelled Death's Touch, as he quickly pulled out his ice gun and shot X in the chest.

X barely saw that shot coming and tried to dodge it, but he was not fast enough this time, the events of the day taking their toll on his speed. The ice bullet slammed into him, right above his heart. The force of the impact caused him to spin in mid-air and crash into the floor.

Sliding his gun back into its holster, Death's Touch grabbed one of the flannel shirts used earlier as part of the disguises used by him and the acolytes. He wrapped it tightly around the wound on his left arm, which just hung there limp, the pain throbbing through his entire arm.

"Are you still alive, X?" asked Death's Touch, softly, staring at the lifeless body of the Secret Agent. The anger and hatred that fueled him seemed to be ebbing away, ever so slowly, now that it seemed his greatest desire had been fulfilled.

Moments passed, then a tiny moan escaped X's lips.

"You are alive. Barely, but you still draw breath," said Death's Touch. "You can die knowing you fought well."

"Not yet," muttered X, unmoving, his face down in the floor. "You owe me answers..."

Death's Touch barked out a short laugh. "You are right, I do owe you answers. After all, you paid for them."

"Were you in the Intelligence Service?" asked X, weakly, his voice barely above a whisper.

"Let me guess...it was the 'disavow' line, correct? It seemed appropriate to me. Besides, I couldn't help but toss that into my rhetoric for the acolytes. They ate it up."

"What happened to you, to turn into this...monster?"

"Death's Touch screamed"

"I'll tell you what happened…Your bosses betrayed me!" shouted Death's Touch, as thoughts of the past rushed through his head. "They sent me off on an impossible mission, where I was trapped in a burning castle on the outskirts of Romania. I nearly burned to death!

"I was found by an ancient band of Gypsies. They brought me back from the brink of death, but I was forever scarred with this hideous visage you see before you.

"I spent many years with them, gaining my strength and learning their ways. They taught me many of the dark secrets they learned from around the world, from ancient Sumerians to Tibetan monks. They are the ones who taught me how to change water into an ice that could be used as a weapon.

"With this knowledge at hand, I set about creating my own network of operatives, under the guise of a religious sect. My acolytes, whom I assume you eliminated downstairs, were eager to do my bidding.

"The Order of the Hand of Death was created, and my mission for revenge upon those that abandoned me began. Your bosses would soon feel my pain."

"What are you talking about?" whispered Agent X, barely hanging onto life. "What do my 'bosses' have to do with you?"

"Did you really think you were the only government-appointed free agent, to be backed by a cabal of secret millionaires?" inquired Death's Touch, shaking his head at X's apparent ignorance. "You are only the latest in a long line of Secret Agents."

Death's Touch paused for a moment, to let what he was saying to X sink in.

"I was Secret Agent X before you."

The realization hit X hard. Being a free agent, he has had no contact with those that appointed him to his task or to those that continue to finance him, so the idea of there being others like him was foreign to him. It was a simple thought that never came up, nor was ever conceived.

Still, could Death's Touch be correct? Was X just a replacement, taking the place of another just like him?

It was possible that Death's Touch was lying, but X honestly believed him. This monster hated him with a fiery passion, and there was little other explanation as to why he did. They had never met before, as X was certain he would remember someone as big as this man. So, the likelihood that Death's Touch was unfinished business from some past case was slim.

What he said made a sick sort of sense, even if his hatred was misplaced.

"Why me?" asked X, his voice getting weaker. "Why go after me?"

"Why not?" replied Death's Touch. "I have no idea who the financiers are, or were. The official who appointed me so long ago died of old age before I could exact my revenge on him. That left me with you, my successor. By killing you, I strike back at them.

"And if they decide to replace you, I will kill your replacement, as well. I will do so until they stop replacing Secret Agents."

"You're insane…," said X, as his voice trailed away into silence.

"I've been called that upon occasion," replied Death's Touch, as he turned his attention back to the window. Outside, one of the President's campaign managers was on the stage and speaking to the large crowd, preparing them for the President's imminent appearance. "Now, if you'll excuse me, I'll let you get back to dying, as I have a mission to complete. Although this job was taken to draw you out, it is still a paying job."

Death's Touch grabbed the ice rifle, the Instrument of Death, as he liked to call it. He checked out the rifle, making sure it was ready. It was working perfectly.

Staring through the sight, He carefully lined up his shot with the podium on the stage, as best as he could with his injured left arm hanging uselessly. Now, all he had left to do was to wait for the President to appear.

An unusual calm washed over him as we waited. He had killed the famed Secret Agent X, the man he should have been. He was about to kill the President, causing the United States to erupt into chaos. His revenge was nearly over. He was victorious!

He was also completely wrong.

As his attention was drawn outside, Secret Agent X silently stood up. A large hole in his coat and shirt revealed the bulletproof vest underneath. The bullet did not reach its target. Instead, X allowed him to think it did in order to discover the truth.

Agent X's eyes burned with a cold fury as he stared at the back of Death's Touch. All of the death and destruction caused today was because this crazy man believed his life was abandoned, left for dead, and then finally stolen by another man. William Galvin died because of the delusions of this maniac. Mayborn almost died, twice.

No one else would be hurt by this monster, this Secret Agent X swore under his breath.

X immediately slammed into Death's Touch with as much strength as he could muster. It was more than enough.

"What?!" exclaimed Death's Touch, who was completely caught by surprise. "No!"

X hit Death's Touch with enough force that he shoved them both through the attic window. The window shattered as they barreled through it, and the Instrument of Death went flying out of the monster's hands. They both grabbed onto the ledge of the ornate roof as they tumbled out, desperately hanging over the edge of the library.

The sound of the glass breaking and hitting the ground far below alerted the crowd of Secret Service and local police to their presence.

The Secret Service snagged the President just as he was about to make his appearance on the stage and ushered him to safety. Apparently, Agent X had acted just in the nick of time.

The local police rushed towards the library. Some of them entered the building, obviously on their way to the roof. Others watched from below, guns drawn, but withholding fire, as they were unsure of what was going on. Regardless, X knew he had only moments left to finish Death's Touch off, once and for all.

X landed several punches to his head with his free arm. He knew it didn't hurt the monster, but it did keep him distracted from getting a better grip on the stone workings of the building. In fact, it was working. Death's Touch only had a tentative hold to begin with, but now his grip was slipping.

"You ruined everything, X!" yelled Death's Touch, whose bad arm suddenly snaked out and grabbed X by the shirt. "I will not die alone!"

Death's Touch let go of the building, pulling Secret Agent X down with him. The added weight of the massive frame of Death's Touch easily caused X to lose his own marginal grasp of the building.

X fell only about a foot before he was yanked to a halt, as someone grabbed his arm. The immediate stop in his drop caused his shirt to rip apart where Death's Touch held onto it. Holding onto a scrap of clothing, Death's Touch continued his descent to the ground, meeting his own demise with a pulpy splat against the brick courtyard.

A relieved Agent X looked up to see who saved him. He saw a friendly face, as a battered and bruised Detective Mayborn pulled him back inside.

"Thanks," said X, catching his breath. "I owe you, again."

"Think nothing of it," replied Mayborn, smiling. "You're just lucky I heard the window break and decided to investigate. You know how hard it is to run when you've been stabbed in the leg?"

The sounds of running echoed through the building, reaching their ears in the attic.

Mayborn stood and helped X get to his feet. "Come on, we've got to get you out of here. The cops will be here any second."

"There's no other way out," commented X as he looked around the attic, hoping that he missed another entrance somewhere. He did not.

They could hear several people charging up the stairs to the attic.

"Don't worry, and follow my lead," said Mayborn, as he threw X's arm around his shoulders, supporting him as if he could not walk on his own.

Suddenly, three beat cops appeared at the top of the stairs, guns drawn. Before they could even yell "Freeze", Mayborn went into his act.

"Out of the way! Move it!" Mayborn yelled, as he moved forward with X in tow. "Can't you see the Deputy Chief is hurt!"

The cops immediately focused on X, who was still wearing his disguise as Deputy Chief Monroe, albeit disheveled. Luckily, that worked to his advantage at this point.

"But…what's going on here? How did he get hurt?" asked one of the beat cops.

"Are you kidding me? You're asking inane questions while a fellow officer is hurt? What the hell is wrong with you?" asked Mayborn, followed by a convincing moan from X.

"Sorry, sir! Go ahead!" snapped the cop, afraid he was going to get into trouble.

Mayborn turned to one of the other cops. "You take charge of the scene. I'll send help up after I've seen to the Deputy Chief," said Mayborn, as they passed the cops and made their way down the stairs.

"Yes, sir!" exclaimed the cop.

As Mayborn escorted X out of the building, they ran into a few more cops, playing this scene out a couple more times. It worked like a charm each time. Within a few minutes, they were outside and walking away from the entire spectacle.

With all of the commotion going on around them, they dropped their act and slipped out into the parking lot and back to X's parked car.

"Nice bit of acting, Mayborn," commented X. "I couldn't have done better myself."

"Thanks."

"You want a lift out of here?" asked Agent X, as he slid into the driver's seat. "It's the least I could do."

"Thanks, but no," replied Mayborn. "I've got to get back and get my story on the record before someone figures out I wasn't even supposed to be here and starts asking too many questions.

"Besides, I could really use a doctor right now."

"Understood," said X, nodding his head as he closed the car door and started the engine. "So long, Mayborn, we'll meet again."

"Of course we will, but will I even recognize you?" asked Mayborn, smiling as he watched his new friend and ally drive away.

THE END

A GUY WALKED INTO A BAR:

BRIAN MEREDITH

•••And the bartender said, "Hey! I haven't seen you in weeks!"

"Yeah, I know, I've been busy. I've been working on a story for a new pulp anthology," the guy replied, as he sat down in his favorite stool at the bar.

It was clear to anyone paying attention in the Northlake Tavern & Pizza House that this guy was something of a regular. The bartender immediately began pouring a pint of the guy's favorite beer (Mac & Jack's African Amber) before he even asked for it. Sliding the cold drink over to him, the bartender asked the guy if he wanted his usual order.

The guy nodded and said, "Yeah, a medium pepperoni, to go."

As the guy enjoyed his beer, the bartender placed his order and returned a few moments later.

"Order's in. It'll be about half an hour," the bartender said. "So, Brian, tell me about this story of yours…"

And with that, I started to explain my participation in this book and the reasons for doing it.

Let me step back for a moment, though. At first, I wasn't quite sure how to approach this afterward. I've never had any luck writing anything in which involved my own personal opinions or inner thoughts. I've always preferred to write about others, fictional or not, rather than myself. Still, I had to come up with something and banging my head against the keyboard was just not getting the job done this time.

It was Ron Fortier, my fellow writer and editor of this fine anthology, who suggested I picture myself in a bar, having a brew with some pals and talking about Secret Agent X. It sounded like a pretty good idea, so I took his advice, but I took it one step further. Instead of imagining what it would be like, I actually went out for a beer (and a pizza) at my favorite watering hole. Since none of my pals were available to go down with me, I told the story to the bartender. Afterwards, he started in with the questions.

"Why did you do it?" he asked. This was easy to answer…I was asked to participate (something that came as a bit of a shock, since I was a writer of comic books, not of prose), and I was not about to turn down a chance to write a story based on an original pulp character.

"Why Secret Agent X?" he asked. Another easy answer to a simple question…I had no choice since he was the subject of the book, but I am so glad that he was. Of course, the bartender didn't know that (hence the question), but it did give way to a more interesting answer beyond the obvious. After all, I could have turned down the assignment and waited for another one with a different subject, but Secret

Agent X was such a complex and interesting character that there was no way I would have done such a thing. In fact, I felt quite fortunate to have been given the chance to add to this character's history.

"Why write about some old character set in the 30's? Why not update it?" He asked. Ah...a double-header question, one worth answering. Once again, it started with a simple answer, but gave way for something a little deep...this anthology was about new stories based off of the old stories, not a re-imagining of what came before into what could be. To change the setting and era of the character would be to change the essence of the character, at least, in my own humble opinion. And frankly, this was not what any of us involved in this anthology wanted. We wanted to be a part of that history, not nullify it and make our own.

Also, I have always had a soft spot for the old pulps, so writing Secret Agent X as it was originally fed my obsession and fondness for the era itself. You see, a part of me has always held a longing for the more simplified times of the 1930's. The world was a lot larger back then, and it still held a lot of secrets and mysteries for those brave enough to seek them out. Nowhere else really showcased those possibilities better than the pulps.

Besides, the moralities and convictions of the characters of that time were not as blurred as you see today. The line between good and evil was clearly drawn in the sand. The good guys were good and the bad guys were bad; it was that simple. You knew who the heroes were, even those like Secret Agent X, who would sometimes be mistaken for criminals. This was what I wanted to write.

"Did you have to do any research?" he asked. I did...with Secret Agent X taking place in the 1930's, it was important that I got the facts right. What kind of guns did they have...? What was their slang like...? Did certain landmarks that exist now exist then...? I spent quite a bit of time researching these types of questions. I told the bartender that a good story was a good story, regardless of when it took place, but it was the little details that would make it believable to the reader.

At this point, our conversation was cut short, as my pizza was ready to go. It sat on the bar between us as I finished my beer, but I left him with one more nugget of my so-called wisdom.

I told him that doing this story was about immortality.

I told him that the original stories of Secret Agent X were written a long time ago under the name of Brant House by several different writers. They thrilled thousands of readers with their tales, but did not get the recognition they were due at that time, thanks to working under this alias.

I told him that it's now over 60 years later, and these pioneers were still known and admired, something I doubt they ever thought would happen. The writers of today have been inspired by their work, enough so that it has been carried on for more generations to come. They live on because of writers such as me.

I told him that by writing this story, a little bit of me would get to live on, too.

ooo

BRIAN MEREDITH is a businessman and freelance writer hailing from the Seattle, WA area. He has been involved in many facets of the comic book industry for years: he is the co-owner of a comic book retail chain called The Comic Stop (www.comicstoponline.com), one of the founders and organizers for the largest comic book convention in the Pacific Northwest called the Emerald City ComiCon (www.emeraldcitycomicon.com), and a published comic book writer. His own brand of pulp-inspired comics, such as Sprecken, Lucifer Fawkes, and Dallas McCoy, have been published though Rorschach Entertainment (www.rorschachentertainment.com), as well as others, such as the horror comedy Steve Lawlis. More information on his upcoming projects can be found at www.microbrewstudios.com.

Chapter 1

Bennett Gardner threw back the covers with one hand and lunged for the bedside lamp with the other. He did this while in the process of climbing out of bed and sent the lamp crashing to the hardwood floor.

Staggering drunkenly around the dark room, Gardner turned this way and that, finally enfolding his dressing gown around his large, stout frame.

The thunder of propellers grew louder outside his bedroom window. The sound rose to a high, thin whine.

The noise added a touch of panic to Gardner's fumblings. He lumbered towards the door, then caromed along the equally dark hallway to the stairs leading to the ground floor.

Even from this location he could hear the strained cry of the overworked engines and it ate at his very soul. The sound should not have startled him. As President and CEO of Allied Airships, the drone of propeller engines was as familiar to him as his own voice.

However, he was not at the office or down at the yards. He was at his elegant ranch house and the close proximity of one of his airships meant trouble. The last time he'd heard the roar of propellers outside his bedroom window had been when one of his captains had come to tell him his wife had passed away. Although crammed with every modern convenience, the ranch boasted no phone, radio or wireless. This was at Gardner's explicit instructions as he wanted the ranch to be a sanctuary from the trials and tribulations of business.

He was at the landing now and flew around the banister to the hall leading through to the cavernous sitting room and the glass double doors that gave on the ten-acre stretch a man of his stature called a backyard.

Gardner's son was in the Navy, his ship currently at sea. His heart skipped a beat as he ran up the corridor at the thought that a second nocturnal landing by one of his ships could only mean catastrophe. He tried to thrust the thought away but it followed him into the sitting room cast ghostly pale by the full moon.

He was outside, the night air cool on his fevered brow, his eyes fixed on the invisible behemoth just starting to take shape above and ahead of him.

He pounded across the cobblestone patio until he was into the high, dew-wet grass that bordered the main house. Blindly he ran, wishing all the while that he could fly up to the bridge and make sure his son was all right.

The airship looked menacing and alien as it emerged from the gloom. Its sweeping gasbag glistened with dew, the light of the bridge like the warm beacon of a lighthouse.

Gardner doubled his speed. A quick glance at the craft told him it was certainly one of his fleet. Tiny faces appeared through the bridge windows, too small to make out, then they were lost from view as his speed put him under the belly of the gondola.

The ship was coming down perilously close to the house. And coming down fast! The whine of the engines rose to an ear-splitting shriek. The airship appeared to be tugged at, drawn down by giant, invisible hands.

He had to alter his angle to the craft lest the airship come down right on top of him.

"My boy!" he cried in anguish as he skirted the ship now just fifty feet above him. He calculated his circuitous approach to bring him to the bridge.

He spied Ritter, the captain of the ship. The man's short, snow-white beard was unmistakable, making him look like an executive Santa Claus. Captain Ritter, working feverishly at the controls, happened to glance up and he spotted Gardner running flat out towards him along the lancing beam of a landing spotlight.

Their eyes locked.

Gardner was taken aback by the confused, anxious expression on the face of the captain. The man held up his hands helplessly.

It was at this moment that Gardner realized that the emergency lay not with his son thousands of miles away but with the airship itself. His long familiarity with this sort of craft also told him that the high-pitched screech of the engines was not the result of the engines guiding the ship down. But rather, they were strained attempting to keep the ship aloft.

The befuddled look on Ritter's face confirmed that this was not a planned descent.

Relief flooded through Gardner. His son was safe!

At that exact moment a low, pulsating whine cut across the sound of the engines. It was a sound Gardner was unfamiliar with. He saw Captain Ritter's eyes widen as he, too, heard the strange noise.

It was the last sound either of them heard on this earth.

The airship erupted into a terrific fireball. In seconds the ship, her crew, the house and Bennett Gardner were reduced to smoldering ashes.

Chapter 2

With one fast jab of a sinewy fist, Secret Agent X put Big Earl Fortune down for the count. But the end of the fight was only the beginning of the Agent's difficulties.

The truck X and his inert adversary were in was careening towards the massive wall of a condemned tenement. X darted a glance at the back of the dead driver whose lifeless foot pressed its dead weight on the accelerator. The man had been the victim of a stray bullet fired at the speeding truck earlier by Fortune's men. Encumbered by Fortune's lolling body, Agent X had no chance of reaching the steering wheel and averting a collision.

Also the driver's lit cigar had been propelled out of his mouth from the impact of searing lead and the stiff breeze from the open driver side window had blown the stogie back into the stacks of crates.

Judging from the smell, X gathered that the flaming tip had nestled amidst the tinder-dry burlap somewhere in the back of the truck and the cramped interior of the vehicle was starting to fill with smoke.

The Agent threw his gaze this way and that for means of escape. A canvas cover draped over one stack of crates was within reach and he snatched it up with the thought of smothering the nascent flames before the fire raged out of control. However, yanking the cloth free revealed the contents of the crates it concealed.

Dynamite.

The first tongue of flame shot up from behind this stack of crates just as the truck rattled across a treacherous section of gravel road. X jounced and swayed, becoming entangled with the unconscious Fortune.

The wall filled the windshield. X coughed from the smoke, saw the wood around the black, stenciled letters spelling out 'dynamite' blacken in turn.

He was seconds from oblivion.

There was only one alternative.

Propping the racketeer's body against a crate, the Agent whipped out the portable make-up kit he always carried on his person. From this he extracted the tube of special molding clay.

Feverishly he worked large dollops of the make-up between his fingers then began applying it to his face. Almost instantly he began to take on the appearance of the ruthless enemy before him. X manically pounded and swiped at his face like a man whose countenance was ablaze, but each blur of motion was executed with immeasurable skill and was guided by years of experience. In seconds he looked exactly like Big Earl Fortune. He splashed hair dye into his brown locks and massaged it in to match the mop of curly black hair Fortune boasted.

The transformation complete, he dropped the kit into his pocket, then wrestled the overcoat from the senseless form.

There was a sizzling behind him as the flames began to eat through the wood of the crates.

He shrugged into the coat, felt the weight of the revolver in the pocket. He didn't search for Fortune's hat, as this had been lost in the mad chase leading up to their confrontation.

Swaying, he fought his way to the rear of the truck. The heat was more intense the closer he drew to the back and he feared his hasty make-up job would smear before he could make use of it.

Finally he was gazing down at the streak of gravel road behind the speeding vehicle. He leaned out precariously over the rear panel and bellowed in Fortune's voice for the man's henchmen.

"Boys! Come get me off this coaster!"

A convertible roadster roared into view. The automobile had been paralleling the runaway truck and the driver had to cut his speed slightly upon hearing his employer's voice. It was the signal they had been waiting for.

The driver deftly guided the car's wide, flat hood to the rear of the truck, until the bumpers almost locked.

X sprang from the truck and landed gracefully on the hood of the car. He teetered for a moment and all seemed lost, but regained his balance and hung onto the top of the windshield.

The driver eased off the gas. After receiving a quick nod from his boss that the man had a firm grip, he turned the wheel to send the car rocketing tangentially away from the truck, which struck the wall with terrific force a split second later. Flames found the dynamite at the same instant and a great fireball erupted to join the burning embers of the twilight sky.

"You all right, Boss?" the driver asked as he continued to reduce speed.

X nodded.

"Did you fix that government clown once and for all?" asked one of the men in the rear seat.

"Agent X is dead," X announced with an evil grin.

The driver shot a look over his shoulder. "Hear that, boys? The Boss got that do-gooder!" A cheer rose up from the back seat. The driver went on, "Three years I been driving the Boss and it looks like our ship has finally come in."

The Agent was stepping gingerly over the windshield of the roadster, glowering at the driver as he did so. He dropped into the empty front passenger seat.

"Save the rah-rahs you bunch of dopes. We've still got fish to fry. What are you slowing down for?" X roared at the driver. "That fireball is visible for miles around. Every cop in the state is already on his way here. You want we should park the heap and wait to say 'Hi'?"

"No, Boss. I was just — "

"You was just being stupid, I know. Now give this chariot some horses and let's clear out."

The roadster surged forward as the chastised driver stomped down on the gas.

X was playing things by ear. He did not know how long he would be able to maintain the deception. Although he'd seen and heard enough of Fortune in the three days he'd observed the man to ape his voice, tone and bearing, he could not be sure his hastily applied make-up job would hold up under close scrutiny. He buttoned the overcoat as if chilled by the wind whistling around the open car, but this was really to hide the fact that he wore a suit of the same color as the recently deceased Fortune but it was of a different cut. The gang leader's had been double-breasted. X wore a single and even the low brows with whom he was presently ensconced could easily detect this given the chance.

Also the wind ruffling his hair might, at any moment, reveal brown roots his hastily applied hair dye had not reached and he was grateful for the concealing fall of night.

If the Agent was going to get out of this jam, he was going to have to keep these lugs thinking of other things.

"Point this heap towards town," he said in Fortune's raspy voice. "We've got things to do."

"Agent X is dead."

The engine whined and the construction site dwindled behind them.

X took a moment to formalize his strategy. His efforts so far today to free the kidnapped scientist had been less than stellar. He'd been fed a false trail out to the site and had gone for it hook, line and sinker. He had almost gotten himself killed in the process.

Retrieving Dr. Paulson Latimer was vital to the security of the country. If he pumped this crowd right, he might tumble to the information he craved.

Chapter 3

"Hey, ain't that the Fair out yonder!" the big, apish goon in the back announced with child-like fervor.

The Agent glanced over at the sprawl of the site at Flushing Meadow east of New York City. The unmistakable lancing Trylon and bulbous Perishpere were a sight familiar to millions of fair goers.

The big man went on. "My sister told me her old man took the family out there the other day. She said it was really something!"

X glared at the man balefully. "You want we should go there now so one of the boys can hold your hand on the Parachute Jump?"

The man looked crestfallen. "Naw. I was just saying."

"Let's stick to the program," X went on. "We've got problems."

"I don't get it, Boss," the driver said. "With Agent X out of the way, we'll get along all right."

"Don't you see," X began. "Chop down one Fed and twenty more'll crawl outta the woodwork. We don't know who Agent X might'a talked to before he went out to the site. And how'd he tumble to that in the first place?"

"Number One set it up good. The Fed took the bait. We punched his ticket."

"Sure about that?" X asked. "You sure he didn't call in before? Sure he didn't talk to Latimer himself?"

The man's eyebrows shot up. "Is that how you figure it?"

"All's I'm saying is I'd like to know one way or the other."

"I'm with you, Boss. We got too much riding on this to take chances now."

"All right," X said, nodding. "I say we pay Number One a little visit. Make sure he's not got something in the works for us down the line."

The men agreed readily, which came as a great relief to X. This Number One was clearly the brains behind Dr. Latimer's abduction. It was vital that the Agent get into the inner circle.

The towering concrete spires of New York stretched across the horizon before them. The driver tooled the car onto the bottleneck entrance to the Queensborough Bridge where they joined with the traffic thickened by people returning from the fair.

X addressed the driver. "Point this heap at Number One's hideout."

The men in the car stiffened.

"Boss — ", the driver began.

"You heard me," X insisted, sensing the sudden change of atmosphere in the car but ignorant of the cause.

"He don't know where it is, Boss," one of the men said. "That's how Number One wants it. None of us know. Except you."

Secret Agent X had made a grave error. His hand glided to the bulge of the revolver in the overcoat pocket. "That's right," he said making a show of rubbing at his forehead. "The damn Fed clipped me a good one before he croaked. I'm still seeing stars."

This seemed to settle the men, except for one who glanced at X suspiciously. "Sure," he breathed. "But like Hardy here says, we can't take no chances. This Agent X is supposed to be a master of disguise. How can we be sure you ain't him? You, at least the real you, once told me you had a scar from a bullet graze on the left side of your neck under the ear. You didn't like it and wore high collars to hide it. How about you show us that scar and that'll settle the thing."

Agent X smiled with Earl Fortune's twisted grin. "Sure thing," he said. "Let me get turned around. I want to make sure there's no mistake."

The Agent shifted, drawing the revolver discretely and keeping it concealed from the driver.

"Okay, Boss," the man said. "Show it to us."

"If you insist." X raised the gun and leveled it at the men in the back seat. "The only movement I want to see is you lot tossing the firepower over the side. Do it!"

Hesitantly, looks of pure hate on their hard faces, the men withdrew their guns and reluctantly pitched them out of the automobile.

X said, "Now — "

The driver lashed out at the Agent's gun hand. There was a stinging blow and the revolver fell from X's grasp to land at the feet of the men in the back seat.

One lunged forward, bending to retrieve the pistol, but a lightning fast chop from X rendered him unconscious. With a groan the man sprawled atop the gun. The other men began pulling and shoving at the dead weight.

The driver struck again at X but the blow was easily avoided now that the Agent was ready for it. With the dense traffic racing across the bridge, the driver had his work cut out for him avoiding a smash up as automobiles darted in and out of lanes, in their haste to get home to what remained of the weekend.

Getting themselves organized, the two remaining henchmen in the back seat went to work. The big, child-like one continued to paw for the gun under the body of their senseless comrade while the other drew a switchblade knife from a pocket, snapped it open and brandished it at X.

Agent X seized the wrist of the man's knife hand and they struggled. Taking the odd smash in the side from the driver when the moment presented itself, X held tight to the knife hand and bent it towards the doorframe. He slammed the hand down on the rounded metal and the fist opened. The knife tumbled from view.

A momentary oasis of clear roadway freed the driver to pummel Agent X in the ribs and kidneys. X fell to one side, dodging a roundhouse punch from the man he'd just disarmed.

The traffic picked up speed and the roadster was once again surrounded by rushing vehicles. X blocked a jab, delivered one of his own, which knocked the man against the rear seat.

Seizing the opportunity, the Agent stood up, put one foot on the doorframe and jumped. He had timed his leap to coincide with the approach of a flat bed truck in the adjacent lane. X sailed up out of the roadster to sprawl on the rough wood floor of the truck.

He slid and rolled precariously towards the edge of the truck but, flailing wildly with both arms, his hands found the canvas straps securing the truck's payload in place. Clutching tightly to one of the straps, X was able to halt his slide. With the grace of a gymnast, he rolled to his feet and whipped his head around in search of the roadster.

The truck was moving faster than the roadster, which X spotted two car lengths behind. The men in the back of that car were both avidly hunting for the gun now. The driver was desperately trying to thrust the vehicle into the left lane where traffic was rocketing past, but no one would yield. X knew that if the roadster managed to come alongside the truck and the men got hold of the gun, he would be a sitting duck.

He had to take immediate action.

The flow of traffic had slowed coming off the bridge. It was almost at a standstill up ahead. It was now or never. X gazed down into the saucer-wide eyes of the driver in the convertible directly behind the truck then he knew what he had to do. He shed Fortune's overcoat.

The truck was carrying iron reinforcing rods in bundles secured to the truck bed by the straps that had saved his life a moment before. He strode over to the nearest bundle, and popped the closure on one of the straps. Rods clattered to the floor at his feet. He seized up one and, holding it like a pole-vaulter, sprinted along the length of the truck.

At the rear of the truck, he turned the rod down and burrowed one end into the rear seat of the open sedan while the driver's mouth dropped open in awe. Pushing off with his muscular legs, X catapulted up clutching the rod, cleared the two cars between the truck and the roadster.

He swiveled at the apex of his arc in order to land feet first.

Beneath him he saw that one of the men had got hold of the gun and was trying to get a bead on the descending Agent. The thug managed a shot that hissed past X's ear, then the Agent was upon them.

His feet burrowed into the stomachs of the two men and the air was crushed out of their lungs. Gasping and clutching their guts, they were no match for X who dispatched them with expert blows to their necks.

Agent X sprang into the front passenger seat to face the driver. The traffic slow down had afforded the driver an opportunity to access the small holster at his ankle. He held a derringer in his fist. However, before he could aim the small firearm, he received a stout jab to the jaw and his wrist was all but dislocated as the gun was wrenched from his hand. He worked his jaw as he stared into the small, menacing bore of his own gun.

"As I was saying," X began as he shrugged his disheveled clothes into some semblance of order. "Let's go see Number One."

"I-I don't know where his hideout's at."

"Sure you do," X said. "You said you've driven Fortune for three years. You expect me to believe you don't know where you've been taking him."

The driver said nothing.

X pressed the derringer to the man's shoulder.

"All right! All right!" the driver ejaculated. "The Boss didn't want anyone to know I knew, said he'd kill me if I spilled. No chance of that happening now, I guess. I'll take you to Number One."

"Good boy." X lowered the gun but kept it pointed at the driver. "Lead on."

Chapter 4

Agent X explained how it was going to work after the three unconscious thugs were dumped in front of the nearest police station. Big Earl Fortune, X learned from the driver, whose name was Petronetti, was expected to know the password to get inside Number One's headquarters. As he did not know the password nor did the driver, X would fake a throat injury and they would both enter the building. The driver would corroborate the whole story and act as his mouthpiece as X told Number One what had happened at the construction site.

Once past the guards, X would have to play it off the cuff. His goal was still Dr. Latimer, but there was something bigger going on and he had to find out what.

"Make it convincing," X cautioned the driver as the roadster pulled up outside the twenty-story spire that housed Number One's headquarters on the top floor. "If I even suspect you're trying to tip anyone off, you'll be the first one that gets it."

The Agent adjusted the scarf he'd taken from the driver, tugged at the brim of the hat and snapped the collar of the overcoat he'd helped himself to from the unconscious men before dropping them at the police station. He climbed out of the car. The driver did likewise.

Walking closely behind Petronetti, X guided the man to the short flight of steps leading to the entrance. They ascended and were met by two men flanking the door. They were dressed as doormen but were too swarthy and rough looking to suit the occupation they feigned.

Agent X and Petronetti pulled up before them.

"Mr. Fortune has got to see Number One," Petronetti said, impatiently.

"Hey, look, Pete," the man on the right said, "a ventriloquist act."

The other man chuckled, his deep-set black eyes boring into X.

"Cut the funnies," Petronetti said, his voice laced with urgency from the gun he knew was aimed at his back. "You're cracking wise to the man who killed Secret Agent X." He paused to see the affect this had on the guards. They straightened and the grins fell from their faces. "The Boss here finished X and would like to let Number One know. Thing is, he caught a hard one in the pipes and they swelled up. I have to do his talking just now."

The men eyed the scarf tied around X's throat, then glanced at each other.

X winced as though trying to speak against agonizing pain and nudged Petronetti from behind insistently.

"Come on, fellas," Petronetti urged. "Don't keep the Boss cooling his heels on the stoop."

The guards wavered a moment then stepped aside. "Go on, then," Pete said.

Inside they hurried to the elevators and piled into the first car that arrived.

The operator also bulged his monkey suit and X saw the butt of a .45 sticking out of his open jacket.

They rode up in silence and stepped out of the car without so much as a glance at the operator. Petronetti motioned X to the ornate door at the end of the hall. If this was the headquarters of Number One and he had all that firepower downstairs and in the elevators, X wanted to know why there were no guards posted outside the door.

"Where's the muscle?" he asked.

"Beats me. Number One normally keeps a couple of gorillas up here."

The Agent glanced around. They appeared to have the floor to themselves. "You're good at keeping alive," he said at last. "Keep it up."

X glided to the door and banged on the thick oak. He didn't wait for an answer but tried the knob. It turned and the door opened.

"You're on," he whispered to Petronetti. "Make it good or else."

Petronetti was sweating. He stepped past X into the room. "Sorry to bother you Number One, but the Boss thought it was important – Cripes!"

At this X flung the door all the way open and leapt inside, gun raised.

He lowered the gun an instant later.

The spacious suite was empty. Bare walls, not a stick of furniture, not even a rug remained on the hardwood floor. However there was one article in abundance in the ballroom-size living space.

Balloons.

Hundred of them bound on sticks protruding from the floor so that the colorful orbs floated at chest height.

Agent X recovered and aimed the derringer at Petronetti. "What's the big idea?"

Petronetti instinctively threw up his hands. "I swear this is the place. The Boss has been coming here regular the last couple of weeks."

"And it looked like this?"

"Yes. No. I don't know. I never set foot in the place. Once the Boss called down for some papers he'd left in the car but I put them outside the door we just came through. That's how I knew about the gorillas. I didn't go in. That's the truth!"

X believed him. Still keeping the gun poised, he motioned Petronetti deeper into the room. They weaved through the balloons. The Agent noticed that all of them stood straight up, the clips holding them to the poles were keeping the things from floating up to the ceiling. They were either filled with helium or hydrogen.

This last thought put X on his guard. He was aware of the flammable nature of hydrogen.

He plucked one of the balloons off its stick. With deft movements of his long, tapered fingers he untied the knot. Holding the opening closed, he motioned Petronetti over.

"Take a hit," X said, extending the balloon to the man.

Petronetti made a sour face but could not argue with the gun Agent X held in his free hand. He took the balloon, put the opening to his mouth and inhaled.

"This is embarrassing," he squealed in a cartoon voice. "Don't tell any of the boys about this, will ya?"

An amused grin played across X's features. From his medical knowledge he knew that inhaling helium temporarily affected the speed and timbre of one's voice because it is lighter than air, the result being the high, squeaky voice his captive was using. Breathing hydrogen would yield the same results but there would be side affects like dizziness and nausea. Petronetti was exhibiting none of these. Agent X was certain the balloons contained helium and were not dangerous. This only deepened the mystery as to their presence in the empty room.

They moved about the room. But there was nothing to see. Petronetti stayed quiet, waiting for his voice to resume its normal timbre. This suited the Agent fine. There was a mystery here he could not fathom. How could Number One run an operation in an empty room full of balloons? It was baffling.

The floor was littered with chips of wood and crumpled up newspapers. A quick look at the papers revealed nothing. X spied a red matchbook peeking out from under a three-inch section of what looked like wall molding. He bent and retrieved the matchbook. Studying it he recognized the EZ Cab Company logo. Other than this he could deduce nothing. X slipped the book into the pocket of his jacket and continued searching.

From the corner of his eye he saw Petronetti easing towards the door with thoughts of escape playing across the man's features. X made him stand against the far wall beneath the picture window.

The Agent prowled around the room. The heat was on and he savored the warmth after the coatless ride into town.

Something came to his attention as he passed close to one of the heating vents. He'd been examining the walls in search of hidden panels or passageways that might explain the enigma of the place. As he'd moved by the other vents, he'd felt the welcome rush of hot air wafting over him, but the rectangular heating vent before him now was cold.

He stooped to stare through the vent grill but could see nothing. A closer inspection of the paneling around the vent revealed a discrepancy to his keen eye. The trim bulged out here more than on the panels surrounding the other vents.

"This is it!" he announced to the sullen Petronetti who smoked by the window.

No release for the panel presented itself so the Agent dug his strong fingers behind the edge of the paneling and yanked with all his strength. He did so again and felt the panel give. A third mighty tug and the panel cracked open.

Agent X looked in at a recessed area containing a stool before an elaborate short-wave radio set. He stepped into the area, his ears tuned to catch the cat-footed tread of Petronetti should the man attempt to escape again.

But what he heard instead was a low, throbbing hum. The noise seemed to be increasing at a rapid rate, the pitch of the noise rising accordingly.

Every instinct Agent X possessed told him that danger was imminent.

Just then the ceiling fan whined to life in the center of the room.

The Agent left the recessed area and turned to Petronetti.

The fan was making the balloons vacillate crazily. The hum behind X was reaching a fevered pitch. Suddenly there was a large clanking noise from under the floor.

The balloons were released. The fan scattered them around the room. Two bounced close to the source of the high-pitched whine.

They exploded in brief bursts of fire.

"What the devil!" Petronetti exclaimed. "It's like some daffy New Year's Eve party!"

"Quick!" X shouted. "The door! We've got to get out of here."

To emphasize the point, three more balloons erupted with gouts of flame. Then another close to Petronetti burst. He jumped. Four more detonated after that.

The fan was blowing dozens of deadly orbs in all directions.

X took a step towards Petronetti but was halted by a squadron of balloons heading towards him like tumbleweeds. Only these rolling spheres could explode any second! There was an explosion above his head, the fire licked out at two others sailing up near the ceiling and they went as well. There was no way to get to Petronetti.

"Run for it!" X bellowed and sprinted for the door.

Like an open field runner he dodged and weaved through the balloons that seemed to be everywhere. Explosions were coming now one on the heels of the other. The whine in the room was ear splitting.

Agent X was almost at the door when a balloon transformed into a fireball behind him and the concussion from the blast pitched him to the floor. He was up in an instant and reached the door as nine balloons exploded at once and set the wall ablaze.

Petronetti was cut off by the mass of balloons pinned to the center of the room by the downdraft of the overhead fan. Explosions all around him convinced him to make a mad dash for safety. Panicked, he chose the most direct route to the door and this took him right through the balloons still clustered in the center of the room. He ran blindly, kicking the things out of his way.

Secret Agent X thought the man might make it, but the whine rose to a screeching intensity and all the remaining balloons detonated at once.

X was flung backwards down the corridor, his eyes dazzled by the fireball that had consumed Petronetti.

Dazed but intact, the Agent hauled himself up. Over the roar in his ears he heard the clank and clatter of the rising elevator. Number One's men were on their way no doubt drawn by the explosions.

X didn't wait to greet them.

He staggered to the laundry chute set back in a small alcove. He yanked it open and was climbing inside when he heard the shouts of the men surging out of the elevators.

Inside the chute, he braced his feet against the smooth tin walls to halt his descent and eased the trap door closed. Like a mountaineer inching his way up a crevice in the rocks, X reversed the procedure and descended three floors.

He stopped at a trap door there, cocked his head to one side to hear if anyone was in the corridor and, hearing nothing, he pushed open the door and clambered out.

Agent X headed for the stairs.

Chapter 5

A service entrance provided the Agent with the means to avoid the guards at the front. Once safely away from the building, he scudded purposefully along the crowded streets.

It was his custom to maintain safe houses all over the city, and the world for that matter, in order to have a secure base to launch fresh assaults on the world or crime. It was to one of these places he headed with alacrity. He hopped a trolley to speed him on his way. His destination lay six blocks from the empty headquarters of Number One, and time was precious.

The tram let him off half a block from his destination, which was an aged brownstone. But X did not enter the edifice. Instead he approached from the rear where a squat garage waited. Retrieving a key from the ring in his pocket, he unlocked the garage. The door rattled up, revealing an automobile.

Agent X climbed inside the stylish speedster, and kicked the starter while the engine thrummed. The sedan rocketed out of the garage under the Agent's expert control.

As he guided the automobile through traffic, he worked the controls on his radio. In his never-ending war on crime, Secret Agent X utilized a myriad of resources. One of which was Harvey Bates.

Bates was a rugged powerhouse standing six feet in his socks. He was associated with the Colonial Research Foundation and this connection gave him access to news and information from around the country — often before the papers got wind of it.

His gruff voice came on the line at once. "Bates talking."

"Report," X quipped.

"None of our standard sources have turned up anything on Dr. Paulson Latimer. All of my operatives have reported in."

The Agent accepted this dead end with a sour expression and then decided to switch his approach. If he could not find the missing scientist, perhaps he could learn the motive behind the man's abduction.

"Anything brewing?

"The mayor and his staff are assessing a number of threats to the fair as well as an extortion demand. All available agents and law enforcement agencies have been placed on round the clock alert since the fair opened. With the air show scheduled for tomorrow morning we are on high alert. The only occurrence has been the mysterious death of Bennett Gardner."

The name struck a chord in X. He knew the man only slightly while in his Elisha Pond disguise. He was unaware the man had been murdered. Three days and nights stalking Big Earl Fortune had kept him away from his normal information sources.

"Tell me about it."

"An explosion, sir. Out at his country estate. The blast destroyed the house, the man and a good deal of the property. The police are sifting through the wreckage. It is not known at this time what caused the blast."

"Motive."

"Also unknown at this time. A side note: one of Gardner's airships is missing. He was CEO of Allied Airships."

X had heard enough. "Keep me posted on future developments. Out."

"This is Bates, out."

The Agent broke the connection and quickly dialed in the frequency of another branch of his crime busting army. Jim Hobbard ran the Hobbard Detective Agency. The big redhead is one of X's chief operatives though he was unaware of this fact. Agent X had cleared the former police officer of corruption charges years ago while in the guise of reporter A.J. Martin and it was under this identity that X kept the Hobbard Detective Agency on retainer. Jim Hobbard took his orders directly from Martin completely unaware that A.J. Martin was really Secret Agent X.

The Agent adopted Martin's voice and spoke into the radio handset. "Hobbard?"

"At your service."

"Get a man over to the EZ Cab Company to see what he can find out. I'm certain they may have ferried Dr. Paulson Latimer's abductors, maybe even the Doctor himself to and from the headquarters of Number One. He is the architect behind this thing. Perhaps the drivers can provide a description of Number One or any of his cronies. Get on that right away."

"Will do, Mr. Martin. When do you want a report?"

"The moment you have it. Out."

The Secret Agent broke the connection and headed for the exclusive Banker's Club across town. The manner of Gardner's death intrigued him given recent events and, disguised as Elisha Pond, he meant to find out what he could.

While he drove, X went about assuming the new disguise. From a hidden compartment on the dashboard he extracted a larger, more elaborate make-up kit than the one he normally carried on his person. From this he pulled a canister of a cleansing chemical and used it to remove the special volatile material that made him look like the late Earl Fortune.

The Elisha Pond persona was, perhaps, his most used identity and it was a cinch to apply the special make-up over his features — a cinch for a man of Agent X's consummate skill that is. He did have to stop briefly in an alley to change into Pond's traditional formal wear. Examples of which were in the trunk of the car as well as numerous other clothing options the Agent might need at any moment.

As he neared the club, Elisha Pond's face slowly, gradually materialized over X's countenance.

The Pond disguise in place, the Agent next handled the container in which he stored the synthetic, concentrated food capsules that constituted his entire diet. He dry swallowed several of these, then returned the container to the hidden dash panel.

The Banker's Club was directly ahead. X tooled the automobile to the front entrance of the impressive structure. He got out and turned the car over to the parking valet and headed up the carpeted steps.

Moving through the revolving doors he was met by the trappings of opulence from the large, ornate reception desk to the crystal chandelier. His feet whispered across the thick carpeting as he strode to the club entrance.

"Ah, Mr. Pond," the man at the desk said, a telephone receiver pressed to his ear. "A pleasure to see you again. This is a most fortunate coincidence. There is a man on the line insisting that he speak with you. Are you available to take the call?"

"Of course. Is there somewhere private where I may do so?" X said in Pond's smooth, haughty tone.

The deskman leaned in to have a word with the operator, then, putting the phone down, escorted X to a small room containing only a desk, chair and a filing cabinet.

"Please forgive the surroundings, sir. You will have complete privacy here, I assure you."

Agent X nodded, waited for the man to leave. When he was alone he glided over to the telephone and snatched up the receiver. He waited to hear the operator hang up before he spoke.

"Yes?"

"I'm terribly sorry to bother you, Mr. Pond. My name is Jim Hobbard and I'd hoped to reach A.J. Martin but his office said he was unavailable. They instructed me to call you."

"That's quite all right," X said, easily. "I can take whatever message you have for Mr. Martin."

"I've a report on the EZ Cab Company."

"Very well," X was taken aback over the how quick Hobbard had completed the task he'd set out for him as Martin but he made no sign. He urged. "Proceed."

"I caught a break. Two operatives of mine were looking into a robbery not a block from the cab operation. I sent them right over. Good thing, too. There's something screwy going on over there."

"Please explain."

"Well, my two boys went in there with some routine questions but they got the bum's rush. No slouches them, they guessed from the icy shoulder that the company had something to hide. So while one of them tried to strong arm his way in, making a ruckus to wake the dead and drawing the dispatcher out of his office, the other snuck round the back. He got in and had a look at the time book. Turns out they've been making regular runs out to the address Mr. Martin gave. Only they ain't been charging for 'em. And each time it's to ride out or pick up a John Smith. My guy got that much before he had to scram. Sounds hinky to me. Enough so that I got to thinking Mr. Martin might want to look into it."

"I see," X said casually. "That is most interesting. I will see that the matter is forwarded to Mr. Martin at once. Goodbye."

The Agent jabbed down a finger on the switch hook to break the connection. He'd memorized the phone number of the EZ Cab Company as a matter of course when he'd inspected the matchbook. He dialed the number in.

"EZ Cabs," a voice garbled.

X, speaking in the deskman's voice so as not to raise suspicion by having a man of Pond's standing calling for his own car, said, "I require a taxi at the Executor Arms. The cab is for Mr. Elisha Pond."

"On our way."

X hung up the receiver and got out of there. It appeared Bennett Gardner's murder was going to have to wait.

Chapter 6

The Agent walked outside. He informed the valet that he was just taking a bit of night air and did not require his automobile. Things were beginning to jump at the club and a steady stream of cars lumbered up to the curb to disgorge the cream of high society. X welcomed this as it kept the valet constantly busy.

He didn't wait long. The Pond name was not without its influence. The fire engine red taxi screeched up to the curb. The cab's slogan was splashed across the door: 'Take it easy in an EZ cab.' X piled in.

"Where to, sir?"

Agent X gave the man an address close to the cab's main depot and the car grumbled into traffic.

X took in his surroundings. It was plainly obvious why the company boasted relaxation. The automobile was a huge Cadillac four-door sedan which would easily sit seven. He could stretch his legs full out where he sat. This was riding in style. X gave the appearance of settling back to enjoy the ride but he was really going over the steps he would have to take when the car reached the destination he'd provided.

On the journey, the Agent made a point of talking with the driver, discussing such mundane matters from the weather to the fair and the big air show in the morning.

A block from the address, X dipped a hand into the inside pocket of his jacket and removed his billfold, palming something else from the pocket in the process.

The cabbie stopped the car at the address X had given him, which was a drug store with an alley along one wall. It was a poorly lit section of this particular street and the interior of the car was cast in stygian shadow.

"Be a buck and quarter, sir," the cabbie announced.

"Certainly."

X leaned forward, billfold in one hand, his small gas gun in the other. The gun contained a non-lethal gas concoction of X's own devising. A cloud of anesthetizing vapor wafted into the cabbie's face and the man's heavy eyelids closed. His chin dropped to his chest and the man's head tilted, spilling the mackinaw onto the seat.

The Agent looked quickly around and, seeing that the car was unobserved, jumped out and came around to the driver's side. He climbed in, shoving the sleeping man over and put the car in gear. With precise turns he guided the car into the alley.

Working stealthily and with skill born of long experience, Secret Agent X donned the cabbie's clothes. As the man was of a much larger frame, X slid the garments over his formal clothes. He then bound the man but left him in the front passenger seat.

Not daring to show a light, X set his make-up kit on the dash and set to work on his transformation from wealthy medical doctor to rough, streetwise cabbie. This he accomplished in a few furious minutes. He snapped shut the kit, returned it to his pocket, then lunged for the registration tag dangling from the steering column. The name on the tag was Andy Russell. This he confirmed against the driving license in the cabbie's wallet on the off chance the man had used someone else's automobile for the pick up.

Satisfied on this score, he quickly practiced the voice and manner he had so carefully observed when conversing with the driver. He had a quick look around to be certain no witnesses were about, then got out of the car and proceeded to haul the sleeping cabbie back to the spacious trunk. X dumped the man in and closed the lid, leaving it open just enough for the man to breathe. Back behind the wheel, the Agent started the engine and glided the large car out of the alley and towards the EZ Cab Company.

Chapter 7

The cab line's offices were located in a jutting structure that resembled the prow of a ship on the corner of Lexington and 89th. There was a cab pulling in ahead of X's and the Agent gained entry by following the lead car and mirroring the actions of its driver. Cars entered and exited from the prow-like extension that housed rows of numbered bays in which the cars were kept while not in use. Although the bays were roofed, as was the dispatcher's office, the center area was open to the night sky, giving the prow the appearance of an elongated donut.

As Andy Russell, X needed to leave his cab in Bay 19. This he did, killing the motor and exiting the vehicle. The Agent adjusted the mackinaw on his head and went to join the men.

"Andy!" a rapier-thin wisp of a man called in a voice too deep for his frame. "That was a quick job of it."

"Well," X said in Russell's voice. "Some rich muckety-muck needed to get across the street. You know what them kind is like."

"Do I ever! We'll be doing likewise before you know it." He smiled, showing a row of small, even teeth and pushed his sweaty fedora back on his head. "Say, what do you make of that ruckus we had with them two fellers snooping around here. You think they might have got wise to what's happening."

X shook his head. "Doubt it. We've got this thing under wraps."

"Well, I'm glad you made it back in time. Word came down while you were on that fare. The Boss is going to say a few words. Tonight's the night!"

"Good," X said, playing along. "I been waiting."

The men were gathered in the dispatcher's office barring X from any snooping he'd hoped to do. The Agent could do nothing else except shoot the breeze with the other men as half an hour ticked by. The men came and went to take the odd fare, but mostly they waited expectantly. Two of them carried in a console short wave radio and hooked it up on the dispatcher's desk to hear the message from the Boss, X assumed.

"What are you going to do with your pile?" the cabbie asked X.

"Get outta this racket for a start," the Agent declared.

"You and me both, brother. Way I hear it, EZ Cabs is going under anyway. If not for the plan, we'd all be out on the street. Time to abandon the sinking ship. Only us rats get to jump in style."

X didn't know what to make of that so he said nothing.

Finally the radio hummed and the dispatcher, a florid man with pale fat rolls under his chin started waving a cold stogie around. "Pipe down! Pipe down!"

From the picture hanging behind the dispatcher's desk, X had learned that the proprietor of the cab concern was named Ezekiel O'Toole – a hawk-face man with wide piercing eyes that glared out from the photograph.

"Shut it you lot!" the dispatcher roared. "That's EZ O'Toole on the line!"

The room fell silent. X inched closer to the radio to be sure he missed nothing.

"Gentlemen!" a voice crackled over the speaker. "This is Number One speaking. We're just a few short hours away from our fortunes. The mayor will give in to our demands, of that I have no doubt. The road has been long and you have all performed to perfection. Now as the final hour approaches I want to thank each and every one of you."

A cheer roared up from the clustered men. X thought he heard something outside but the yelling drowned it out.

"You have all kept our secret and you have kept it well," the voice of EZ O'Toole went on. "And for this you will be handsomely rewarded or the city will tremble in fear."

The cheer went up again. This time X was sure he heard a low rumbling.

"Already they approach, like flies into the spider's web. This close to the end we must be certain that nothing foils our plans. Nothing."

X definitely heard the noise now. It was a low rumbling like an airplane engine heard from a great distance. The sound seemed to grow louder in the seconds he listened. He needed to put some distance between himself and the group so he could hear clearly. X headed for the door.

"Hey, Andy," one of the men came after him. "What gives?"

"Going for a smoke and some air," X replied with a reassuring smile. "I'll be just outside the door. Keep it open so I can hear."

The man let go of the Agent's arm and used a battered ash stand to prop the door open, then rejoined the others.

X made a show of lighting up while keeping his head cocked to hear O'Toole's voice.

The sound was louder out here under the open roof. X waited for a trolley to grumble by, then focused his hearing on the noise. He glanced up and saw stars twinkling in the night sky. Another cheer made him look back in the direction of the dispatcher's office. He took one last drag on his cigarette and was about to toss the butt and re-join the others when a dark shape obliterated a section of the night sky.

The humming engine sound grew louder.

Agent X backed into a pool of shadow and, unseen by the cabbies, craned his neck to look up. The long, sausage shape was unmistakable.

It was an airship.

And it was descending rapidly right over the building.

X recalled the room full of balloons that was supposed to be the headquarters of Number One. He knew now that Number One was EZ O'Toole. He could not begin to grasp what O'Toole's scheme was but he did know that both party balloons and airships could be filled with helium. O'Toole had somehow managed to ignite the helium in the balloons, that much the Agent had witnessed with his own eyes.

He watched the descending airship fill the opening.

If the balloons could be ignited, so could the airship.

What had O'Toole said? 'We must be certain that nothing foils our plans.'

Like a bunch of loud mouth crooks posing as cabbies, X realized.

The airship blocked out the sky. The drone of the engines was so loud the men could hear it now over the sound coming from the radio. A couple poked their heads out but could not see the cause of the engine noise from where they were.

"Clear out, men! We've been double-crossed!" X had time to issue this one warning. Then he heard the low whining sound he'd heard back in the balloon room.

The airship would explode any second.

X tossed his cigarette aside and sprang into action. While the others scattered towards the exits only to find them closed and barred from the outside, Secret Agent X snatched up a coil of thin chain hanging from the wall and yanked the top off of an engine stand. He tied the chain around one prong of this star shaped metal object and stepped out beneath the sloping expanse of airship obliterating the sky.

X played out some of the chain and took hold of it with one hand. He began to whip the chain and the crude grappling hook whistled as it cleaved the air. After a few turns, he launched it up at the airship. A moment later the star shaped hook clattered to the cement at his feet.

The whine was reaching a fevered pitch. An explosion was imminent.

He picked up the hook, twirled it again, then let fly.

This time one prong bit into the skin of the ship. The Agent pulled on the chain once to be sure it held. It did.

With a great leap, X shimmied up the chain. In seconds he was clear of the roof and was at the side of the great ship. As he passed the gondola, he could see the crew frantically trying to raise the ship, but clearly they could not.

"Get out while you can!" X roared from outside the open window. "The ship is going to explode!"

But the crew just stared at him blankly, blinded by the sure knowledge that helium was non-flammable. The sudden appearance of a man outside the window just added to their confusion.

With a disgusted grunt, X climbed up to the roof of the gondola. Reaching up he shook the hook loose and coiled it again, his hands a blur of motion.

The airship dropped another ten feet and drifted to the left. X found himself facing the sheer wall of a skyscraper not fifteen feet away.

The chain whirled in his hands and he let fly. Only this time he pitched the hook straight out towards the building. It shattered a window and hooked on the frame.

Without hesitation, he leapt from the top of the gondola and began arcing towards the building. The wind whistled in his ears, but he could clearly hear the now high-pitched whine all around him. He adjusted his swing and hit a window two stories below the one his hook was affixed to.

The glass shattered and flew in all directions. X tumbled into the vacant office, rolling into a filing cabinet. The impact knocked the wind out of him, but he regained his feet, and collided with the door. He pawed at the lock, got it open and crashed into the hallway.

It was at this moment that the airship exploded.

A hurricane blew through the shattered window, a wave of searing heat right behind it. X dove to one side, performed a tuck and roll and regained his feet. Sprinting full out, he could not escape the gust of rapid air behind him. It picked him up and carried him towards the hallway window and certain death on the street below.

But the angle was wrong. Instead he hit the palm tree standing next to the window, then he impacted against the unyielding wall behind the plant.

The wind was crushed from his lungs.

Then everything went black.

"...the gust of air....carried him towards....certain death on the street below..."

Chapter 8

The next thing Agent X was aware of was an intense ringing in his ears. He flung his eyes open and was blinded by a shaft of sunlight stabbing through the shattered window above where he lay in a heap. Dust drifted in the air. There was a weight on him. A brief inspection revealed that this was the palm tree and a section of the fractured ceiling tile.

X squirmed out from under these obstacles and rose to his feet, swaying slightly. The sunbeam bothered him and for a moment he could not determine the cause of the distress. He dimly recalled being there the night before, listening to a speech...

Then he had it!

Agent X sprung into action.

He stumbled over the shattered glass and twisted metal past the office doors blown off their hinges by the blast and, doubting an operator was on the job for the elevator, headed for the stairs.

The Agent tottered down these as fast as he could manage. He breathed deeply during the descent and gaped his jaws to counteract the affects the blast noise had had on his hearing.

At street level, the noise and commotion he'd dimly heard above grew dramatically louder. He stepped through the front door of the office tower, shading his eyes against the blazing morning sun.

Police and firefighters were dashing here and there around the smoking ruin of the EZ Cab Company. The rubble from the destroyed building had been strewn outwards by the downward thrust of the explosion and was fanned out into the roadway and piled up against the foundations of businesses across the street with shattered front windows. Broken glass carpeted the area. Thick, glistening hoses snaked in all directions. Ambulances came and went, their sirens wailing and shrieking.

The Agent spotted Inspector John Burke and made his way towards him. When he was close enough for the man to contact him discretely, X emitted a strange whistle-like sound he used to identify himself as Secret Agent X to those who knew him. The note was eerie, melodious, like the call of some wild bird, yet pitched in a minor key.

Burke whirled around and glared with his gray eyes at the Agent who was still in the guise of cabbie Andy Russell although the impersonation was quite a bit the worse for wear.

"Agent X!" Burke shouted, his pale sharp-featured face turning crimson. "I should have known you'd be tied up in this!"

"There's no time for personalities," X interjected. "It is imperative that you locate and detain Ezekiel O'Toole."

"And why in the Sam Hill should I do a thing like that?"

"He is the man behind last night's explosion. And I'll lay odds he murdered Bennett Gardner in the same fashion."

The Homicide Chief eyed him suspiciously. "Now how would you know about that?" X made no answer, but Burke went on. "Skip it. As for O'Toole, we're trying to locate him, sure, but only because it was his business that got blown down."

"I tell you, he's behind it."

"You're dreaming. An airship lost power and came down. That is all."

"Which ship? From what line? Find out and get in touch with them. I guarantee you the ship that exploded was filled with helium, not hydrogen gas."

"So what if it was?"

"Helium is non-flammable," X said, looking around. "Making what happened here impossible."

"It sure looks real to me."

"Get in touch with the line."

"Even if I didn't think everything you told me was a load of hooey, I couldn't reach the line. Must be every ship on the Eastern Seaboard heading here right now for the big air show at the fair. Every airship office is a madhouse right now."

The Agent suddenly got an idea.

"How will the airships get to Flushing Meadow? What approach will they take?"

"Right over the city. The skies over New York are going to be filled with ships inside of two hours."

"Don't you see?" X blurted. "The mayor's office has received demands for money from someone calling himself Number One. O'Toole is Number One. He means to terrorize the city. He has the means to bring down and explode every airship that flies over. He must be stopped!"

"You're cracked! Why would he blow up his own business?"

"To throw off suspicion, make himself look like a victim. Locate O'Toole and ask him these questions."

Burke wavered as he considered what Agent X had told him. Despite his animosity towards X, Burke was a good policeman and those law enforcement instincts were putting the fragments of fact together to fit the picture the Agent was painting.

"Well, even if there is something to what you're saying, no one can find O'Toole."

"A man of his standing must belong to a dozen social clubs and have offices all over the city. To say nothing of his personal residences."

"You think New York's finest doesn't know its job? We've checked all them places. No sign. O'Toole has vanished. And awhile ago, too. The clubs haven't seen hide nor hair of him and his houses were stripped bare."

This made X recall the empty headquarters he and Petronetti had visited. Where could Number One be?

Agent X could see that further discussion with Burke would accomplish nothing. He made as if to leave the man's side.

"Where do you think you're going?" The inspector's jutting eyebrows lowered menacingly. "I've got a pile of questions for you!"

"They will have to wait."

X glided away.

Burke bawled out to his men to take X into custody, police whistles shrilled, but Secret Agent X faded around a fire engine and there was no sign of him when the bulls closed in.

Agent X felt completely exposed. As Burke's men searched for a disheveled Andy Russell, the Agent had swept the man's appearance off his own face and moved through the crowd with his true face visible for all to see. Since no one knew what he really looked like, it was the perfect disguise.

He reached the opposite corner at the edge of the gathered, gawking throng and sprinted full out for a passing crosstown and took the car. X paid his fare to the impassive conductor who bawled up to the motorman with an 'all clear'.

The streetcar lurched as the steam tanks gurgled and clanked. Agent X watched the scene of devastation recede as the red-faced, snub-nosed streetcar nudged its way through traffic.

As the trolley rumbled and slewed, Agent X worked on deducing O'Toole's plan. For the man to explode airships, he would require some apparatus to do so. But where could such a device be located? With the main depot of EZ Cabs destroyed along with most of the concern's fleet of automobiles, the device could not be concealed there. The empty headquarters as well as O'Toole's vacated holdings were a mystery he must solve.

The device, whatever it was, needed to be designed and manufactured somewhere, it required power to run, and O'Toole must have a way to coordinate his minions.

How was this being done?

The conductor strode by and something on the man's uniform caught his eye. The Agent called him back and eyed the badge as the man approached. The badge designated him and the car as being part of the E.Z.O Line.

"Is this trolley line owned and operated by Ezekiel O'Toole?" X inquired.

"Sure thing," the conductor quipped, then made as if to move on.

X put a restraining hand on his arm. "You heard about that business with EZ Cabs?"

"Did I ever, sir. Terrible thing."

Although the Agent's outward manner seemed relaxed and conversational, his mind was in turmoil as a hint of the truth danced before his mind's eye.

"Was the trolley line attacked? Has service been disrupted in any way?"

"Not at all, sir. All cars are running smoothly."

The conductor headed up the aisle, leaving X gazing out the high, open window, deep in thought.

Why would O'Toole try to cover his tracks by destroying the cab line, gut his dwellings and offices, yet leave the tram line intact? Number One hadn't batted an eye at murdering his crooked cabbies, so why keep the streetcars running?

An idea tickled at the Agent's capacious intellect.

This time he got up and, steadying himself with the seat backs, went to join the conductor in the rear.

"Is there a radio on this car?" he asked.

"You are a curious one, aren't you?" the conductor replied with a smile. "No, sir. No radio. If we need to check in we use the call boxes at the switchback points. I have to climb down to switch the poles at any rate and the box is right there. We're twenty minutes from the next one. Is there some kind of emergency?"

There most certainly was, X mused, but none the man could help him with.

"I see," was all X said.

The Agent's gray cells throbbed now with this new information.

"One more thing. Are the EZ Cabs running at all this morning? Or were they all destroyed?"

"From what I've heard, there're some about, but no dispatch. I wouldn't try to flag one if I were you."

X nodded his thanks to the man and got out at the next stop. He dashed with newfound purpose to the curb.

The cabs! With their two-way radios! That was how O'Toole was keeping in touch with the men he'd recruited from the ranks.

This solved one mystery but brought him no closer to finding Number One.

It being Sunday, the drug stores were closed. Agent X needed a telephone. It was urgent he make a call.

Frantically turning his head this way and that, he hit on the answer.

He ducked down an alley and, his hands a blur of motion, re-applied the face of Andy Russell over his own. An airship droned by overhead as he was finishing the transformation. Soon the sky would be full of ships! So many floating bombs in the hands of Number One!

Once again disguised as Andy Russell, X went back out to the street, waved down a checker and dove inside.

"Where to, Mac?"

"I'm new in town," X said, putting on a Boston accent. "Ride me around, will ya?"

"It's your coin, fella."

The cab began moving through traffic. Minutes ticked inexorably by as X, under the ruse of being a wide-eyed tourist, scanned the surroundings.

He spotted his quarry.

X tossed a dollar at the startled cabbie and climbed out. The light was red up ahead, the traffic at a standstill.

The EZ cab was in the next lane, fifty yards from the checker he had just vacated.

The light turned green as the Agent lunged for the door. He noticed the man's flag was down even though the car was empty. X piled into the cab.

"You've got the wrong pew, friend," the driver turned and spat at the Agent. "Go land yourself another chariot."

X leaned towards the cabbie.

Sudden recognition dawned on the cabbie's face. "Andy! Sorry didn't know you at first. What the blazes! The news, they said — "

"Yeah, well, I've got something to say. That skunk O'Toole double-crossed us. Blew EZ sky high!"

"What are you saying?"

"Did you get the call last night?"

"Yeah, sure. But I had a fare and you how the boss feels about keeping up appearances. Had to haul out to Jersey. I — "

"We all got the call. O'Toole pulled us in and blew the place."

"But, why? He can't finish nothing without us."

That was what X had been hoping to hear.

"Pull the heap over," he urged. "Somewhere private. We gotta talk."

The cab pulled into Central Park. The driver put the machine under one of the many footbridges and killed the engine. Airships floated overhead.

The cabbie turned and leaned over the back of the seat. "Okay, Andy, what gives?"

The Agent extended his gas gun. But his reflexes were still off from the battering he'd taken and his hand bumped the top of the seat. The gas gun fell from his grasp. With blinding speed, X chopped down on the man's neck but he struck only a glancing blow, which momentarily stunned the man.

The cabbie groaned but there was still a lot of fight left in him. He lashed out at X with his elbow and struck the Agent on the cheek.

X reeled back and blocked a second blow delivered as a feinting move as the man turned and heaved himself over the seat. The two men grappled in the cavernous passenger area. X blocked another blow, then drove a short jab at the man's jaw. Dazed, the driver kicked up, striking X on the outside of his thigh, knocking him to one side.

Agent X recovered and directed a series of punches at nerve centers in the cabbie's torso.

The man's face twisted in agony and his limbs flailed.

The fight was over.

"You will regain control of your limbs in a few minutes," X explained.

This did not calm the man at all. He fought to move one arm deliberately to the rear of the front seat. The hand flopped and slid down the leather to the base of the seat and fumbled beneath it.

X, ready for anything, watched the man.

The hand found what it sought. X heard a click.

Without warning, the entire back of the seat rolled up like a window shade, revealing a concealed compartment.

The Agent stared in amazement at what the compartment contained. Revolvers hung from pegs with spare clips of ammunition. A large two-way radio was set into the back of the seat, the handset dangling.

The cabbie was struggling to reach a pistol. X retrieved his gas gun and dosed the man who was unconscious in seconds.

X examined the find unmolested.

He found the catch under the rear of the front passenger seat. But here the back of the seat dropped down instead of rolling up. The panel locked when horizontal, forming a broad table. Behind this, in the hollowed-out seat were all the makings of a miniature laboratory. Test tubes and beakers, vials of chemicals a Bunsen burner and rubber gloves were just some of the things he found.

Looking over the contents, X also learned why no one had been able to find Ezekiel O'Toole. And why his home and holdings were vacant.

Number One was using EZ Cabs to carry out his plans. X was certain that all of the spacious automobiles were roving headquarters, housing hidden compartments like the ones before him. In these could be hidden all the devices or comforts O'Toole might need. He could go anywhere in the city, his resources always immediately to hand. On the streets of New York no one noticed taxicabs. They were as anonymous as streetlights. While the police searched for O'Toole, he was right under their noses, being driven around the city streets.

Number One had destroyed the cab line to cover his trail, sparing only the ones with material he needed to complete his plan.

X had not forgotten the ever-increasing rumble of airships overhead. Time was critical.

And O'Toole could be anywhere in the city. Agent X had no clue where to find him.

Chapter 9

X could not afford to squander precious time trying to revive the unconscious cabbie. Instead he pawed at the man's jacket to find his wallet. The identification inside revealed the man to be one Kenneth Ames.

Recalling the man's voice, X thumbed on the radio, which warmed quickly. It was time for a desperate play. Clutching the handset in a white-knuckle grip, X said, "This is Ames reporting. Come in."

There was a tense moment of crackling silence on the other end before a reply was forthcoming.

"What is it?"

"I-I think I'm being followed," X stammered. "I'm sure of it. I need to lay low. This isn't my usual route. Where's the nearest safe house?"

"Wait."

The Agent listened to the airships overhead. People were starting to pour out of buildings to gather on the street, necks craning, to watch.

"I have the directions," the voice said over the speaker. "Just give me today's code word for confirmation."

X was stuck. He'd gambled and lost. He tried to bluff.

"I don't have time for that stuff!" he shouted.

"Wait."

Agent X's eyebrows rose in surprise as he wondered if the ruse would work.

Then poison gas hissed out of the radio console.

X had barely a second to take a deep breath and hold it. He flung the door open just as the other three locked automatically and tumbled out, pulling the sleeping cabbie with him. They sprawled on the pavement. The Agent sprang to his feet after kicking the door closed. Not trusting the proximity to the automobile, he dragged the cabbie a safe distance away.

An attempt had to be made to revive the man. The skilled fingers of X kneaded and pressed certain nerve clusters on the man's neck and shoulders. He worked in the hope of raising the man's consciousness to a near dream state, which would allow him to answer questions. Twenty minutes ticked by, each second like the stab of a dagger in the Agent's gut, while he continued the precise massage.

Ames moaned, his eyes fluttered open and fell until finally he stared up at the sky through half-lidded orbs.

"Ames!" X barked. "Where is Number One?"

"Don' know," the man replied dreamily.

"He means to threaten the city with exploding airships!"

"Yup."

"How does O'Toole explode the ships?"

The man's head rolled on the litter-strewn pavement and X feared he might lose his only source of information at this critical juncture.

"Lati- Latimer…" Ames spoke groggily. "Elect… beam…"

Ames was out until the gas wore off. There would be no awakening him now. Agent X sat back on his haunches and poured over what he'd learned. The use of a beam made sense as a means to ensnare the airships, but electricity would not ignite helium. What had Ames been trying to say? He rubbed his jaw in thought. There had been something he recalled reading in the file of Dr. Paulson Latimer while he was preparing for the mission. Among other things, the man had been experimenting with creating bubbles in gases while in liquid state. Injecting electrons into them, then exploding the electron bubbles with sound waves.

Had Number One forced Latimer to develop this line of experimentation, only as a weapon? Advance the research to explode helium in gaseous state with some sort of electron beam? It made sense. But such a device would require great energy to deliver and would have to be aimed at targets floating hundreds of feet above the ground.

X beat a fist against his thigh in frustration. He had the answer now, knew who was behind the threats and why. But his unseen enemy could be anywhere at this moment, could strike from ten thousand different locations in the city.

He considered the cabs, but large as they were, it would be impossible to carry a beam canon undetected in the vehicles. Besides the majority of the automobiles had been destroyed in the blast.

A streetcar lumbered past on the avenue barely glimpsed through the trees of the park. The racket the trolley made pulled X from his ruminations. The pole wheel sent out showers of sparks from its connection to the overhead power lines. The glow from the sparks was lost in the bright morning sun. He vaguely recalled hearing a streetcar shortly before the car barn was destroyed…

Secret Agent X leaped to his feet and dashed to the wall surrounding the park. He vaulted this to stand in the street staring after the bulbous rear of the streetcar.

When the car slewed around a corner X could see the front of the trolley.

And, at last, he had solved the mystery.

He ran as fast as his feet would carry him in the opposite direction the streetcar had taken.

Chapter 10

The building X sought was on the far corner. He wound his way through the staring pedestrians with their fixed gazes on the sky. Inside the building, an elevator was just disgorging its passengers. When the car was empty, X seized the operator by the tie and yanked him into the lobby. The Agent then sprang inside, clattered the gate closed and got the car moving.

X burst from the elevator at the top floor and scudded to the stairwell that led to the roof.

His shoes crunched over the gravel rooftop. His destination was a long, wooden, padlocked shed in the center of the roof. The Agent had the key in his hand and popped the heavy lock.

Agent X swatted at the light switch inside the door and the shed lit up revealing a canvas-covered shape. Like some great stage magician, the Agent whipped off the covering and gazed at the autogyro that lay underneath.

A button affixed to a post near the craft next drew the Agent's attention. He pressed the button and the roof opened.

The gyro and hangar were more of X's mission materials he used in his battle against crime. The machine was always kept in tip-top operating condition, ready to take to the sky at a moment's notice.

Agent X hopped in and jabbed the starter, which fired smoothly. The rotors whirred, began to turn. In seconds they were a blur of motion above his head. He worked the controls and the autogyro ascended into the sky.

His timing could not have been better. Once clear of the surrounding skyscrapers, he saw a vast spread of airships before him — all shapes and sizes flying above the city. Airplanes darted and buzzed like flies around the massive crafts.

However, no sooner did this incredible sight appear before him, that the airships began to plummet. Like Icarus in the ancient myth, they hurtled from the sky. First one, then two more, then half a dozen more — O'Toole was implementing his scheme.

The Agent grabbed up the handset of the special transmitter and dialed a frequency known to only two individuals in the entire world.

"K-9," was all X said.

In Washington, a high-ranking government official, who was the only other man alive who knew the frequency, spoke from his shadowed office.

"What is it, Secret Agent X?"

"A most grave emergency, sir," X spoke hurriedly yet respectfully. "It is imperative that you locate and disable the electrical generating station that powers the streetcar lines in New York City. All power must be cut off or hundreds, perhaps thousands, will perish. I do not have the authority to issue the command."

"How certain are you of the threat?"

"Absolute certainty, sir."

"I will authorize the action."

The transmitter went dead. X gave the briefest sigh of relief. Now if only it could be done in time.

The EZ trolleys were the key, he'd surmised back in the park. Not only were the cars large enough to accommodate the electron generator but the poles could be modified to house the beam emitter. As trolleys only used one power pole at a time to draw electricity, the free pole need only be raised from its housing to its normal position: pointed at the sky. The electron beam could then be unleashed on any airship that passed overhead, bringing it down to be destroyed. Scattered about the city, streetcars were as innocuous as taxicabs, who would notice either on the teeming streets? The Agent glanced down and could see the sausage-like streetcars amidst the teeming traffic, the poles of each raised, one to the power lines, the other to the sky.

It was an ingenious plan, one that could still be carried off if K-9 could not cut the power to the cars and their electron beams.

The Agent was not idle as he waited for K-9 to take action. Something else had occurred to him when he had deduced the terrible scheme. He had reasoned that O'Toole was maniacal enough to want to see his great plan put into action should the mayor not give in to his demands, and yet still have the freedom to flee safely in the ensuing chaos. There was no way to do this on the ground. However, up in the sky, all could be observed and escape was easily obtained. These conclusions had led Secret Agent X to take to the air.

The gyro darted and skipped, swerved and cut around the airships descending everywhere. X kept one eye on these behemoths while he scanned the swarming airplanes. Most of the planes contained photographers or sightseers who had rented open ships with the intention of experiencing the spectacle like a bird in flight.

There were a few closed aircraft in the sky as well and these drew the Agent's attention. It was his guess that O'Toole and Paulson Latimer were in one of these.

The gyro dipped under a falling airship and into the path of a huge craft descending rapidly to choke the concrete canyons of the city. X hauled back on the stick to rise above the sinking craft. The landing wheels of the gyro scraped and rolled along the taut skin of the airship as it cleared the top of it.

The sun lanced into the cockpit momentarily blinding him. Dazzled, he pawed at his eyes and thought he caught a glimpse of a large airplane with the sun at its back. Its immobility drew his attention.

X could hear the yells and shouts rising up from the masses below. The swarm of planes had also been affected by what was transpiring. The lazy circles they had been flying had given way to bursts of speed and determined aeronautic maneuvers. Some had turned back, others moved closer, but all were agitated. The high-flying craft he'd glimpsed continued to loll through the sky as though oblivious to what was transpiring.

The gyro surged forward under X's control.

Cautious lest he tip his hand, the Agent directed the autogyro on a loose, sweeping approach. This was easily done as the last of the airships were falling all about him and he had to navigate his way around them.

He placed the gyro beneath the larger plane and matched speed.

Slowly X raised the gyro using the fuselage of the plane above to cover the action from the occupants of that plane. He came up under the other craft undetected.

He halted his ascent dangerously close to the underbelly of the other plane. If it should dive unexpectedly, the two craft would collide with deadly results.

The air was momentarily free of other planes.

It was time to act.

But it was not going to be so easy.

Before X could but twitch his control stick, the airships began to rise slowly back up into the sky.

K-9 had shut off the power. The electron beam had been rendered useless!

O'Toole, realizing the gig was up, opted for escape. The plane above the gyro canted to one side and slid from view. The Agent banked the gyro in a tight turn and caromed after it.

O'Toole's plane headed east, the gyro in hot pursuit. X threw a glance over his shoulder and smiled grimly at the sight of a sky once again filled with airships. He then turned his attention back to the chase. X knew what he had to do but needed the right set of circumstances to pull it off. It didn't look like he was going to get them.

The World's Fair spread out beneath them now. The aircraft swooped in low just missing the spire of the Trylon. Faces on the ground turned up at the pass, wondering if this was part of the air show.

X opened the throttle and his smaller, lighter craft was able to gain ground. The tail of O'Toole's ship now loomed before him.

A side door opened on the plane and a man protruded clutching a gun.

The Agent did not hear the shots, but he heard the whine of bullets as they careened off the gyro. One punched a hole through the windscreen six inches from his head.

X made as if to ram the craft, forcing the pilot to bank sharply. This almost tumbled the gunman out of the plane and he quickly retreated back inside. The door snapped shut.

The autogyro dove back under the plane. The empty fields around the fairground would serve for a crash. He swung the gyro like a pendulum beneath O'Toole's plane. Gasps rose up from the fair-goers, the pavilions forgotten for the moment.

With one last check that the nose filters he'd taken from a pocket were in place, X went into action.

The gyro swooped up on the left, slightly ahead of the other craft. As they drew dangerously close together, X shifted out of his seat and kicked the door of the gyro open. He had locked the stick before vacating his seat, putting the autogyro in an arc above O'Toole's plane.

At the precise moment when the wings of the two planes passed each other, inches apart, X leaped. He struck the wing of O'Toole's plane, his weight making the ship dip crazily.

The Agent had a cargo hook in each hand and he buried the sharp metal barbs into the skin of the wing. Scrabbling crab-like he approached the fuselage behind the pilot. The gunmen inside dared not fire for fear of hitting the pilot.

X reached the wing's support strut and lowered himself to wrap his legs around it.

The pilot, eyes wide, stared in horror as X approached. Desperately he swung the craft this way and that trying to shake off the Agent but the cargo hooks held fast.

Agent X was at the door directly behind the pilot. He raised one of the hooks and smashed in one corner of the glass. Through this he tossed two gas pellets.

He followed close behind the erupting pellets. He entered unchallenged.

The first order of business were the gunmen. He dispatched the coughing man with a swift judo chop. A second gunsel was attempting to draw his weapon while immersed in a cloud of the swirling vapor, but the gun fell from his grasp and he pitched over.

X saw Dr. Paulson Latimer already asleep from the gas in the rear of the plane.

O'Toole sat in the front seat. He was reaching back desperately to get at the door there in the hopes of flinging it open to clear the air.

X launched one of the hooks at him. It struck the man on the back of the head. His hat flew off and a spurt of scarlet splashed against the windscreen. O'Toole slumped forward, dazed.

The plane took a sudden nosedive as the pilot collapsed over the stick.

The Agent used the momentum of the dive to propel himself over to the front of the craft. He somersaulted across and came to crouch between the pilot and O'Toole. He pulled the limp pilot out of the chair and dropped into the seat.

X put his hands on the controls, then a million stars exploded on one side of his head.

O'Toole, with one last surge of strength, had struck the Agent.

Although the blow only fazed X for a second, it had dislodged one of the nose filters he wore against the gas.

For a lethal moment, X inhaled the knockout gas!

The plane continued to hurtle downwards. The windscreen was filled with patchwork farmer's fields. Fighting grogginess, his actions slowed, X fumbled with the controls. His vision swam, his limbs would not obey his commands.

The ground loomed.

He pulled feebly on the stick. Black dots danced before his eyes.

Somewhere in the foggy depths of his mind, he recalled the cargo hooks, one of which was in his lap. He seized it up and smashed out the pilot window.

Cool air rushed into the cabin.

The Agent's mind cleared.

With every ounce of strength he could muster, X pulled back on the stick.

At first all seemed lost. The plane continued to rocket towards the ground. But then the nose slowly started to rise up. With gritted teeth, X fought the controls and the numbing affects of the gas and continued to pull. The nose rose, the plane leveled, the wheels inches from the fallow fields.

Agent X cut back the throttle and bumped and bounced the plane down onto the field.

A stand of trees loomed ahead but the plane's speed had been cut sufficiently and the plane came to a complete stop with room to spare.

Chapter 11

Distant sirens heralded the arrival of the authorities. X pulled the occupants from the plane and dumped them unceremoniously in the dirt. He bound the unconscious men with their ties and belts, then carried Dr. Paulson Latimer from the plane. The affect of the gas pellets was not as long lasting as the gas gun X usually utilized and the fresh air quickly revived the doctor.

The man came sputtering up to consciousness. He was a tall, lanky man with close-cropped gray hair and a bushy mustache. His intelligent eyes fixed on X behind his spectacles.

"It's all right, Doctor," X soothed. "You're safe now. The police are on their way."

"What? Who are you?" Latimer stammered.

"A friend."

This seemed to calm the man. X helped him to his feet.

"As it would be best if I'm not present when the police get here, I was hoping you could answer a few questions. The State Department will need to know these things."

"For the man who saved my life, anything!"

"Very well, what was the nature of the device O'Toole had you construct?"

"I had developed a way to observe electrons in gases. It was all most innocuous I assure you. By injecting electrons into liquid helium they are repulsed by helium atoms which push them away, forming a sphere. A bubble is formed inside the gas with the electron at its center. Then, using sound waves, the bubble ceases to expand and collapses with tremendous force."

"Sound waves? Cavitation."

Latimer nodded eagerly. "Precisely. O'Toole learned of my research and fixated on one facet of the work. You see, when the bubbles collapse, they compress the matter inside, this raises the temperature to several thousand degrees in the surrounding gas, which emits light, much like a star. However this takes place on a microscopic scale. I never thought of the method as a weapon of any kind. But O'Toole was right, by performing the procedure on an immense scale, he could use the beam to increase density then ignite the helium in airships. He forced me to create such a device and test it out in the country. I shudder to think of the implications."

"Bennett Gardner," X said to himself, then addressed Latimer, "Have no fear. O'Toole meant to use the device but he was stopped in time."

"Thanks to you, I have no doubt."

X made no answer to this.

"But what did O'Toole hope to achieve?"

"As with all such ilk, his needs were base. Money. Power."

"And it would have worked if not for you!" This was from Ezekiel O'Toole who had regained consciousness and glared at X from where he sprawled on the ground. "With the electron beam and my streetcars to deliver it, I would have been invincible. Damn you!"

"A man of his standing," Latimer sighed. "I don't understand it."

"O'Toole was financially strapped," X declared. "Isn't that right, Number One?"

O'Toole turned his gaze to the sky. "Yes, I'd lost everything! Swindled! I would have had my revenge on the city and made a fortune in the process."

"If you had used your electron beam to create chaos," the Agent went on, "you would have reaped no fortune."

"Ah, but here was a weapon any nation in the world would pay handsomely for."

X shook his head at such base avarice. He turned to Latimer. "Thank you for your cooperation, Doctor. I will see that this information reaches the right people in order that this threat may be neutralized. The police will see that you get safely back into town."

"What about you?"

Agent X chuckled. "The police have other plans for me."

"But you're a hero, you saved my life. From what I gather you saved the city."

X looked away. "I did my job." He made as if to go, then paused to listen to the sirens growing louder with each passing second. He reached out and traced a large X on one of the dusty plane windows.

And with that he turned and walked towards the fair grounds and the thousands of faces behind which he might hide while he secretly waged his never-ending war on crime.

The End

"I did my job."

X MARKS THE PLOT:

ANDREW SALMON

Being invited to contribute an X tale to the revised edition of this anthology was a thrill. As a relative newcomer to the world of pulp, there is still a lot I've got to learn about the wealth of characters from the Golden Age and their rich history. But when I first learned of Secret Agent X, I knew, without having read any of the original novels, that this was a character I hoped to one day write.

Thus, I got my hands on some original X tales as fast as I could and devoured them. In doing so, my desire to write the character only strengthened. When Ron asked if I wanted to take a stab at an X tale, my answer was an immediate yes. It felt like I'd been waiting a lifetime to work with the mysterious agent.

But what the heck was my Secret Agent X story going to be about?

For inspiration I cast my mind back to those glory days of the 1930s. The first thing to jump out at me was the 1938 World's Fair. This has always been a fascination of mine and Doc Savage's romp through it in the *World's Fair Goblin* is one of my all-time favorite Doc adventures. I wouldn't set my tale at the fair as that had already been done but something related to the fair sounded right.

Airships. Another important image from the time. A bit of head scratching and I latched onto the idea of a criminal mastermind somehow being able to explode airships over New York City as part of an extortion scheme.

Okay, now we were cooking with gas. And that was the problem, gas. You see I like to infuse my pulp tales with just enough reality to counter the suspension of disbelief. One of the things that stayed with me from *World's Fair Goblin* was that Doc and crew had been running around an actual historical event. This simple little fact has colored all of my pulp work since: I like to put a little reality into my tales of the fantastic.

And the reality was that by 1938 most airships were filled with helium. The highly volatile hydrogen had given way to this much safer gas in the United States. So how could my evil genius get airships to blow up if they couldn't blow up?

Got to love the Internet!

While poking around for information on helium and a means to make it explode, I stumbled upon some actual scientific work being done with exploding electrons in helium while in liquid state. Of course this work was being done on a minuscule, safe scale. But pulp is, by definition, over the top, and it was no great leap to up the ante. If small explosions could actually take place in helium in the real world, then they could blow big in pulpdom.

Unless Secret Agent X could stop the mastermind behind it.

Sounds like the plot of a pulp story.

That's what I thought, too.

All that remained was for the evil mastermind to have a way to deliver the electron beam.

While pondering this I happened upon the cover of a recent Shadow double volume reprint. It featured the Shadow swinging over a city street. The 1930s street depicted had the usual stores with neon signs and vintage cars driving by, but beneath the Shadow's feet are the long lost streetcars of the time.

I've become very well acquainted with the trolleys of yesteryear. Where I live in Vancouver, a group of dedicated enthusiasts have restored two hundred-year-old trams to pristine condition and run them on weekends in the summer. My wife and I practically live on these clanking, hissing time machines and at $1 a trip, it's an experience that can't be beat.

Or, rather, it used to be.

With the approaching 2010 Winter Olympics here, the powers that be decided to build the Olympic Village right smack dab where these restored streetcars ran. Because of the construction, the line had to suspend service. No more rides into the past for this pulpster.

So I was very much missing this experience when I spied that Shadow cover. And, seeing as I've ridden streetcars of the kind depicted in the painting, I felt I had first hand experience in writing about them. Also these glorious wooden monsters traveled all over the cities of the past. They might catch the eye today, but, back then, who would notice them? The perfect way for my villain to go about his villainous pursuits.

And that was it.

You've just read the result and I hope it has given you some pleasant, edge-of-your seat moments. It was a hoot to write and hopefully a hoot to read.

If you like what you read, there's more on the way.

I've got a Jim Anthony tale slated for that upcoming anthology and it's been my great honor to write the Ghost Squad with the modern master of pulp, Ron Fortier. Both will be published by Airship 27 and Cornerstone Books. And I'm not done there. An all-new space hero is set to blast across the stratosphere. His name is Mars McCoy and I'm pleased to have a story in the forthcoming anthology of space opera excitement. This will be a joint Airship 27/White Rocket Books endeavor. Keep an eye out for it.

And Airship/Cornerstone will be releasing THE LIGHT OF MEN. This is a non-pulp, harrowing novel of mine that I'm most proud of. It's a powerful time-travel tale set in a Nazi concentration camp.

I would like to thank Ron for allowing me to play in the universe of Secret Agent X and I hope I get the chance to do so again somewhere down the road.

Thanks for reading.

•••

Ellis Award nominee **ANDREW SALMON** lives and writes in Vancouver, BC. His work has appeared in numerous magazines including *Storyteller, Parsec, TBT and Thirteen Stories.* He also writes reviews for *The Comicshopper* and is creating a superhero serial currently running in *A Thousand Faces.*

He has published three books to date: *The Forty Club* (which Midwest Book Reviews calls "A good solid little tale you will definitely carry with you for the rest of your life"); *The Dark Land,* the first of a series ("a straight out science-fiction detective thriller that fires on all cylinders" — Pulp Fiction Reviews); and *The Light of Men,* his first work for Airship 27/Cornerstone.

Andrew's work will also appear in the upcoming all-new Jim Anthony collection, and the new Mars McCoy adventures. He is also co-writing the Ghost Squad with Ron Fortier for the line. He is set to release *Wandering Webber,* his first children's book, in the spring. To learn more about his work check out the Airship 27/Cornerstone store and the following links: www.Lulu.com/thousand-faces and www.LuLu.com/AndrewSalmon.